the
illusion of
ecstasy

the next dose in the Thizz series.

NICOLE LOUFAS

This is a work of fiction. Names, characters, places, and incidents are either the product of the author's imagination or are used fictitiously. Any resemblance to actual events, organizations, or persons, whether living or dead is entirely coincidental.

THE ILLUSION OF ECSTASY

ISBN: 978-0-9964946-2-5

Copyright © 2016 by Nicole Loufas

www.nicoleloufas.com

Editing by Holly Kothe with Indie Solutions, www.murphyrae.net

Cover design by Murphy Rae, www.murphyrae.net

Except for the original material written by the author, all song titles and lyrics contained in this book are the property of the respective songwriters and copyright holders.

Drink Coffee

Because drugs are bad for you.

October 2006

The moment Matt lifted the plate off that chest, everything I thought I knew about my father changed. Words like integrity and honesty could no longer be used to describe the person he pretended to be. All the missed birthdays and interrupted holidays so he could tend to his pro-bono cases. Helping the helpless. Fighting for equality and justice. It was all bullshit.

Will Walker has already admitted to paying my father to lose Devon Brown's case. The police have questioned some of his former clients. They've all given statements on how much they paid for his "pro-bono" services. This has prompted an IRS investigation. One I told them I would fully cooperate with when I though my father was innocent.

In order for them to prove he took the money, they have to find it. The IRS has tax returns, bank statements, and payroll records. They know every penny that my parents earned for the last ten years. I can't just walk into a bank and deposit this money. Hell, I can't even use it to buy books or pay my tuition. They're watching everything I do.

"What about the note?" Matt asks.

Beneath the cash was a note for my mother on where to find more. There are two addresses. One is a self-storage place on Brannan Street, and the second is a post office box in Eureka. My father assumed my mom would be the one to find this chest if something happened to him. He was wrong. His actions cost both of their lives.

"We'll go to Brannan Street tomorrow," Nick says.

I'm overwhelmed. I don't know if I want to throw up or jump around for joy.

"I can't think about Brannan Street right now. This is already too much." I gesture to the cash spread across my attic floor.

"As long as this money stays hidden, you have nothing to worry about," Nick assures me as places the last three stacks inside the chest and replaces the false bottom my father created to hide the cash.

Nick stands and walks to me. I'm keeping my distance from the money. I don't want to get too attached.

He rubs my back and kisses the top of my head. "Don't worry, we're gonna fix this."

I like Nick's confidence, but I really don't see how he can help. The insurance money I collected will run out eventually. Once that happens, I'm screwed unless I can sell the house. I can't do that until the IRS investigation is over. That could be years. I'm basically sitting on a pile of cash I can't use or let anyone know exists.

I watch Matt pile old baby clothes and photo albums on top of the money. "What if someone robs the house?"

"They won't steal this stuff." Matt holds up an old stuffed animal then drops it into the chest. He closes the lid and replaces the lock.

"It's been up here for years," Nick adds. "It'll be okay for a few more days."

He walks to the stairs that lead down to the hallway, and pulls the string above his head. The light bulb goes out.

"We found it, and we're not that bright." I toss a drop cloth over the chest. Then place an empty suitcase on top.

"I think it'll be fine, but if it makes you feel any better, we can stay here tonight and guard it," Matt suggests as he climbs down the ladder.

I take one last look at the chest and part of me wishes I didn't know what was hidden inside. Not because the money can cause a whole heap of new problems for me. That money means my father wasn't the man I thought he was.

I climb down the ladder and retract the stairs into place. As I walk towards the living room, I look at the pictures hanging on the wall. The faces are familiar but I have no idea who these people are. I stare at my parent's wedding photo. Although I've seen this picture every day for most of my life; I no longer recognize the man standing beside my mother.

Did she know what he was doing? Is that why she did so much charity work? Maybe she thought doing good with some of the money would clean her conscience.

If my parents weren't the people I thought they were, what does that say about me? Am I a fraud, too?

I find the boys huddled in the kitchen. They break apart when I walk in. I know them, they're plotting something.

"If we're going to stay the night, I need get grab some stuff from my apartment." I open a cabinet and look inside. The house has been well maintained, but it's just a façade. The cabinets are empty. The only thing filling this house are old lies, and dirty money.

Matt gives Nick a desperate look; like a shut-the-fuck-up kind of look.

"I can't stay," Nick finally says. "I have an early class tomorrow. I'll pick you guys up after so we can go check out the storage unit."

"Okay," I say and follow him out of the kitchen. I look back at Matt; he's staring into the sink like he's going to puke.

I walk Nick outside and watch him get into Matt's Mustang. He doesn't even turn around to say goodbye. He closes the door and drives away. Something weird transpired between them in the kitchen, and I'm one hundred percent sure it has everything to do with me.

I lock the gate and pause for a second to prepare myself for whatever is about to happen. The realization that I'm going to spend the night alone with Matt slaps me across the face.

I go back upstairs and find Matt standing in front of the living room window. He turns at the sound of my footsteps on the hardwood floor. The expression on his face makes me nervous. I turn from the hallway into the kitchen to avoid the intense look in his eyes.

"There's no food here, but we can raid my mom's wine rack downstairs. I just need to go to my apartment and grab my toothbrush," I ramble. Because rambling feels safe. "We can stop at

Golden Boy and get a pizza on our way back." I open the refrigerator hoping to find a bottle of courage sitting on the top shelf.

"Are you hungry?" he asks.

"Uh, not really." I close the door and we lock eyes.

He looks sexy as hell leaning against the doorframe. Pizza and my toothbrush are the last things on my mind as he steps towards me.

"Me either," he says.

He reaches for my hand and pulls me into his arms. I try not to think about what this means or what will happen tomorrow.

He leans in and kisses me. Even though our lips touched in the past; the emotions I'm feeling right now weren't fueling that moment. *This* kiss wasn't instigated by a dare. We have no audience. Nothing holding us back. I relax into Matt's arms and let this thing between us finally take over.

Ten minutes after Nick leaves, Matt and I are naked in my childhood bed. My first sexual experience without ecstasy is surreal. Not totally in a good way. It's quick and sort of sloppy. I've never been this present during sex. I'm not saying Matt is a bad lover. You know that feeling when you finally get something you've been craving, and the idea of it was better than the reality?

Yeah, that.

Dani

Thanksgiving 2006

Matt stops in the circular driveway of the Marino estate and turns off the ignition. I know this is the last place he wants to be. His parents called last night with news that Ashley's fever had spiked. In a normal child a fever isn't a big deal, but Ashley is getting chemotherapy, so her weakened immune system makes her susceptible to all kinds of bad.

"Your mom will call when they have news," I assure him. My words are meaningless, nothing can soothe his anguish.

"I know." His blue eyes are cradled in dark circles. "I just don't feel like doing this." He gestures to Nick's house. "Can we just go back to bed and sleep until the holidays pass?"

This isn't the first Thanksgiving the Augustine family has spent in the hospital; it is the first Matt has spent without them.

"You just want to sleep?" I rub Matt's thigh. He half smiles as he leans over to kiss me.

Kissing Matt in Nick's driveway feels a little naughty. Not as bad as the truth-or-dare kiss at the beach or the time I told Matt I loved him on Nick's birthday. Such a dick thing to do. There was also that time we danced in his room. Nothing happened in reality, but the thoughts running through my head were bad. So bad. Having Matt within my reach was torture, especially when I was high. There were times I wanted him more than air. More than Nick. And now that I have him, it isn't quite what I imagined. We've been officially dating for about six weeks, and even though we've known each other a lot longer, we're still in that awkward new stage.

"Come on, I want to get this day over with. Don't forget the bag," Matt reminds me as he opens his door.

I reach into the back seat for the duffel bag filled with my father's cash.

Money laundering is not listed on the JM Developers website, but that is exactly what Mariann and Nick are doing for me. Mariann Marino gives away hundreds of thousands of dollars in scholarships every year. I didn't win one of the JM Developers young apprentice contests or apply for a Marino Education Scholarship. If Mariann is going to give me money, there better be a good reason, otherwise it will give the IRS an open invitation to investigate. That's bad for everyone.

Matt walks around the back of the house to the kitchen door. This place is like a second home to him. He even has his own room. Well, the room he stays in when he's in town. His parents sold their house when they moved to Colorado. Matt hasn't said anything, but I can tell he feels lost. It's the same way I felt when I moved to Eureka. Lucy's house wasn't my home, and it never will be, but it feels nice to know you have a place to go. One filled with people who love and care about me. At the end of the day, that's all that matters. Matt doesn't see it that way. He feels abandoned. It isn't like his parents are dead. They may have moved out of state, but he can call them at any moment to say hi. He doesn't realize how lucky he is. It's really hard for me, and Nick, to sympathize.

"Matt!" A plump woman in a black dress with a pumpkin-colored apron greets us at the door. She gives him a kiss on the cheek and comments on his weight. "You're not eating. What's wrong?"

"Nothing, geez." He kisses her cheek and closes the kitchen door. "Georgia, this is Dani."

Georgia playfully shoves Matt out of her way so she can fold me into her arms. "Dani, it's so good to finally meet you." She smells like rosemary and onions. "I've heard a lot about you and my boys."

"Georgia, don't harass my guest," Mariann says from the doorway on the opposite side of the enormous kitchen.

Georgia releases me, and I turn to greet Mariann. I'm surprised to see her in a pair of jeans and a white cashmere sweater. She's far more casual than I thought she would be. We're practically wearing the same outfit. Except mine came from Old Navy.

"Matthew Augustine, will you ever use the front door?" She walks to Matt and gives him a big hug. "Parading Dani through the back like she's the help."

"Excuse me?" Georgia says with more attitude than I give Heather when she's being a brat. "Are you implying something, Ms. Marino?" Georgia sounds like she's offended, but the smile on her face tells me this is just a game they play.

"Oh shut up, Georgia. You're burning the gravy." Mariann takes my hand. "How are you, Dani?" She gives me a quick hug, then leads us out of the kitchen. "Let's get out of here before Georgia makes us chop something."

"You know full well you're not allowed to touch anything in my kitchen," she yells to Mariann as we escape into the dining room.

"Georgia has been with me forever, don't take any of our banter seriously," Mariann explains.

"No, of course not," I say and take Matt's hand. He slowly pulls it free then shoves his hands in the pockets of his dress pants. I try not to take it personally. Neither of us likes to flaunt our relationship in Nick's face.

"Matt and Nick were practically raised by that woman." Mariann places her hand on Matt's shoulder. "Weren't you, Matthew?"

He turns to Mariann with a smile. "Yeah, she taught me how to tie my shoes, and she gave me and Nick the sex talk." His face flushes. "We were about eight. She walked in on us looking at a Victoria's Secret catalog. God that was embarrassing."

"I remember," Mariann laughs. "Nick couldn't pass that store for two years without turning ten shades of red."

"I still can't!" Matt admits, and they laugh. I haven't seen him laugh in weeks.

This realization makes my heart hurt. Things have been really stressful with Ashley out of remission, and my IRS problems. We are finally together, and everything else in our lives is falling apart.

Mariann leads us into a formal living room. Lucy, Johnson, and my baby cousin Marguerite are in the corner, admiring the lights on an enormous Christmas tree. Nick is speaking to a man in a suit, and beside him is Haley. She was one of Heather's former minions. Tiny blades stab at my chest when I see her smile at Nick.

Did he bring a date?

9

"Dani!" Lucy calls my name, and everyone turns in our direction.

I walk straight to my family and say hello. I haven't seen them in a month. Not since Johnson helped me remove the floor boards in the attic to retrieve the rest of the money. The note we found in the chest led us to a storage unit, where three bags of money sat in a metal container. With the money was a key to the post office box, which held a single letter. It was addressed to Lucy and contained a drawing of her attic. Beneath the floorboards, under my bed, was the last thirty thousand dollars.

I tried to convince Lucy to keep the money, but she refused. She says it's mine even though it was in her house. I don't think it has anything to do with me. Lucy would never keep the money, knowing where it came from. She has morals, something I seriously lack.

"The baby looks like she doubled in size." I grab her hand and kiss it. It feels like a wet piece of dough.

"She's an eater," Lucy says. "In fact." She grabs her right breast. "I think it's about that time." She takes the baby to the sofa and pulls out a privacy blanket thing. She puts it around her neck and unbuttons her shirt.

"Lucy, you don't have to cover up in here," Mariann says. "We've all seen a boob."

"Speak for yourself, Grandma," Nick disagrees. "Seeing one of Lucy's boobs is not on my bucket list."

"It better not be," Johnson warns.

Everyone in the room laughs, except Johnson. As far as Johnson is concerned, Nick will never be more than the punk kid who almost got me killed.

Lucy ignores the remarks about her boobs and leaves the blanket in place. "Thank you, Mariann. But I don't mind. As long as the baby is happy, I'm happy." Her face glows as she looks down at her daughter.

I watch Nick and Matt retreat to a corner to talk, but also because breastfeeding freaks them out. They still view boobs as something created for their pleasure, not a food source. Matt looks at me, then slides Nick in front of him. News flash, I'm not a lip reader or an idiot. I can tell when something is going on. I walk across the room to put a stop to their whispering, but Mariann foils my plan.

"Danielle, come and meet Mark."

I reluctantly change course and wipe the scowl from my face. Time to play pretend.

"Mark, this is Danielle Batista." She steps to the side so we can shake hands. "You'll be handling her trust until she graduates from college."

That is a Marino family rule. Nobody gets money until they earn a degree. If we want to pull this off, I am no exception. I have to follow the family tradition.

"She is currently pre-law at CAL," Mariann tells Mark.

"Actually, I'm switching majors," I correct her. I look back at Lucy and Johnson. I might as well get this over with now. "I'm considering a degree in social science."

I've always wanted to be a lawyer. Researching case studies, filing motions, writing opening arguments, picking juries, and wearing really awesome pantsuits was my dream. None of that sounds appealing to me anymore, especially the suits. I don't want to believe it has something to do with the fact that my father wasn't the man I thought he was, or that the money paying for my education was given to him by men like Will Walker.

In my heart, I know my father had good intentions. One day he crossed a line and couldn't go back. Will that be me if I follow in his footsteps? Will it be Matt? He's still pre-law. His dream hasn't changed. Matt's focus is inspiring. Hopefully, some of that inspiration rubs off on me.

"What kind of jobs do social science majors get?" Johnson asks. He is trying to hide the irritation in his voice and failing miserably.

"Oh, I know," Haley interjects. "I read somewhere that the number one job for sociology majors was managing a Starbucks." She starts to giggle and the rest of the room grows quiet.

I look at her clueless face and I wonder why I'm not mad. She was obviously putting down my career path, but it was kind of funny. I loved my job at Eureka Coffee. Making coffee is the only thing I'm qualified to do.

"Haley, why don't you go see if Georgia needs a hand in the kitchen," Mariann suggests. Haley quickly exits the room. After she's out of earshot, Mariann apologizes. "Sorry, I'm breaking in a new assistant. She hasn't learned the art of polite conversation."

Everyone sort of nods like they get it. I don't. Haley is Mariann's new assistant. How the hell did that happen?

"So, Haley isn't going to college?" I ask Mariann.

"Sadly, no. I'll help her get a degree if that's something she wants to pursue. She has a little bit of growing up to do, and a lot of refining."

Mariann tells the room that she had her last assistant for sixteen years. "She recently got married and moved to Vermont. I figured I'd get a young one. It'll be years before she's ready to settle down and have a family."

"You never know with kids these days," Mark says. "I had a client that dropped close to half a million on his daughter's wedding. Two years later, she was divorced and asking him to pay for a second one."

"That's just ridiculous," Lucy says as she switches the baby to the other boob. "When we get married," she pauses and looks at Johnson. He rolls his eyes. "I want a cozy backyard wedding. One where nobody wears shoes and we sip cocktails out of mason jars."

"That sounds beautiful. You know, there's a clearing about three hundred yards into the woods. The trees and the flowers that surround it are beautiful and perfect for that kind of wedding. You just name the day." Mariann smiles at Lucy and holds up a glass of wine.

"I think I might take you up on that," Lucy says and nudges Johnson.

One of the helpers stops in front of me with a tray. Three wine glasses sit on top; two red, one white. Nick calls their domestic staff "helpers." He thinks it's less demeaning.

"Take the white," Nick suggests from over my shoulder. "It's more your style."

"I don't have a style."

"I know." He kisses my cheek and walks away.

I look at Matt to gauge his reaction to Nick's show of affection. It's just show, nothing more. Matt isn't even looking my way; he's too busy refilling his wine glass. The only thing on his mind is getting drunk.

The meal is served in the formal dining room. The chandelier dangling above the table looks like it belongs in the San Francisco opera house. T and Georgia join us for dinner. The table sits all ten guests and a high chair. There are several smaller tables set up; they remain empty. I wonder if Mariann was expecting more people.

The food is laid out buffet style. After we fill our plates, I notice the helpers line up to get food then leave the room.

"Where are they going?" Lucy asks as she returns to her seat with a new plate after the baby spilled water on the first one.

"I ask them to join us every year, and they decline." Marian gestures to the empty tables. "I won't give up hope."

"They're in the kitchen, where the conversation is a lot more fun," Nick adds. "And they have beer." He smiles at his grandmother, and she winks back.

"I have a no-beer-at-my-table rule. It's one rumor about me that's true." She holds up her wine glass, and Johnson makes a grunting noise.

I catch Lucy's eye, and we smile because we know how much Johnson hates wine. He's being a pretty good sport about it. He wasn't too thrilled to spend Thanksgiving with the Marino's; he's only here for me.

"Thank you for sharing this holiday with Nick and me. We truly appreciate all of you and hope to see you in years to come." A photographer snaps a picture of Mariann, another of Nick and I, then one of the entire table. He nods to Mariann to let her know he got his shot, then walks out of the room. That picture was the reason my family is eating dinner at this table. It's part of the plan we devised to help me use the money.

"Thank you for having us," Lucy says and lifts her glass to Mariann.

"It's my pleasure, really. It's always been my dream to have a large family." She looks at Nick, and he looks at his plate. "I hope this isn't the last meal we share together." The guests mumble various forms of appreciation to Mariann. She smiles graciously at them all then says, "Let's eat."

The meal is amazing. Even the wine is good. Nick was right, white is my style. After dinner, Lucy and Johnson leave to have dessert with Johnson's family. They ask me to join them, but I decline. I'm not here just for the food, we have to finalize paperwork for my trust.

"I'll be home tonight," I tell Lucy as I kiss the baby goodbye.

Lucy wasn't totally on board with our plan, but she didn't come out and say so. I see it in her eyes. She's worried about me. In some way she thinks everything that happened with Will was her fault. Like she dropped the ball or missed the signs. She knows I used ecstasy, but not how much I used. I did everything I could to keep her in the dark. Ecstasy is probably the easiest drug to hide. Being in a good mood all the time doesn't raise many flags. You really have to know what you're looking for, and after a while your behavior on ecstasy becomes the norm. Since Lucy's schedule was opposite from mine, we rarely spent much time together. She really has no idea how dependent I was, and I'd like to keep it that way.

"Don't forget, we're going shopping tomorrow," Lucy reminds me.

"Ugh." I slump my shoulders like a pouty teenager.

Johnson pats my back. "Better you than me, kid." He gives me a hug and kisses my forehead. "Call me if you need a ride." He looks back at Matt, who's on his sixth glass of wine.

15

"I will," I lie. I would never call him for a ride; he'd never forgive Matt for being irresponsible. Right now I'm batting zero for two in the boyfriend department with Johnson.

After Lucy and Johnson leave, we go up to Mariann's office to finalize the paperwork and hash out the details of my life for the next few years.

We're seated at a round table covered with papers that have my name on them. My attention is focused on the portrait of Jake Marino hanging on the wall in front of me. Nick looks so much like his grandfather. Matt told me they were really close. He died two years before Will Walker came into Nick's life. If Jake Marino were alive; Nick never would've fallen into Will's grip. Who knows, maybe my father wouldn't have either. I shouldn't think that way. It isn't fair to put the future of so many people of the fate of one man's life. Nobody should have to carry that much responsibility.

"Mark will send monthly updates on your account balance. You should meet every quarter or so to go over investments and general financial expectations." Mariann shuffles more papers in front of me. "Right now her major financial burdens are tuition and books. Her rent is covered until the end of the year, is that right?"

It takes a beat to realize Mariann is asking me a question. Everyone has been talking at me, around me, over me, for the last hour. "I paid a full year's rent with the insurance money. It's paid until next July."

"Hopefully, we can get her into a condo before her lease is up so she can start earning equity," Mariann tells Mark. They've been speaking in foreign terms ever since we came in here to discuss my financial security.

"The market is tricky right now, but I'll keep my eye open for something worthwhile," Mark says.

"I don't really want to live in a condo," I tell them. "I like my flat. I have the option to extend the lease."

I live in North Beach, not too far from where I grew up. It's my neighborhood. It's all I have left of my former life. I don't want to leave it.

"Buying a condo is a good financial investment. It also gives you a nice tax break." Mark explains. "You don't have to worry about any of that. We'll handle all the boring stuff." Mark seems like a good guy, kind of sleazy in the way people who manage money for a living are; but nice.

"Leave it up to Money Mark." Nick slaps Mark on the back. "He's got you covered, Dani." Nick sits on the arm of my chair. "And if he doesn't." Nick makes a throat-slicing movement.

Mark laughs. Sort of.

"Nicky, please." Mariann points to an empty chair. Nick plops down beside me.

Nick and Matt have been on the couch in the corner listening and whispering, throughout the meeting.

"I think that's all we need," Mark says as he looks over his checklist.

Nick takes my hand and I force a smile. It hurts. I can only imagine how Matt feels.

"Great, I'll call you if I have any issues, but it all seems pretty standard." Mark stands and shakes my hand. "Welcome to Alexander

Investment Management, Danielle," he says. "Nick, nice to see you as always."

Nick stands and shakes his hand. "Do your thing, Money Mark."

Mark and Mariann start towards the door, then he stops. "One more thing, when is the wedding? Will I need to account for expenses?"

I stop breathing. Nick freezes beside me. Matt makes a grunting sound from the couch.

"They're planning on having a long engagement." Mariann ushers Mark out of the office.

I exhale. Nick rubs my back and moves away. I gather all of my papers and shove them in the envelope along with one thousand dollars in cash Mariann handed me in front of Mark. It's to hold me over until my bank card comes in. I wonder if this is from the bag of cash I gave her. It doesn't matter anymore, it's clean and accounted for.

Haley walks into the office with a cell phone in her hand. "Is Mariann in here?"

"She just walked Mark to the door," Nick tells her. "She's headed towards the foyer."

Haley twists her face in confusion. "Where is the fo-yay?"

Nick sighs and shakes his head. "Come on, I'll show you." He closes the door as he leaves.

I finally look at Matt. He hasn't said a word this entire time. He's standing near the window, looking into the night sky.

"I hate this," he says softly.

"Hate what?" I ask, even though I already know. I'm playing stupid because I want to talk about it. We used to talk all the time. Talking was our thing. Now we say as few words as possible.

He turns around with his hands in his pockets. His eyes find mine and he frowns.

"I hate that you're engaged to Nick."

Matt

"It isn't real," she says.

I turn back to the window and look at her reflection behind me. "We know that. The world doesn't."

Pretending Nick and Dani are engaged so Mariann can set up a trust, one the IRS won't get suspicious over makes sense. Not telling Mark the truth is understandable. If the IRS ever comes around asking questions, Mark will think their relationship is on the up and up. I get it.

But why the fuck did they take engagement photos? Did they really have to announce it in the newspaper? It's fake. It's all fucking fake.

It doesn't feel fake.

Nick had a lot of firsts with Dani. Being engaged to her was not something I thought he would add to the list.

"Mariann thinks it will only be six months to a year at most; then we can call it off," she says. "This is the only way I'll be able to use the money."

I've heard it all before. It doesn't change the sick feeling I get when I see Nick take her hand or kiss her cheek.

"We can't give the IRS any reason to investigate the trust." She stays on the other side of the room, clutching her paperwork. Like the paperwork is her salvation. "This is the only way."

"Yeah, I know," I sigh. "Can we just get out of here?"

She knows there is more behind my wanting to leave. She doesn't ask. I don't tell. I can't even admit it to myself. It's embarrassing. I'm not the eleven-year-old boy crying for my mom because she spent another night at the hospital with Ashely. I'm a fucking man now. I need to act like one. I grab my suit jacket from the back of the sofa. It's the same suit I wore to Arnie's funeral. I don't want to wear it to Ashley's.

Dani doesn't say anything as I walk past her. We live in a silent fear. Afraid one of us is about to drop the hammer. Say the thing we both know is inevitable. Being with Dani is so much harder than just being her friend. I'm responsible for her feelings, her well-being. Isn't that what I signed up for? What I fought for the day Nick used her as bait to bring down his uncle?

I told Nick he didn't deserve her. I thought I did. I don't know if that's true anymore. Dani isn't a prize to be won. She isn't an arm wrestling contest or a drag race. She's a person. A beautiful, sensitive person. Maybe that's it. Her fragility scares me. I don't want to break her.

This situation with Nick doesn't make things any easier. He's still part of her life. A very relevant part. He's also the only family I have right now. I don't know how Nick put up with me and Dani hanging out all the time. That's not true, I know how he did it. Thizz.

I'm not against dropping a pill every now and then to take the edge off. Dani isn't into it. Getting high reminds her of everything she lost. She blames thizz for her parents' murder. Will Walker was vying for power; that's why he hired her father to lose Devon's case. He needed Devon in jail so he could control the drug empire they built together. Now Devon's dead, and Will Walker is probably going to jail for life. Meanwhile, we're still living with the consequences of their actions.

Dani doesn't blame her father, but I do. He took a lot of money from people like Will, some worse than Will. If he were an honest man, Dani would have her parents. She would have the life she deserves.

I pull in front of Lucy's, and Dani asks me to stay the night.

"Yeah, right. Johnson will cut my dick off if I sleep with you in that house." I'm not trying to be dramatic. Johnson told me he would cut my dick off if I slept with Dani under his roof.

"You can sleep on the couch." She rests her head on my shoulder.

We don't get to spend many nights together. She lives in the city, and I'm in Santa Clara. We see each other a few times a week. My schedule is only going to get worse once I'm on a full class load. I'd love to fall asleep with her in my arms.

I kiss her head, and she looks at me with her big brown eyes. Out of habit, I watch to see if they ping-pong from side to side like a cartoon character on too much caffeine. They don't move. They just look tired. She looks tired. So am I.

"I love you," she says. The words still make me feel like the luckiest bastard on the planet. Why am I even debating on whether or not I should stay? Dani is the only reason I'm here. I could've gone to Colorado to see my family, but I stayed for her. She's been really stressed since we found the cash. She needs me, and I want to be here for her.

I pull the emergency brake and reach for the ignition. Holding her on the couch doesn't sound like a horrible way to fall asleep. I think Johnson will be cool with that. Clothes on, feet on the floor. I won't even use a blanket.

"If you don't want to stay here, maybe I can go back to Nick's with you. I've never slept at his house before." She sort of laughs.

The thought of her at Nick's makes my stomach burn. I release the brake and rev the engine. "No, I'll just see you tomorrow."

Her eyes narrow as I place my hands on the steering wheel. I wait for her to say something. To fight me. She doesn't.

"Ok," she says quietly and opens the door. She steps out with her paperwork secured in her left hand. "Goodnight, Matt."

I exhale and look at her. "I love you." I emphasize my statement with a smile. "Goodnight."

Dani closes the door with a little more force than needed, then stomps towards the house. I wait until she's inside before I take off.

This is so hard. It doesn't have to be. I could go back. Tell her I'm sorry. Explain why I'm being such a jerk. It isn't her. It's Ashely. My parents. It's the weak feeling I get when I see her and Nick in the same room.

My cell buzzes in the cup holder and I pick it up. It's Nick.

I answer on speaker phone. "What's up?"

"Duuude." Nick's voice is muffled, like he's cupping the receiver. "I'm in your room, and you are not here." He laughs and I hear something fall on the floor. "Oops. I hope you didn't need that lamp." He's high already.

"It's your lamp, Nick."

"Damn, you're right. Shit."

"I'll be there soon," I tell him as I blow through a yellow light.

23

"Matty, wait!" Nick yells. "Is Dani with you?"

My ears get hot at the excitement in his voice when he says her name. Or maybe it's just the fact that he's high and I'm not.

"No, I dropped her off at Lucy's." Thank God. I don't want her anywhere near Nick right now. "Meet you in the cottage?" Nick moved back to the main house; we use the cottage as a hangout when we're home from school.

"Yeah, hurry up man. I'm bored as fuck!"

I hang up and press the gas pedal to the floor. It's been months since I took a pill. Nick pulled me aside earlier tonight, right before dinner, and asked me if I wanted to pop. My first thought was hell yeah. Then I looked at Dani and pictured her and Nick together. Even though I wasn't high yet, it killed my buzz.

As much as I love Dani and I want to spend time with her, I really need this. Just a few hours with my best friend, not worrying about whether or not I make her happy.

Two hours later

We're lying on the floor, with our feet on the couch, having a serious discussion.

"Nah, man. My Chevelle would've walked on your Mustang!" Nick tosses a tennis ball at the wall. It bounces right back into his hand like a yo-yo. It's fucking magic. To the wall, to the hand. He never drops it. Nick never drops the ball.

I take a puff on the joint and pass it to Nick. "My Mustang is geared better and makes more torque." The ball flies out of Nick's hand, hits the wall, and hits me in the face. "Fuck, dude."

"Sorry." Nick laughs and hands the joint back.

"Where did you get the weed?" I ask. It isn't like he has a hook-up anymore. I can't really see Nick going to one of the dealers in town.

"Haley," he says and springs off the floor. He walks to the kitchen.

"Her uncle grows it, right?"

"Yeah," Nick says. "Don't bring him up around Haley. She doesn't really like the dude."

I remember the summer before sixth grade Haley's parents went to jail after a huge drug raid. She's lived with her uncle and grandmother on and off ever since. In all our conversations she's never had anything nice to say about her uncle.

"Haley said he sells to a co-op now." Nick tosses me a bottle of water. It lands on my stomach. It doesn't hurt. Nothing hurts right now. "It's pretty good shit, right?"

"It's alright." I sit up and place what's left of the joint on the table beside the couch. We both know it doesn't come close to the bud Will used to get.

"How much thizz do you have leftover?" I crack open the water and drown my insides.

The day Will was arrested, Nick told the cops all the drugs were packed in Will's duffel bag. It gave the cops no reason to search his place. Nick was fully cooperating in order to stay out of jail, they didn't suspect him of hiding a stash of pills. They wouldn't have found them anyway, because he buried the bag under a garden gnome.

"I still have a couple hundred." Nick sits on the couch and runs his hand through his hair. "It's fucking tempting, dude."

"What is?" I swish the water around my mouth and realize I need flavor. "Don't you have any beer?" I stand and go the kitchen.

"Selling the rest of it, just for fun," Nick says.

I walk back to the couch and hand him a beer. When I see the look on his face I realize he's serious. "You're fucking serious?"

"Yeah," he shrugs. "Don't you miss it?"

"No," I yell-snort. I can't control the volume of my speech when I'm thizzin'. "Are you seriously asking if I miss almost getting shot, or worse, busted?"

Yes, being arrested is scarier to me than being shot. If I get shot and die, that's it, I'm dead. If I were arrested, it would mean a life of hell. Even if I didn't do jail time, my record would be fucked. No law school. No career. No Dani. That is a fate worse than death.

"I mean the parties and shit." Nick stands up and sort of dances around the room. "I want that rush again. I want to walk into a room and have everyone high on my shit." Nick always got off on the glory. He lived for it.

And Arnie died for it.

"It won't be the same without him," I say. We don't say Arnie's name. It hurts too much. I even hate using his name to call Dani's dog. I usually just end up calling him dumbass. Which is ironic, since I also called Arnie the same thing.

Nick sits on the couch and takes a pull on his beer. "Yeah."

We watch the trees rustle outside the cottage. Each of us lost in our own fucked-up worlds for a few minutes. I wonder if Dani is asleep. I left my cell in the car on purpose. If I had it, I would call her. I would tell her every single feeling and thought I'm having right now. I want her here and I don't want her here. I just want to see her smile. Her face lights up, she fucking beams. I haven't seen her smile like that in months.

"Are you thinking about her?" Nick asks. I look at him and he shrugs. "I know the look, dude." He knows because he misses her, too. Being high without Dani sucks.

"She doesn't want to pop pills anymore," I tell him and take a pull on my beer.

"She told you that?" Nick questions.

"Yeah."

"When?"

"I don't know, right after everything." I try to recall the exact moment Dani said she didn't want to get high. I can't. Did she say it? Did I assume?

"Oh," Nick says.

I can tell from the way he said oh that he knows something. I nudge him with my elbow and give him a what-the-fuck look.

"She just said something to me last week," he shrugs. "She sounded like she wanted to get high." Nick glances at me, then to the open door. "So, you guys haven't dropped at all since you started going out?"

Nick is trying to ask me if I've had sex with Dani on thizz. I know why. He has. He knows what she feels like when your senses are on high alert. He's touched her, kissed her, he's done it all. I haven't.

"Have you ever been with her when you weren't high?" I sound like a dick. I don't care.

"Hmmm?" Nick contemplates my question. "We did it so many times, I really can't remember." He cracks a smile, and I feel like cracking him in the jaw.

"Fuck you, dude." I stand up and go to the bathroom. Thinking about Dani and Nick is making my heart race the way it does before something bad happens. I fill the sink, then dunk my head under the cold water, and try not to look in the mirror. I can't face myself right now.

Nick is on his phone when I return. He hangs up and shoves the phone in his pocket. He's trying not to smile and failing.

"What?" My high is starting to fade. It's midnight, I dropped my pill at nine. Nick probably took two to the face. Maybe even three. He's still up. Way up.

"You're welcome," he says and walks to the kitchen to throw his empty beer bottle in the trash. He walks around the room, picking up trash and rearranging shit, then pushes the coffee table back into place. Once the front room is back in order, he goes to the closet and pulls out a set of sheets. He sniffs them and grins at me.

I follow him into the bedroom. His king-size bed barely fits in this small space. Arnie used to joke about making the room wall to wall mattresses. He had big plans for our graduation night that included this room, whipped cream, and hot girls. I almost bring it up, then decide it's not the right time. Especially because Nick is obviously up to something. He pulls the blue-and-white striped comforter off the bed and tosses it on the floor. The sheets go next. I don't know why he's changing them; he hasn't slept out here in months.

"Do you have any idea what the fuck you're doing?" I pick up the clean plain white sheet and jump over the bed to help him. The space between the bed and wall is minimal, I barely fit.

"I can make a fucking bed," he says. "I'm just better at unmaking them." He throws a pillow at me. I pick it up, jump on the bed, and smack him across the face.

"Oh, it's on!" Nick grabs the other pillow and jumps on the bed feet first. Like a fucking ninja. "Let's see what you got, Matty."

28

Nick and I circle each other for a few minutes. I wait for Nick to make the first move. He always makes the first move. To my surprise, he just keeps circling and smiling. Finally, I go for it. I lunge, and he falls against the padded headboard. Wood cracks. I keep wailing on him with the pillow. Nick grabs me around my knees and takes me down. He tries to pin me using a move I taught him. He has no chance. I arch my back and twist my body. Before Nick can take his next breath, I've got him flipped over. We're both breathing heavy. I hold Nick by the neck, not too hard. I don't want to hurt him. Not really. I'm lying on my back, my arm wrapped around his neck as he's lying beside me, sort of in front of me. I feel his hand tap out at the same time the screen on the front door squeaks open and then slams shut.

Nick starts to laugh when Dani appears in the doorway.

She takes in the room. The comforter on the floor, the sheets askew. Nick in my arms. She's trying really hard to keep a straight face. "Am I interrupting something?"

"Just working out some aggression," Nick jokes and breaks free.

I want to ask what she's doing here, but I suspect Nick had everything to do with it. The phone call, changing the sheets, it makes sense now. That thoughtful motherfucker.

"I can come back later," she teases and breaks into a huge grin. Her face lights up. She only beams like this when she's high. There is only one person who could've given her pills.

Nick jumps off the bed and wraps Dani in his arms. He pulls back and kisses her on the forehead. Her eyes flutter closed, and all I can think is—karma is a bitch.

Dani

I never planned to take ecstasy again. But finding the money sent my anxiety levels into outer space. I can't concentrate. I can't eat. When I sleep, I dream. Bad dreams. I don't want to believe my father is the sleazy, money-driven asshole Will Walker says he is. The stacks of money I found hidden in our attic would beg to differ.

Last week I met Nick and Mariann for lunch. It was the start of our charade. If we want to pull this off, we have to start acting like we're together. Doing things publicly, like going to events, shopping for wedding dresses. All the things a normal couple would do. It's easy to pretend when Mariann is there. It's weird when it's just the two of us.

After lunch, Nick drove me home. He asked if he could hang out for a little while until traffic died down, so I invited him into my apartment. We were sitting on the couch, watching the fog roll down the street, and I said, "I really wish I had some thizz right now." I don't even know why I said it. Boredom, or just to make conversation.

When Nick reached into the front pocket of his jeans and pulled out a bag. I didn't realize how much I wanted it. Needed it. Until he dropped two pills in my hand. Neither of us said word. He just stood up and left.

I didn't tell Matt about the pills. I didn't hide them either. Matt was busy with school, we both were. When I packed for this weekend, I don't know why I brought the pills. Having them made me feel better. Holding them is like holding happiness.

After Matt dropped me off to an empty house, they were the first thing I thought about. I went straight to the attic and pulled the pills from the side pocket of my backpack. I placed them on the bed in front of me and stared at them. They looked just as harmless as they did the first night I took one with Nick. I never would've believed something so small would become so significant in my life.

I've been staring at these pills for over an hour. I've come up with twenty reasons not to take them, and only one reason I should. My life isn't as monotonous as it was four months ago. College is a lot more challenging than I anticipated. Popping a pill means three or four days of recovery. I have papers due, a test on Thursday. Taking this pill puts my future in jeopardy. And still, I want it. I want to have all the amazing feels again. This time with Matt.

I know in my heart that I care for him. I wanted him before thizz. He made my heart pound, my hands sweat, he was everything I ever wanted. A single smile would keep me high all day. I didn't know him then. He was just a crush, a stupid high school fantasy. The reality is a lot more complicated.

Matt and I don't seem to mesh. Meshing is important in a relationship. Meshing is everything. I want to mesh with Matt. We don't mesh as often as I did with Nick. Is it wrong to compare them? They are the only two men I've ever slept with. I have no other frame of reference.

My phone buzzes on the desk and I get up to answer it. The caller ID tells me it's Lucy.

31

"Hey, Lucy."

"Hey sweetie, we're going to stay the night at Johnson's old place. Will you be ok?"

Johnson still has his house in Arcata, the one his grandfather built. He's lived there his entire life. He can't let it go. I don't blame him.

"Yeah, I'll be fine." I pick up the pills. "I was just about to go to bed," I tell her as I walk downstairs to the kitchen.

I hear Lucy muffle the phone. "Is Matt with you?" she whispers.

I pull a glass from the cabinet and fill it with water before I answer. "No, he went back to Nick's." I place the pills in my mouth and take a gulp of water. "I can have him come back if that makes you feel better."

I know it will make me feel better.

"Just make sure he's gone before we get home in the morning, which reminds me," she pauses. "Raincheck on the shopping. The baby is really fussy. I think she's coming down with a cold."

I let out a silent yes and fist pump the air. "No problem, give her a kiss for me."

"I'll call you before we leave tomorrow just in case Matt makes a surprise appearance later tonight," Lucy teases.

"Goodnight, Lucy."

"Nighty-night."

I hang up and skip up the stairs, back to my room, and wait for the magic to happen.

I'm scribbling in my journal when my hand starts to tingle. I'm not gonna lie, I missed the fuck out of this feeling. I'm happy I took both pills because it makes this moment even more intense. I close my eyes and let my body drift into the euphoria. I feel everything. Every breath, every nerve, every tear.

Why am I crying?

I'm not really crying. My eyes are watering, like when I'm around a cat for too long.

My breathing hitches. Almost like a sob. I'm sobbing. It feels good. It's a good cry.

I put a CD into my boom box and hit play. It's a CD Nick gave me. I left it here on purpose. There was no room for it in my new life.

Hearing our song makes me miss him. Not being with him. Just the time we spent together.

Shut up, Dani.

I'm just being nostalgic. I don't want to be with Nick, but it's okay to remember the good times. Isn't it?

I could call him. No.

I should call my boyfriend.

Matt.

He's my boyfriend.

Holy fuck.

Why is that so funny? It is.

It's fucking hilarious.

"I'm with Matt. We're in love," I say to the room.

The room doesn't give a shit.

I'm so fucked up.

I'm so fucked.

I'm scribbling more nonsense in my journal when the phone rings. It's Nick. He shouldn't be calling this late. Only boyfriends call this late.

"Nick?" I distort my voice like I was sleeping.

"Hey girl, what are you doing?" The tone of his voice gives away his condition.

Even though I know telling Nick is probably a bad idea. I do it anyway. Thizz won't let me lie.

"I'm rollin so hard right now!" I laugh and jump off the bed to look out my window. How many times have I done that, looking for Nick?

His laughter explodes through the phone and I almost start to cry. Happy tears. Ecstasy is way better when you share it with someone, so when he tells me he's sending T to pick me up, I don't ask why. I say, "Okay, I'll be ready in ten minutes."

"Cool, see you soon," he says.

"Wait," I yell before he hangs up. "Matt?" Just saying his name makes me nervous. Not scared-nervous. Like, I-really-want-to-see-him-but-I-might-puke-and-cry nervous. "Is he? Did you both?"

"Yep."

This news makes me extremely happy. I hang up and run downstairs to brush my teeth. Why am I not surprised Matt is high? Why didn't we get high together?

Because we don't talk anymore.

We suck as a couple.

We can fix that tonight.

At Nick's house. Oh God.

I stand over the toilet, lift the seat, and puke.

I jump out of the SUV and run to the cottage. The first thing I hear is grunting, followed by laughter. I have no idea what I'm going to see when I walk through the door. I open the screen and let it slam behind me so they know I'm here. The room turns quiet. My head is spinning, my eyes are tweaking, my heart is kicking the inside of my chest as I walk into the bedroom.

Nick, Matt, a bare mattress. I don't know if I'm turned on or horrified.

Nick jumps off the bed and lands in front of me. The laugh waiting to escape my chest is muffled by his embrace. Even though it's only been a few hours since I saw him last, it feels like a lifetime ago. Maybe that's because I haven't seen this Nick in months. The thizz version of Nick. He buries his face in my neck; I feel his lips brush my skin before he lets me go.

"I fucking missed you," he whispers. He missed the thizz me.

"I know," I reply, and throw my arms around his neck for one more hug. Nick lifts me off the ground, and I look at the bed as Matt scrambles to his feet. I know that look. He's nervous. Surprised. My jaw tightens, and I remember that he didn't know I had pills.

Nick sets me down and steps aside.

"Hey Matt," I say, like he's just Nick's friend and not my boyfriend. We've never even talked about taking ecstasy. I just assumed that part of our lives was over.

He steps forward and hugs me. His lips find my forehead, and my body goes limp in his arms. Being kissed by Matt sets my body on fire. He trails kisses down the side of my face until he reaches my neck.

Chills line my arms, because my body has no idea how to react. I hear the bedroom door creak and then click shut. Matt resurfaces. He takes two backward steps and sits on the bed with me standing between his legs. This is real. I get to feel the way I feel and be with Matt.

Somebody slap me.

I look over his head at the bare mattress. The sheets are piled in the corner. "What happened to the bed?"

Matt looks back and says, "We were fucking around."

"Really?" I raise my eyebrow. I know he doesn't mean it in a sexual way, but it's fun to tease him. "I'm sorry I missed it."

Matt grabs my waist and pulls me on top of him. "Is that like a fantasy of yours?" His words don't have a playful tone. "You want to have me and Nick at the same time?" He sounds like he's accusing me, not teasing me.

"No." I push back, letting my contempt for his remark be known in the simple one-syllable word.

Matt ignores the waves of disdain flowing from every pore in my body and begins kissing my neck. "Take this off." He starts to unzip my hoodie.

I stand up and take it off in a very unsexy way. This doesn't mean I have forgotten about the cheeky attitude he was giving me a few seconds ago. I'm undressing because I want to.

I pull down the zipper and realize I'm wearing Nick's old Eureka High basketball shirt. I left it at Lucy's along with a bunch of other unwanted clothes. When I was changing tonight I pulled it out and put it on. Not for sentimental reasons. It's just really comfortable.

"Definitely, take that off." He starts to pull my shirt up.

"Is everything okay?" I ask him.

36

Matt huffs when I don't lift my arms. "I'm fine. I just don't want to fuck you while you're wearing his clothes."

His tone isn't friendly. He isn't even smiling. He doesn't look like he's having fun at all.

"You have no problem fucking me in his bed though," I snap and back away.

Matt sits up and rubs his hand over his face. He won't meet my eyes when he speaks. "Have you ever had sex with him in here?"

"No," I snap. I'm offended by the question, but I kind of understand. If Matt's parents hadn't sold their house, I might have had an issue sleeping in Matt's old bed, knowing he shared it with the cousins.

He looks at me, and I see nothing but pain and anguish in his eyes. Thizz is supposed to be fun. This isn't fun. "I don't mean in this bed. I mean in the cottage."

"Not that it matters, but no." I pick up my hoodie and put it back on. The room just got really cold. Matt contemplates my reply. Then he stands and starts to make the bed. I watch him for a moment before opening the door. He doesn't say a word when I leave.

I walk to the kitchen, and a chill runs down my back. The last time I was here, so was Will Walker. He isn't getting out of jail anytime soon. It doesn't stop me from feeling like someone is watching. I look out the front door, and through the screen I see movement. It's just the wind.

I move into the kitchen and open the refrigerator. It's stocked with drinks. Rows and rows of bottles and cans. Water, soda, beer, iced tea, and juice. I pluck a mango-flavored alcoholic beverage from the door, then search for a bottle opener. I open and slam drawers as I think about the tone of Matt's voice. The look on his face.

All those nights on the beach, in his room, on Nick's birthday when we had to hold back. The torture of having to refrain from acting on the feelings we can openly admit to having now. We're finally together, yet something is still keeping us apart.

I open and slam another drawer. I'm not even looking for the bottle opener anymore. I just want to slam things.

I keep my eyes on the door, waiting for Matt to appear. He doesn't. Suddenly, the screen creaks open and Nick peeks around the door.

He sees me and smiles. "Is it safe?"

I hold up my drink, and even though Matt just pissed me off, I smile. Nick made me smile. I'm so fucking confused. "I need a bottle opener."

Nick closes the front door and joins me in the kitchen. He opens the only drawer I didn't check and pulls out the opener. "Here you go," he says and pops it open. He tosses the cap in a jar with hundreds of others.

"What are you doing here?" We turn and see Matt's frustrated face glaring back at us from the bedroom.

Nick looks at me with an apologetic smile and then moves towards the front door. "I just realized that I left the front door open. I didn't want you guys to freeze to death, so I came back to lock up. I didn't think you'd be, uh, finished."

I choke on the sugary liquid when I realize what Nick is insinuating.

"Sorry, dude." Nick laughs as he realizes his comment is sort of a dis to Matt's love-making skills. "Shit, I've only been gone fifteen minutes." He looks at me and I start to laugh. Not because he's right. I laugh because he's so wrong.

Matt doesn't laugh. He doesn't move from the doorway. He's watching me and Nick. His eyes bounce between us. Words sit on the tip of his tongue. I want to hear them. I want him to tell me what I already know. If there is anytime I can take his rejection, it's right now with an abundance of serotonin flowing through my veins. It will make the pain bearable, at least for tonight.

"I think we need to talk," I say to Matt.

He narrows his eyes and gestures to the couch.

I walk to the sofa and sit down. Matt moves towards me, and Nick heads to the door.

"No," Matt says. "Stay."

Nick looks perplexed. "Why?"

"Because we'll both just tell you what happened later, so you might as well hear it firsthand." Matt sits beside me. "Do you care if he stays?" He finally looks at me. His eyes are weary, like he's ready to tell me what's been weighing him down.

I lean in and kiss him, because regardless of how this night ends, I love Matt. And right now kissing him is the most important thing in the world to me. I keep my eyes open. The moment our lips touch, his flutter closed. I need him to know that my feelings haven't changed, no matter how fucked up things have gotten.

His hand moves from the back of the sofa to my neck. He pulls me to him and kisses me again. His tongue slides against my lips. I part them and allow him inside. Something happens that I can't describe in words. My body starts to dissolve into Matt's. We are barely touching, but I feel him everywhere.

I climb onto his lap and take his face in my hands. I don't want this kiss to end. I want to feel his lips on me forever. This is my Matt.

He grabs my hips and holds me in place as he kisses down my neck. I moan. Matt moans. Then someone coughs.

"Sorry," Nick says and clears his throat. "I didn't mean to watch, but goddamn."

Matt places me on the couch beside him. "It's alright." He composes himself and picks up my drink. He downs half the bottle. "Just got carried away."

"I know," Nick says softly.

He sits on the other side of me.

Matt sort of smirks at Nick's comment.

"Is it weird?"

"A little." Nick rubs the back of his hand on the side of my thigh. I feel his warmth through my jeans. His eyes find mine and he says, "It hurts." I watch him swallow the emotion his eyes can't hide.

Although Matt can't see my face, he can see Nick's. He knows his eyes are locked on mine, so I look away. Nick picks up my drink and finishes it off.

Matt leans forward to look at Nick and runs his hand over his face. "Sorry, man."

"Don't be. I had my shot. I blew it." Nick stands up and rolls his neck. He turns around and regards Matt and me on his couch. "You guys look good together." He smiles. It's a legit smile.

Matt stands and tells Nick he loves him. They hug. A tear forms in the corner of my right eye. It's the leaky one. The one that always fills with water when I watch a sad movie or hear my father's favorite song. Now, as I watch the only two people I've ever loved hug it out, I can't keep the tear from slipping down my cheek. I sniffle and wipe it away.

"Ah man, you made her cry." Nick pushes Matt in the chest and reaches for me. I shake my head. I don't want to ruin their moment.

"Come here." Matt holds his hand out.

I shake my head again. Tears fall faster. I bury my face in my hands. I'm a horrible person. I'm every awful word you can say to a girl. I'm a dumb girl. A really dumb girl. I fell in love with best friends. What kind of idiot does that? I don't deserve either one of them.

Nick sits on my left side, and he puts his arm around me. "Hey, don't cry. I'm good."

Matt sits on my right side and rubs my thigh. "Come here," he says, and gently pulls me out of Nick's arms. He kisses my head. "I'm sorry I've been weird lately. It isn't you." I look at him because I want to see his eyes when he finally tells me the truth. "It's hard to be away from my family," he admits. "I feel like I'm missing time with Ashley. It's killing me."

This wasn't the truth I was expecting to hear. I know Matt misses his parents and Ashley, but I didn't think it was affecting him so strongly. This makes me feel even worse. I'm a selfish asshole. Of course I assume everything is about me.

"If you want to go see them, I'll cover your airfare." Nick reaches for Matt and pats his shoulder. "For both of you."

"Nah, man. It's cool." Matt hates taking handouts from Nick. "You've done enough."

Matt is referring to the house in Santa Clara. Nick was able to get a place close to campus for them to share. He covers the rent and all the utilities. Matt's on full financial aid, so he needs to save wherever he can. He still has the money Nick paid him from his cut of their last buy. I suspect most of that money came from Nick's trust.

41

Matt does too, but there is no use arguing about it. Nick will deny it. Since Matt doesn't have a job, that money is all he has to live on.

"I'm always here if you need anything, dude." Nick holds his palm up. Matt takes it and they do their handshake. It's cute. It makes me giggle.

"What's so funny?" Nick places his hand on my leg, threatening to squeeze. He knows it's my tickle spot.

"Nothing," I laugh and brace for him to apply pressure. When I feel nothing but the warmth of Nick's palm through my jeans; I realize he isn't trying to tickle me. He's just copping a feel.

"Are you touching my girl?" Matt asks with phony exasperation.

"I was thinking that maybe I could keep this area." Nick swirls his free hand over my thigh. "You don't need it, do you?"

I bite my lip to hold in the traitorous grin trying to escape. I'm not with Nick. That doesn't mean I don't find him attractive and I still care about him. Falling out of love with Nick has taken a lot longer than falling in love with him.

I slap Nick's hand away and shrug Matt's arm off my shoulders. "First of all, I'm not some piece of real estate you can divvy up for your own personal use. I'm a human. I say who gets what and when."

They look at each other, and silently agree on something. Nick and Matt have like a twin thing. They always know what the other is thinking.

"Ok," Matt says. "Who gets what?"

My heart jumps up and slams against my chest. The idea of having both of them makes me sweat. I unzip my hoodie, and Nick takes off his sweater. Matt looks at Nick like what the fuck?

"It's hot in here, dude." Nick tosses his sweater on the floor. He's excited, like a kid about to blow out his birthday candles.

Matt doesn't look as enthusiastic, but I can tell he's intrigued. I like having their undivided attention. I'm going to take full advantage.

"You guys are the only two people I've ever had sex with," I say, just to gauge their reaction.

"Good," they say. At the same time.

We laugh.

"You know I have to ask," Nick says.

Matt covers his face with his hand. "Don't do it, dude."

"What?" I ask, confused.

"Maybe I shouldn't," Nick reconsiders.

Matt leans forward to look around me and says, "You shouldn't."

"What the fuck are you guys talking about?" I move from the couch and sit on the table in front of them. I need to see both their faces at the same time.

Matt explains that Nick was going to ask which one of them was better at sex. I suck in a breath and choke on my spit. I haven't had sex with Matt on thizz. I haven't had sex with Nick sober. They're even.

"You're even."

They smirk at the same time. The same way, because they really are the same in every way. This makes me laugh so hard I cry. They think I'm crazy. I probably am. I'm sitting between the two people I promised myself I'd never come between again. One little pill, and here we are. Okay, two pills.

I stop laughing and sigh. Then I decide to ask Matt the question I've been holding in for weeks. I take his hand. He threads his fingers through mine.

"Are you happy with me?" The smile drops from his face. He wasn't ready for me to hit him with something his heavy. "I mean, are you happy with us? Is it what you thought it would be?"

Matt contemplates my question. He doesn't just spit out the expected answer. I don't know how that makes me feel. Nick sits back and waits for Matt to answer too.

"I'm happy that we're together," he says. "I love you more than you even know. The timing just sucks."

It feels like someone just drop-kicked my heart. "What does that mean?" I ask quietly. Quiet voice is the only thing I have right now. Anything louder than a whisper will be a scream.

"I feel like I abandoned my family," he says. "We don't know how long—" his voice cracks.

"Dude, it's okay," Nick says so Matt doesn't have to finish. "It sucks being away and it's making it hard to appreciate what you have." Nick looks up at me and says, "We get it."

I nod in agreement, but my heart is breaking.

"It doesn't mean I don't want you, Dani. I do. But my head is fucked up right now."

I hear Matt saying he misses his family. He is saying he wants to spend time with Ashley. How does this affect our relationship? Our life together? Our future?

"It's the holidays, man. They fuck with everyone," Nick interjects. He stands up and walks to the kitchen. He rummages in the refrigerator, comes back, and hands Matt a beer.

"We'll all go visit at Christmas." Nick rubs my leg and raises his eyebrow for me to say something.

"Yeah, it'll be great," I mumble. I know a visit isn't what Matt needs.

Matt smiles and thanks Nick. "Alright, dude." He pulls me back onto the couch between them and holds me in the crook of his arm. "We can show Dani how awesome we are on a snowboard."

"Hell yeah!" Nick springs from the couch and starts bouncing around at the idea of snowboarding in Colorado.

I get a little excited too. "I'm pretty good, you know." I stand up to walk to the kitchen for a drink since Nick didn't bother to get me a beer.

I push past Nick, and he pulls me into his arms. My hands go around his neck out of habit. Hugging Nick feels like the most natural thing in the world. Like riding a bike. He lifts me over his shoulder and grunts like a caveman.

"Hey!" I yell, and he sets me down.

"I was about to carry you into the bedroom until I remembered you weren't mine anymore," he admits with a sad look in his eye.

"I'm still your friend." I wrap my arms around his torso and hug him. "Actually, I'm your fake fiancée."

"That's right!" Nick exclaims. "In that case, let's go." He pulls me towards the bedroom a few steps. We look at Matt, and he just sits back and takes a pull on his beer. "You're not going to stop me?"

"Did you ever stop me?" Matt replies.

Heat rushes to my ears. Nothing happened between us when I was with Nick. We flirted, we hung out, that's it. Matt doesn't owe Nick anything.

Nick squeezes my hand. "I should have." His hazel eyes find mine. "I never should've let her go." He lifts my hand to his mouth and kisses my knuckles.

The honesty flowing through the room freaks me out. I slip my hand free and return to the couch where I belong.

Matt takes my hand as I sit down and turns to face me. His expression makes my stomach hurt. I can tell he's about to drop some seriousness on me.

"Do you want to sleep with Nick?" There is no emotion in his words. He's not angry or hurt. Just curious. I'm appalled.

"Dude," Nick protests.

"Let her answer." Matt doesn't break eye contact with me.

I look at Nick; he shakes his head ever so slightly. He wants me to say no, even if that's not the answer I want to give. Luckily, Nick and I are on the same page.

I take Matt's beer off the table and drink it. It's disgusting, but my mouth has turned abnormally dry. I place the can back on the table and turn to Matt. His eyes narrow. Doubt starts to creep onto his face. He expects me to choose him. He wouldn't have asked otherwise. You shouldn't ask questions if you aren't prepared for the answer. I already know what I'm going to say, I just want to drag it out a little. The tease gives me a rush like you wouldn't believe.

"If I say I want to be with Nick, what would you do?" I test him. A fresh set of tingles washes over my body at the thought of walking into that bedroom with Nick. It's just a thought, nothing more.

"I'd leave so you can be together."

He's testing me. Maybe he's getting off on the rush too.

"It's that easy for you?"

"Hell, no." He smirks. "But I don't want to stop you from being with the man you really love."

The slut in me grins. "This has nothing to do with love."

Matt's eyes flit to Nick, then back to me. "Do you love her, Nick?"

"Dude," Nick says.

"Answer the question," Matt demands.

"Why are you doing this?" I ask. "I was joking."

Matt ignores me. "Nick, are you still in love with Dani?"

Nick sighs, and although I'm not looking at him, I know he's running his hand through his hair. I know him. I know them both. "I'll always love her, man. But she's yours."

Matt looks up with a fierceness that burns through me. His glare makes my chest ache. "If she weren't mine?"

I don't say a word. I deserve this. I asked the question.

"You already know," Nick says.

Matt nods. "Tell her."

Their banter has me curious now. I turn and look at Nick.

"No," Nick answers quickly. "If you want her to know so bad, you tell her." He leans in the doorway to the bedroom. He isn't plotting anything; he's just keeping his distance.

"The day we found the chest," Matt starts, "Nick told me he wouldn't fight to get you back. Not until I had my shot. He said if I blew it, if I couldn't be the man you needed, he would be."

I look back at Nick, he's wearing the saddest smile I've ever seen. As much as I love and care for Nick, if Matt and I broke up, I wouldn't go running back to him. It perturbs me that they assume I would.

"I love you, Nick." I smile at him, and his eyes smile back. I feel Matt's hand slide from my leg. I turn back to Matt and look into his crystal-blue eyes. I place my hand on the side of his face and kiss him softly. "You are the only man I need. I don't want anyone but you."

The grin on Matt's face lights up the room.

I don't realize that I've just gutted Nick until I hear the front door open and close.

Matt

Christmas Eve 2006

Nick and Dani decided not to come to Colorado with me. Nick doesn't want to leave Mariann alone, and Dani doesn't want to miss Marguerite's first Christmas. It's for the best. I just want to spend time with my family. I don't want to entertain Nick and Dani. I sure as hell don't want them to entertain each other.

Ever since Thanksgiving, me and Dani have been good. So good. I think we both needed a healthy dose of honesty. It worries me that we needed a pill to sort things out. We didn't stop that night. We've done it twice since then.

Nick has been distant. He doesn't tag along as often when I go to the city. In the back of his mind, he probably thought he'd have Dani again. Part of me thought he would too. I know now that she wants me. Just me.

They still have to play pretend engagement. Mariann has them attending events with her so they're seen in public. Anything to legitimize their relationship. The more pictures and memories they make, the better. Dani hasn't heard from the IRS. No news is good news.

I walk off the plane and through the Denver airport. It's Christmas Eve, so the terminal is crowded. I switch my phone on, and it rings immediately. I love that it's Dani.

"Hey babe, I just walked off the plane," I tell her as I grip my carry-on and follow the signs to ground transportation.

"I just wanted to hear your voice," she says.

"I'm really glad you called, but I can't talk and walk right now." I sidestep a lady with a luggage cart stacked with presents. "I'll call you when I get to my parents' house." It's their house. I don't have a house. I live with Nick at school. I stay at the Marino estate when I'm in Eureka. I crash with Dani in the city. I am homeless.

"Give Ashley a hug for me," she says.

"I will. Bye." I hang up and shove my phone in the pocket of my ski jacket. I don't plan on hitting the slopes, but it's the only thing I have to combat the Denver cold.

My parents are waiting on their front lawn when the taxi pulls to a stop. It's a modest single-story house with a two-car garage. The last time I spoke to Ashley, she said Mom was repainting the room they saved for me. The blue wasn't quite the same color as my old room. It's the third time she's painted it since they moved in.

Mom runs to the cab as I get out. She hugs me for a long time. The longest anyone has ever held me. I watch my dad pay the driver as he takes my bag out of the trunk. The taxi leaves, and my mom finally lets go.

"Hi Dad," I say, and he gives me a brief but firm dad hug. "Where is Ashley?" I look towards the front door.

"She's at the hospital." Mom walks towards the house. "I promised her we'd head over after dinner."

I don't want to wait until after dinner. She's the reason I'm not with Dani. The guilt I carry for not being here with my sister is killing me. I can't enjoy my life knowing hers may be ending. "I ate on the plane," I lie. "I want to see her now."

This hospital is like every other she's been in. Cold and antiseptic. No matter how many colorful decorations they hang, it will still be a place where people die. I don't make eye contact with anyone in the halls or elevator. I can't stand to see pain on the faces of strangers. The least I can do is give them a tiny bit of privacy.

We pause at a door. My mom looks at me like she wants to say something, then changes her mind. A warning, I think. So, I brace myself before I walk inside.

Ashley is thin. Really thin. Scary thin. She's lost all her hair. She looks like she's dying.

"Matty," she says softly and forces a huge smile. "You made it."

I walk to my sister's bed with a smile so painful I feel like I need the morphine pumping into her arm. I lean in and hug her. She smells of sweat and lemongrass. I look on the nightstand and see my mother is burning oils again. Ashley told me once that she hates them, but she lets Mom think they help.

"I brought this for you." I pull a black San Francisco Giants beanie from my pocket. I place it over her bald head. "You gotta represent."

Mom makes an adjustment to the beanie. "You look great, honey."

"I look like shit," Ashley replies. "But I love the hat, Matt. Thank you." She reaches for me, and I lean down so she can kiss my cheek.

My parents leave so I can visit with Ashley alone. As soon as they walk out of the room, she asks about Dani.

"So, you guys are like, officially a couple? Like boyfriend and girlfriend."

"Yes." I smile. "We hold hands at the movies and everything."

Ashely laughs, but it looks like it hurts. Not just the pain in her bones. My sister doesn't think she'll ever find someone to hold her hand at the movies. Her biggest fear is dying before she has a chance to fall in love. I always thought it was so lame. Such a girly thing to want. I get it now.

"Are you okay?" I stand up and check her IV. I have no clue what I'm looking at.

Her eyes close, and she takes a deep breath. She presses the button on a little trigger that dispenses her pain medicine. "I'll be okay." She smiles, and I know it's just for my benefit, because there is nothing in my little sister's life to smile about.

I only visit with her for fifteen minutes before she falls asleep. I sit in the chair beside her bed and start to cry. This isn't something anyone should have to watch or go through alone. I want to be here for her, for my parents.

My mom walks in and takes me to the cafeteria. I don't speak as I walk down the hall. The people I pass take one look at me and turn away to allow me to grieve without an audience. It's a common courtesy.

I sit down while Mom gets our coffee. She places a white paper cup on the table in front of me and takes the seat opposite from mine.

"She looks bad, Mom." I try not to get choked up.

Mom rubs my hand and tells me she's getting better. "You missed the worst of it. We didn't want to worry you during your first semester of school."

They're still keeping me in the dark. I'm old enough to handle the truth. "So, the treatment is working."

"Yes, she's responding well. When you come back for spring break, she'll be her old self." Mom smiles confidently. If my mother believes Ashley will get better, that gives me a little hope. My mom never lies.

I can read people fairly well. It's one of the reasons my dad knows I'll be a good lawyer. I can see through bullshit. It's how I know Dani isn't lying about loving me. Or the fact that Nick still wants her.

"Do you have any plans for your birthday yet?" Mom asks. A group of nurses waves at her as they exit the cafeteria. She knows everyone here, just like she did back home.

I haven't given my birthday any thought. It isn't until March. "No." I sip the shitty hospital coffee and think of Dani. She's staying with Lucy until after New Year's. I wonder if she'll see Nick. He's steered clear of her since Thanksgiving, but now that I'm not around, she might feel comfortable hanging out with him. It's a crappy thing to think, especially right now. Ashley should be my main concern.

"Well, you know we'd love to spend it with you." Mom stands up and tosses her cup in the trash. "Come on, let's go home and get some dinner. It's Christmas Eve."

"I don't want to leave her alone." I stare at my hands. "There's a couch in her room."

Mom kisses the top of my head. "Okay." She gets it. There was a time when she didn't leave the hospital for weeks. She refused to let my sister spend a single second alone. She didn't want Ash to feel abandoned. I hated her for it.

My parents didn't leave me. They came here for Ashley's treatment. But I can't shake the feeling of being left behind. I feel like an eleven-year-old kid again. They have a house, jobs, cars, a lawn, they have a life here. A life that I'm not part of. I want to be. I want to be part of this family.

 Dani

December 31st, 2006

I roll over and check the clock. It's two 2:28 in the morning. The baby is screaming. Again. I pull a pillow over my head and moan. She has a fever or a stomachache or both. She's on hour four of non-stop crying. I'm fully awake, and now I have to pee.

I bump into Johnson in the hall. He's a zombie.

"Sorry," he grunts as he walks toward the baby's room with a bottle in his hand.

"What's that for?" I point at the bottle. "I thought Lucy said the nipple would confuse her?"

"She's desperate," Johnson says without any further explanation. Lucy's been storing breastmilk for emergencies. Like her boobs are going to go out of service or something. This would definitely be considered an emergency.

I use the bathroom then head down to the living room. Maybe a little distance between me and the screaming will help. The baby's room is right below the attic; her wailing travels through the floor right into my ear.

As soon as I settle on the couch, the baby quiets. The bottle must have worked. Great. This is going to kill Lucy's mommy-self-esteem. My eyes close. The heaviness of sleep starts to overcome me, then BAM! Loud angry baby strikes again.

I can't stay here.

Nick pulls up in the SUV. I jump off the porch and run to the truck. The heater is on full blast.

"Thank God!" I place my hands in front of the vent to thaw out.

"Why are you waiting outside?" Nick asks as he pulls away from the curb.

"I'll take my chances with frostbite over spending another second in that horror show."

Nick looks at me for a second then turns back to the road.

I realize he is checking to see if I'm high. "What?"

"Nothing," he says. He focuses on driving back to his place.

"I'm not thizzin," I tell him. "You can just ask. I have nothing to hide from you."

Nick scoffs. "True. But old habits and all that."

I know all about old habits. There is something about Eureka, because ever since I stepped foot in Humboldt County, I've wanted to get high.

"Are you hungry?" Nick asks as we pass the twenty-four-hour diner.

"No, I'm good."

"Thirsty?"

I smile into the darkness. "Nope."

"Is there anything you might want before going to bed?"

I just laugh as Nick hits play on the stereo, and our song comes on. I reach over and turn it off. I look at him, and he smiles his Nick Marino smile.

"You know I'm playin', right?" Nick turns onto the private road leading to his house. The last time we drove on this road, in this SUV, he was taking me to Will Walker. He was using me to get his uncle to confess to killing my parents. Those memories are never far from my mind.

"You're just being Nick. Only now your charm doesn't work on me."

Nick laughs like he doesn't believe me, then he says, "I would never disrespect Matt. Or you." The serious tone in his voice is sweet. As much as he tries to convince everyone he's an arrogant asshole, I know better.

I place my hand on his shoulder and say, "I totally trust you. I wouldn't have called if I didn't."

"I'm glad someone has faith in me." He raises his eyebrow, and I sock him in the arm.

Nick puts the SUV in park then jumps out to open the back gate. We usually go through the front, but I guess Nick doesn't want to wake T at this hour. Nick gets back in the truck and pulls inside.

"I'll lock it up later." He drives to the back of the house and parks near the path that leads to the cottage.

I look at the trees rustling softly against the night sky. It's a silent sway. I don't hear anything except the soft hum of the engine, and the sound of Will's voice in my head.

Your daddy took a job, and he didn't come through...

"Do you think about that day?" he asks.

I look at Nick; his eyes are focused on the darkness in front of us. I realize he's just as traumatized as I am. "Yes."

"Me too. Every time I use that gate." Nick cuts the engine and opens his door.

For some reason, his confession soothes me. It's nice to know I'm not the only one still affected by what happened. We both lost our parents, and we were both hurt by Will Walker. Nick and I may not ever be together again, but we're connected in ways that will never be broken.

As we approach the cottage, I turn to go inside, and Nick keeps walking.

"Where you going?" he asks.

"Let's go in here," I suggest. I don't really want anyone to know Nick picked me up in the middle of the night.

"Are you sure?" Nick looks a bit apprehensive.

"Yeah, come on. I'm freezing." I pretend it's not a big deal. If I don't make it an issue, then we can pretend hanging out alone in the middle of the night is totally okay.

Nick unlocks the door and turns on the light. As he adjusts the thermostat on the wall, I go to the bedroom and take the comforter off the bed. I drag it into the main room, and Nick starts to pace.

"Just come up to the house, you can stay in Matt's room." He walks from the wall to the front door. "Come on, you're gonna freeze in here."

"Once it warms up I'll be fine." I sit on the couch and pull the comforter over me.

"At least let me stay with you. I'll crash out here and you can take the bedroom."

"I'll be okay. I just want some peace and quiet."

"The house is quiet," he argues.

I kick my Vans off and tuck my feet beneath the comforter.

"Matt is going to freak if he finds out I let you sleep here alone."

He's right. I don't want him to think I ran over here to be with Nick the first chance I got.

Nick and I decided to let him go to Colorado alone so he could spend quality time with his family not so I could sneak over here in the middle of the night.

Nick's phone rings, and he pulls it out of his pocket. He checks the caller ID and holds it up for me to see.

"It's Matt." His voice raises an octave and he runs his hand through his hair. "What should I tell him?"

For a split second I think he knows I'm here, then something even worse crosses my mind.

"He wouldn't call this late for nothing." My pulse races as Nick realizes I'm right. Our thoughts turn to Ashley. "Answer it."

"What's up, Matty?" Nick says. "Is everything okay?" I watch Nick closely, waiting for any sign that something horrible has happened. Just a few seconds pass and he gives me a thumbs up. "Nah, I wasn't asleep." Nick laughs at something then says, "No, actually, um. Dani called." He pauses and listens to whatever Matt is saying. "She couldn't sleep—"

Nick listens for a long while without saying a word. Then he walks into the bedroom and speaks low into the phone.

I strain to listen to the one-sided conversation. The only word I catch is goodbye. Nick comes back in the room and sits near my feet. He runs his hand through his hair.

"How is he?" I ask.

"He's good." He shrugs. "Just wanted to remind me to pick him up from the airport."

"You're such a liar." I check the time. "Why isn't he sleeping?"

"Why aren't you?" Nick counters.

"A crying infant."

"Matt's going through some shit. He's good though. For real." Nick feels for my foot under the comforter. I pull it away. He smirks and takes his hands off the blanket. "Sorry. Habit."

"That isn't habit. I've never slept on your couch before."

"You should have," he says. "I should've brought you here when we were going out. I was just, I don't know, fucked up back then. I thought I was protecting you, but I treated you like a side chick."

"You did not," I laugh. "You were a great boyfriend." I stop myself from saying anything else.

He places his arm on the back of the couch. "Not good enough."

I don't want to talk about us. I switch the subject back to Matt. "Did he say anything about Ash?"

"Yeah, he said she looks really bad, but they say she's going to make it."

"That's good news." I haven't spoken to him all day. He promised to call before he went to sleep. When he didn't, I figured he was busy with his family. "Did you tell him I was here?"

"No. I didn't get a chance." Nick runs his hand through his hair. "Is that bad?" The question is rhetorical.

"Just tell him I was asleep."

"I should've told him you were here." Nick lets his head fall back and hit the wall. "I fucked up."

"Then we won't tell him." I sit up and look at Nick. He opens one eye. "He doesn't need to know. Nobody does. I'll stay here and you can drive me home in the morning before you go to the airport."

Nick mulls it over for a minute. Then he says, "Okay, but I'm staying here with you."

I hold out my pinky, and Nick loops his with mine.

"Deal," I say.

"Deal."

New Year's Eve, 2006

I yawn as I walk out of the terminal at SFO and into the chilly mid-morning air. I spot Nick waiting at the curb. As I approach the SUV, I hear music bumping through the rear speakers. I open the passenger door and hop in.

"What's up, dude?" He holds his hand out, and we do our handshake.

"I hate flying," I tell him as he cranks the stereo during the rise of "Lucky Go Leah." My ears ring. Flying always gives me a headache. "Are you ever gonna get sick of Audiodub?"

"Fuck no! They rule, dude." Nick pulls away from the curb and heads towards the highway. I didn't expect him to say yes. Dani loves Audiodub too. Even though they discovered the band before they knew each other, it's something they share. They will always have Audiodub.

"How's the fam?" Nick asks as he pulls onto Highway 101 North. "What's Colorado like?"

"Cold as fuck. My parents are good. They say Ashley is going to pull through, but she looks really sick this time. I don't think I can handle it if something goes wrong and I wasn't there." Nick is the only one who knows what I've been contemplating. It isn't something I even want to admit. Stanford has always been my dream. Not to mention Dani. I have everything I've ever wanted, and I'm ready to walk away because I miss my sister. My family. What kind of man does something like that?

"You're a plane ride away, Matty. If something bad happens, Mariann will let you use the jet. You know that, right?" Nick steals glances my way as he drives. He's so fucking loyal it makes me feel like an asshole.

"So, what's the plan tonight?" I change the subject to the annual Marino New Year's Eve party. I'm tired of the pity party I've been throwing myself the last few days.

"The usual suspects. Business contacts, a bunch of Mariann's friends, and basically anyone who decides to show up. Mariann has that open door policy on New Year's Eve. Anyone from town is invited."

"That's pretty cool," I admit. "How come we never went to one of these parties before?"

"Cause we weren't interested in hanging out with a bunch of old people." Nick laughs. "If we were smart we, would've at least gone for the free booze."

I think about how we spent last New Year's Eve: smoking weed and drinking at a house party. That was the last day Dani spent with her parents. They were murdered the next day by Nick's uncle. I wonder how she is holding up.

"Have you talked to Dani today?" I ask in an it's-not-a-big-deal kind of way.

"What?" Nick clears his throat. He lifts his hand to run it through his hair then stops himself and adjusts the rearview mirror instead. He's hiding something.

"Did you talk to Dani?"

"Oh, um yeah, for a second this morning. She woke me up and made sure I wasn't late to come get you." He turns on the air-conditioning. "Is it warm in here?"

"No, it's freezing." I flip the vent in front of me closed. "You know her parents died on New Year's Day, right?"

Nick nods his head and runs his hand through his hair. "Yeah, man. I know. How could I forget?"

The tension in the car turns thick. I don't know if it's because I brought up Will, or because Nick has something to hide.

"Did she ask you for a hook-up to like, help her through the day?" I watch all of Nick's mannerisms closely. I don't think he'd lie to me, but Dani might have asked him not to tell. I lied for her all the time when they were dating.

"Nah, man. She didn't ask," Nick says. "And if she did, I'd tell you. For real. I would've told you about the pills I gave her before. I didn't think it was a big deal. That's why I gave her two. One for both of you."

I believe Nick. He wouldn't go behind my back. I'm the douchebag who fed his girlfriend pills. I'm the one who can't be trusted. I didn't fight for her. I didn't even admit I liked her. I let Dani fall in love with him instead of me. I was wrong. I was the one who didn't deserve her, not Nick. I'm the loser.

"For the record," Nick states, "I would never give her pills again without telling you."

"Thanks, Nick," I say and hold my hand out. He shakes it to solidify his statement. If there is anyone I trust with Dani, it's him. The insecurities I feel when they're together are my issues. Nick has never given me any reason to distrust him.

It's one hour until midnight. I just spoke to my parents in Colorado. Ashley made it until eleven-fifteen then fell asleep. I walk into the main room to rejoin the party and look for Dani. I've barely spent time with her or Nick in the last two hours. The JM Developers lead council has been talking my ear off. He offered me an internship in their Fort Collins, Colorado office this summer. I'm sure I have Nick to thank. It's a shit position, mail room and filing, but it's something. The guy's name is Jim Jameson. He's here with his second wife, and he's currently divorcing his third. He called it wife recycling. He's kind of a douche.

"It's been twenty minutes, have you made your decision yet?" Jim says as I walk past him towards Nick and Dani.

"Still thinking about it." I point at him like I'm a douche too, and keep moving. I can't help but think I'll be dealing with guys like him for the rest of my life.

Nick and Dani have been sitting at a table in the corner near the bay windows for the last hour. Haley drifted in and out of their conversation. She was trying to coax them to dance, at Mariann's request. She's been working the room all night, looking for volunteers to join her on the dance floor. Yes, there is an actual dance floor laid down just for tonight. The doors between this room and the formal living room are open making it one large space. The furniture has been replaced with pieces you would see in a fancy lounge or night club. A black curtain has been hung to hide the fireplace. The bar has been set up in front of it. Flickering lights bounce off the curtain behind the bar to give the room a snowy effect. I can hardly tell this is the same room we gathered in for Thanksgiving.

"Matty," Dani yells when she sees me. "Did you bring me a new glass?" She holds up her empty wine glass. She's been drinking white wine all night. It's her new favorite thing.

"I forgot," I lie. I don't want her to drink anymore.

She makes a pouty face and spins on her stool towards Nick. "Will you get me more wine?"

I watch his eyes drift from her eyes to her mouth and back. It's a quick look, but nothing gets past me where Dani is concerned. Nick smiles his perfect smile and slides off his stool with her empty glass in his hand.

"You want something, Matty?" he asks as he brushes past me.

I shake my head and say, "She's had enough."

"What!" Dani says way louder than she needs to. "You aren't the boss of me," she slurs. "I want one more glass, then we move on to something stronger." She winks with half her face.

Nick smiles at her then turns to me. "She wants to pop a pill. Are you cool with that?"

Something tightens in my chest. Fuck no. I don't want Dani to discuss popping pills with Nick. I can't say what I feel out loud. At least not here. Dani will blow up if I say no. "Let's get her out of here." I take the empty glass from Nick and place it on the table.

"We can't go until after midnight," Nick says. "It's only forty-five minutes, we'll keep her happy until then."

We will keep her happy, he says. Like it takes both of us to make Dani happy. I don't know where this bitterness is coming from. It's me. Yesterday I was eating cheeseburgers with my family around Ashley's hospital bed. I was really happy there. I left them because I missed Dani. Now that I'm here, I feel like I should be there.

Nick leaves to get Dani a glass of wine and a bottle of water. I sit beside her and stare into the black window in front of us. You can't really see beyond the darkness. The window is a reflection of the party happening inside. I see Nick stop in front of Haley and take her to the dance floor. The DJ is playing an old Motown song. A lot of people get up and dance. Dani and I remain in the corner.

"I missed you," she slurs and leans towards me. Her head rests on my shoulder, and she runs her hand down my back. She slips it under my sweater and scrapes her nails against my skin.

Nick and I are wearing almost the exact same thing. A white t-shirt under a black V-neck sweater, except Nick's sweater has a gray stripe wrapped around his chest. We have on the same Calvin Klein jeans and white Nikes. Dani drags her nails across my back, and I wonder if she did the same thing to Nick.

My mind is playing dirty tricks on me. Nick isn't after Dani.

"You look beautiful," I tell her. "I love that dress on you." I kiss her head and put my arm around her bare shoulders.

"Thanks." She sits up. "Mariann bought it for me." She looks at her chest and makes some adjustments. "I had to pose for the formal picture." She shrugs.

I think about the Marino family picture hanging above the table in the foyer. It's updated every few years. Mariann included Dani to reinforce the lie we're all living. Dani has become part of Nick's family, and there is nothing I can do about it. Her heart is mine, but the world thinks she belongs to Nick. Nothing has changed.

"Are you okay?" she asks.

I wipe the scowl from my face and lie. "Yeah, I'm good. Just thinking about taking that dress off of you later."

Dani giggles and leans in for a kiss. It's a sloppy drunk thing that makes me pull back.

"Stop, we can't do that here," I remind her.

"You like that, don't you?"

"Like what?" I look at her cleavage and smile.

"You like that we still have to sneak around. Does it turn you on?" She tries to kiss me again, but it's more for show than pleasure. She leans too far over and slips off her chair.

I grab her wrist to keep her from falling on the floor. "You're wasted."

"That never stopped you before," she snaps.

"Why are you acting like this?"

"Why are you?"

I almost say I'm normal, but that would be a lie.

Nick returns with Haley. "Let's go dance," he says. When he sees the look on my face, he tells Haley to take Dani to the bathroom. Neither girl protests.

"What's up, man?" Nick asks.

"I'm tired. Time change and shit." Colorado is only one hour ahead of California, but Nick probably doesn't know that.

"We only have thirty minutes, then we're out." Nick checks his watch. "If you don't want to party later, that's cool. You guys can still have the cottage." Nick socks me in the arm.

The cottage was a bust last time me and Dani used it. When we finally got down to having sex, we were both crashing. I fell asleep in the middle of it. It was bad. As far as Nick knows, we had mind-blowing thizz sex all night. Porn-level shit.

"Thanks, man." I pull Nick in for a bro hug. "What's up with you and Haley?" I ask when I see her practically carrying Dani back to the table.

"I don't know, could get freaky later." Nick smirks.

"Mariann is okay with you screwing the help?"

Nick laughs. "The help has never looked this good."

At midnight we join the rest of the guests on the dance floor for the countdown. Dani is standing between me and Nick. Technically, they're together, so he kisses her first. Just a friendly peck on the cheek. Dani turns to me half a second later and throws her arms around me.

"I love you, Matt," she slurs in my ear and kisses my neck.

I can't kiss her, not in front of all of these people. As far as the world is concerned, Dani and Nick are in love.

Nick taps my shoulder and we break apart. "Let's get out of here."

Dani's face lights up. "Yes!" she cheers.

Nick and Dani walk around the room, hand in hand, saying goodnight to the guests. I wait for them by the door. When they're finished working the room, we head to the cottage, and Nick tells us he's meeting Haley in an hour.

"You're going to fuck Haley tonight?" Dani inquires.

Nick runs his hand through his hair. "Maybe," he says like it's a challenge. "What are you going to do about it?"

"Nothing!" Dani's voice echoes into the courtyard.

69

"Shhh!" Nick wraps his arm around her neck and covers Dani's mouth. She laughs and tries to wriggle out of his arms. Her heels don't help her balance, so she just leans further into Nick.

I hate that he's touching her mouth. "You don't have to walk us," I tell Nick and pull Dani towards me. "We know the way."

"I know," Nick says and lets Dani go. "I need to get some shit." He raises his eyebrow at me.

I can't see Dani's face, but I know she's smiling. Thizz always makes her smile.

We get to the cottage, and Nick unlocks the door. He flips the light on and goes straight to his stash hidden under the stove. Dani leans on the counter and watches Nick pull it free. She taps her nails against the granite in nervous anticipation. I don't know a single person who looks forward to a shot of tequila with the same enthusiasm as popping a pill.

The few moments before you put the pill in your mouth are almost as thrilling as when the drug hits. It's like being next in line for a roller coaster. Only this ride lasts for hours. Sharing the feeling with someone you love, well, nothing in the world even comes close to that.

At least that's what I thought until I watched my sister eat an ice cream cone. She made it look so good, I had to get one too. Eating ice cream with Ashley was the most fun I've had in a long time. No pills required.

I don't feel like I can tell Dani I don't want to get high tonight. I've never felt peer pressure like this before. It isn't even about taking drugs; it's about making sure I don't ruin Dani's mood. It shouldn't be like this. We shouldn't be like this.

Nick places the bag on the counter and opens it. "How many do you want?"

"I don't know." She turns back to me. "What do you think, babe?"

I'm babe now? I want to tell her she doesn't need it, but I'm not sure if that statement is true.

"Whatever you want."

Dani winks at me and tells Nick six. Six? She must be stashing some for another day, just like before. Old habits.

"Damn, girl." Nick places the pills in front of her. "What's the most we ever did?"

"You mean together," she says in a slightly sexy tone. As sexy as she can be in her condition. I grind my teeth together to keep from saying some really horrible shit.

"Yeah." Nick seals the bag, leaving a dozen pills on the counter.

I'm waiting to hear what I have to contend with. Every pill increases sensation—I don't even want to think about the level of pleasure they experienced together.

"Two. But the most I did in a day that we, uh, saw each other." Dani looks back at me. "Sorry," she says, apologizing for the extremely uncomfortable conversation. "I think it was four."

"That was my birthday," Nick says. The smile on his face turns serious. Focused. He lifts his hand and brushes it against her cheek. I watch them share the memory of their first time. Dani's first sexual experience, period. I want to put my fist through the wall.

"I'm tired," I say instead of what I really want to say. "I think I'm just gonna crash. If you guys want to stay up and pop, that's cool." *Motherfuckers.*

71

Nick and Dani start to protest.

"Come on, man," Nick calls as I walk to the bedroom.

"There's no way you're more tired than me," Dani yells. "The baby kept me up all night. I finally had to run away."

Nick makes a noise and Dani stops speaking. I turn around and watch a silent exchange take place between them.

"Dude, I forgot to tell you," Nick starts.

"Nothing," Dani interjects.

"I can't lie to him."

"It's not a lie, it's an omission of events," Dani argues.

My body temperature rises as I prepare for what Nick is going to say. I expected something like this would happen. I squeeze my fist together and brace for the pain.

"Dani called last night and asked me to pick her up."

She rolls her eyes and turns around to face me. "I slept here, it's no big deal," she insists.

"She was here when you called. I didn't tell you because you were going through some shit," he says.

The fact that he didn't tell Dani why I called leads me to believe he wasn't trying to fuck me over. What stings is Dani's attitude. She didn't want me to know. It's the same desperate plea she used when I wanted to tell Nick about the pills I was giving her or even about just us hanging out together while she was at work. She hasn't changed.

I walk to the counter and look at the pile of blue dolphins. I take two and swallow them without water. I walk back to the bedroom and slam the door.

Dani

January 1, 2007

So, 2007 totally sucks.

Matt is still pissed an hour later when my pills have kicked in. Nick left to meet Haley as soon as the first rush hit. I'm jealous. Not because he's going to sleep with her. I just wish I could enjoy every sensation I'm having with someone else.

I sit on the floor near the front door and watch the trees sway in the moonlight. A year ago today I was on Lucy's couch. My parents were asleep upstairs, unaware that this would be the last day of their lives. I want to change so many things about that day. I'd say good morning for one. During the drive home, I would've sung old rock songs with my father. Listened to my mother rattle on about the charity event she was planning. I didn't know I only had hours. I thought they'd be around to annoy me for years.

I don't appreciate the things in my life until they're gone. Matt is in the next room and I'm sitting out here. It doesn't have to be this way. I have the power to change the things in my life that I don't like. I just need to get off of my ass and do it.

I crack open the bedroom door and look inside. Matt is lying on the bed, staring at the ceiling. His sweater and shoes are off. I'm still in the strapless dress Mariann bought me. My only other article of clothing is a pair of black lace panties. I plan on using them to my advantage.

"Can I come in?" I ask softly as I chew on my cheek. "I'm cold."

"Come here." Matt holds open his arms, and my body tingles.

I skip to the bed and crawl into the space beside him. Matt presses me into his chest. I close my eyes and steady my breathing to match his. My feelings for Matt only make sense when I'm high. Sober words cannot properly describe the euphoric sensation of being in Matt's arms. "I love you so much," I whisper.

"I know," Matt whispers back.

"I want you to be happy."

He lets out a long breath then says, "This is hard, Dani."

I nod and bite the inside of my cheek.

"It's so much harder than I thought. I catch myself feeling jealous a lot more than I have a right to be."

"You have a right to your feelings," I say to him.

"That's just it. I think I have a right to my feelings, but I don't want you or Nick to have a right to yours." He moves his arm from around me and sits up. My head falls onto the pillow. "You and Nick were together. You have feelings for each other. My ego can't handle it."

"We *had* feelings for each other," I correct him. "I don't want him the way I want you."

"I know, but I still want to break things when I see the way you look at each other. He knows you in a way that a guy shouldn't know things about his best friend's girl."

"You're being a hypocrite," I remind him.

"And you're being a whore," he spits back.

All the air in the room is sucked into my lungs. I almost don't believe what I've just heard. I want to cry and scream, and punch. Too many emotions at once make it impossible to act on any of them.

"I'm sorry." He turns around quickly. "I didn't mean that." He leans over and tries to hug me. Repeating the word sorry over and over again. But it's just a word. A meaningless word.

I cover my eyes with my hands to prevent them from bouncing back and forth. I only took one pill, but it's still affecting my eyesight. The light behind my eyelids swirls in various colors. A kaleidoscope of reds and purples. I focus on the colors to keep from screaming or crying or both.

He thinks I want to have sex with Nick in the same way I wanted to fuck him when Nick and I were together. He thinks I'm weak and emotional. He doesn't know me at all. Or maybe he knows me too well.

Suddenly Matt's lips are on mine, and I don't stop him. I want him. Only him, and I'll prove it. He rests himself on top of me and peppers my face and neck with kisses.

"I love you so much, Dani." He sucks my neck gently. "I want to be a better man for you. I have to work through my shit to get there. Don't give up on me." His voice cracks.

I grip the sides of his face and hold him still. His eyes ping-pong, but he stays focused on me. "I will never give up on us." I grit my teeth and fight back tears. "Ever."

Matt crashes into me with his mouth, our teeth knock together. He lifts the bottom of my dress, slips his finger into the side of my lace panties, and pulls them off.

He pulls his t-shirt over his head. I get up on my knees and turn around so he can unzip my dress. He does it slowly, kissing my bare skin as he goes. When the zipper hits my lower back, tiny bumps cover every inch of my body. I turn around and fall onto the bed. Matt tosses the four-hundred-dollar cocktail dress on the floor.

Nervous excitement and my erratic body temperature cause my teeth to chatter. "Your turn," I say and try not to bite my tongue.

I feel his hands between us, working on his zipper. We break apart so he can pull his jeans off. I'm on the pill, so there is nothing stopping us now.

My body is electrified. The slightest touch on my arm ripples through my entire body. The blue pills sitting on the counter create a reality where thoughts are swaddled in rainbows, and feelings become living, breathing things. Matt's lips are on my neck. I feel the vibration on my inner thighs. He is everywhere because ecstasy is everywhere. We found the missing piece to our puzzle. The thing that makes us whole.

Matt moves at a steady pace above me. I open my eyes, his are closed. He is lost in me. I'm lost completely and totally with him.

March 2007

I wake up to the smell of Dani's shampoo. I open my eyes and see her naked body walk across the room. She closes the blinds and removes the towel from her head. We took our last hit of thizz yesterday and swore this was the final time until summer. Our grades are suffering, but our sex life is off the hook.

I'm ready to be done with it all, but Dani still enjoys it. I'm hoping I can show her that we can be just as awesome without thizz. We don't need a pill to be happy. To mesh, as she calls it. I also want to know that I'm good enough. That the girl I'm going to love until the day I die, doesn't need a pill to show me she loves me.

Dani slides back into bed and wraps her naked limbs around me. Her cool, slightly damp skin feels good against my warm sleep-deprived body. It takes some control not to smile when she peppers my face and neck with kisses. I resist the urge to moan as her hand glides over my bare chest and down my stomach. She stops at the top of my boxers and lets her fingers linger for a few seconds to see if I move. When I don't, she slips them under the waistband and makes tiny circles; crop circles, she calls them. I'm at my breaking point, and she knows it. I let out a little moan. She giggles, then her hand slips lower and she grabs me. I'm on top of her two seconds later.

"Heather is home," she warns.

"So." I rip the sheet off and go to work on her neck. She moans softly. I pull back to look at her face. She's glowing in this light. Her wet hair clings to her damp skin. I move it back into place. She's so fucking beautiful. So perfect in every way.

"It grosses her out when we're loud," she says.

"You're kidding me, right? After the dude that sounded like a horse giving birth to a cow last week?" Heather dates some really weird men.

"What do you think you sound like to her?"

"I don't even want to know. Plus, you're the loud one."

"Am not."

"Do you want me to prove it?" I push against her and she whimpers.

"Yes," she says, breathless already. Just the way I like it.

I win our debate when Dani is screaming so loud the gay guys that live downstairs are cheering. I hang out with them sometimes when I'm waiting for Dani to get back from school. They're extremely cool and gave me the best tips on manscaping. I like them way more than the douchebags rooming with me and Nick. I'm all for a *real* college experience, but the guys renting the spare rooms in Nick's house take things too far. I don't even think the loudest one is a student at Stanford. He never goes to class or even gets dressed. Last time I was home, he was naked in a kiddie pool in the backyard with a bag of weed and a six-pack of beer the entire day.

I take a quick shower and get dressed while Dani heads down to Columbus Avenue for coffee and Arnie's morning walk. I check my phone for the time. My train is in an hour. I have to catch it or else I'm waiting three hours for the next one. The Sunday schedule sucks, but I wouldn't give up morning sex with Dani for anything in the world. I'd walk back to Stanford if I had to. Hell, I almost had to walk since my car is in the shop because of a factory recall. Nick offered to drive me up, but it's like having your dad drop you off for a date. Awkward.

My phone buzzes with a text from my mom; she wants to know what time my flight lands. I'm going to visit them for my birthday. Ashley emails weekly pics of her hair growth. I told her I'd cut my hair to match hers while I'm there. Her hair is probably an inch off her head, so it looks like I'm getting buzzed. I don't care, I'd do anything to see her smile.

My sister is getting healthy, and I have the girl of my dreams. Other than worrying about money, my grades, and how I'm going to afford tuition next year and still eat, my life is perfect.

The front door opens, and I hear Arnie scamper up the stairs. His nails scrape the hardwood floor as he runs to the kitchen for water. I open the bedroom door and find Heather hugging Dani in the hall. "What's wrong?"

"Nothing," Heather says and walks down the stairs and out the front door.

Dani goes into the kitchen and places her coffee cup on the counter. She lifts Arnie's water bowl and fills it. "Heather is happy for us, that's all." She turns around with a smile on her face. "We're fucking awesome."

I cross the kitchen and kiss my girl. She is, without a doubt, the one. There isn't another person on this planet that gets me in the way

79

she does. One look and I'm done. I'm hooked. Dani is a high I'll never get tired of. I never feel closer to her than the morning after we thizz.

"I have to go," I tell her.

"I know." She grips my waist and squeezes. "One day, you'll stay forever, right?"

I lift her chin and kiss her softly on the lips before I answer. "Yes, one day soon."

I haven't told her this, but I've looked into transferring to UC Berkeley. My rival. The school I've loathed for most of my life. I'm willing to give up Stanford for Dani. That's how much I love her. CAL is also half the cost of Stanford, and moving in as her roommate will look a lot less suspicious.

We're still sneaking around in case the IRS is watching. It's been nearly five months, and we haven't heard a word from them. I'm starting to think the fake engagement is overkill.

I finally make it out of Dani's apartment, and run down to Columbus and Union to catch the 30-Stockton. It will take me right to the Caltrain station. The bus stop is in front of a produce market, where two old Chinese ladies are gossiping near the mangos. A little boy comes running out of the market with a toy plane in his hand, and they yell at him as he runs by. He doesn't stop until he bumps into a young Indian couple coming around the corner with their morning coffee. This street is a microscopic version of the world. Nobody is the same race or color. The only commonality is our love of this city.

"Excuse me," a voice says.

I instinctively move aside. The sidewalk gets crowded around the bus stops. I step closer to the building behind me and turn towards the voice. Two men in black suits and sunglasses are standing before me. I move, but they stay in place.

"Are you Matthew Augustine?" one of them says.

"Yes," I say and notice the car parked in front of the bus stop. It's a tan Crown Victoria. Total cop car.

"I'm Special Agent Freeman, this is Agent Lee." They flash badges at me. "We're with the IRS Criminal Investigation Division."

I swallow hard and nod. The attorney Mariann hired for Dani warned her about these guys. He called them CI and told Dani not to speak to them under any circumstances.

"We have some questions for you regarding your relationship with Danielle Batista," Agent Lee says. "Do you have time to speak to us now?"

"I have to catch a train," I say and look up the street for the bus.

"You attend Stanford," Agent Freeman says. "I'm a Stanford alum. Class of ninety-nine."

"Cool." I force a smile like I give a shit.

"Were you in town visiting Danielle?" Lee asks. His tone isn't accusatory. He's trying to sound casual. I know every single question they ask is premeditated. "Do you visit often?"

If they're questioning my relationship with Dani, that means something. "We're good friends," I say. There is no use lying. I'm two blocks from her flat at nine-thirty on a Sunday morning. They were probably watching her place and saw me leave. Lying will only make things worse. "And her roommate is pretty cute," I add.

The agents laugh. Then Freeman says, "How about we give you a ride to Caltrain? That way we can chat for a few minutes and clear up some things we found during our investigation that involve you."

"Am I being investigated?" I ask officially.

81

"No," Agent Freeman assures me. "There are a few things that don't add up in regards to Miss Batista's trust fund and her relationship with Nick Marino. Since you seem close to both of them, maybe you can help."

I adjust my backpack nervously and look for the bus. It's late. At this point I'll probably miss my train anyway.

"Your name seemed to pop up a lot, so we thought we'd talk to you directly. You might be able to clear the air about some of our concerns. We don't want to bother Miss Batista any more than we have too. She's been through enough trauma."

My defenses are on full alert, and I know the last thing I should do is talk to these assholes, but I don't really feel like I have a choice. If I tell them to fuck off, it only makes me look guilty. "What kind of concerns?"

"Well for one, you visit Miss Batista quite a bit without Nick. Sometimes just for the night." Agent Freeman leans on the wall beside me. "Are you two messing around behind Nick's back?" He follows the question with an evil little laugh. Agent Lee joins in, and I even offer a fake little chuckle.

"It's not like that," I start to say, and then I realize they've been watching us; I don't know what they've seen. "Dani and I are really close friends. Sometimes we get friendly when we drink. That's it." Freeman looks at Lee to see if his partner is buying my bullshit.

"So, Danielle and Nick are really engaged?" Agent Lee asks.

"Yes." I make sure my tone is clear and confident. "They've been together since we were in high school."

"You've never dated Danielle?" Agent Freeman pulls a notepad out of his pocket and starts to flip through pages like he's reading otherwise.

"No. We're just friends," I reiterate. It hurts to say that out loud. Dani is the most important thing in my life. It pains me to tell these assholes that she means nothing to me. That I'm nothing to her.

"Do you want to tell us why you purchased a ring two weeks ago?"

I feel the blood drain from my face. Nobody knows I went to Shane Company to look at rings. Not even Nick. That means they're following me. I didn't buy an engagement ring or anything. I can't afford one. The ring I bought doesn't compare to the fake engagement ring Nick gave her. That thing is some kind of antique that's worth more than my car. I just wanted to give Dani something special. She made me promise not to buy her anything for her birthday, so I was saving it for a random Tuesday or something. The less special the occasion, the more Dani will appreciate it.

"The ring wasn't for Dani," I lie. "I bought it for my sister. I'm going to visit them for spring break."

They seem to believe me but continue asking questions about Dani, and a few about Heather, which I tell them I can't answer. I check my phone for the time. Even if the bus comes right now, I'll barely make my train.

"Let us give you a ride," Freeman says. "I don't want you to miss your train." He turns to escort me to their car, and I follow him, because once again, it doesn't really feel like I have a choice.

Agent Lee walks ahead of us and gets into the driver's seat. Freeman opens the door, and I get it in the back. As soon as he closes the door, my cell phone buzzes. It's a text from Dani. I close the phone and shove it in my pocket. If the IRS doesn't believe their engagement is real, then they don't believe the trust is real. That's a problem.

Will Walker and some of Bill Batista's other clients have already confessed to paying him a for legal services that were supposedly offered for free. The IRS has been trying to find that money ever since. Bill was careful. Everything they owned was paid for legitimately. He even took out a personal loan for seventy-five thousand dollars to update their kitchen. From what we found hidden in the attic and the storage unit, he didn't spend much of the quarter of a million dollars he illegally collected from his clients. He knew better than that. Sometimes I think Dani is worse off now that she found the money. It complicated the shit out of her life, my life, everyone involved.

Mariann broke the law the moment she took Dani's money and funded her trust. It isn't one of those back alley money laundering operations you see on cop shows. It's the same crime nonetheless. At this point, Nick and I are accessories.

These agents probably don't even give a shit about Dani's father. JMD are the largest real estate developers in the country. They have real estate deals in every state, dozens of government contracts, and they're starting to delve into the global market. Busting them would be a huge score for the IRS. Nick and Mariann would lose everything. If I can't convince these agents that nothing is going on between me and Dani, we're all fucked. If we aren't already.

April 2007

Matt sent a mushy text during my last class of the day. I read it again as I walk down the hall and someone bumps me from behind. I stop and he moves in front of me.

"Let me see your phone," Zack demands as he holds out his hand. "You only smile that stupid when Matty sends a good one." I roll my eyes and hand him my Blackberry. He scrolls through the text and smiles. "He deserves a blow job for that one," Zack says and hands my phone back. "I swear all the good ones are still straight."

"You better not let Antonio hear you say that," I warn.

"Antonio knows he's just my bitch." Zack laughs and walks away.

"Hey," I yell after him. "Don't forget to take good notes for me tomorrow. I need an A to get my GPA up."

"I got you." He waves me off and disappears into the crowd.

Lucy and Johnson's wedding is this weekend. We're driving up to Eureka tomorrow. I can't wait to see them and the baby. Lucy emailed me new pictures; Marguerite has tripled in size since the holidays.

I'm also excited to get away. I've only seen Matt once since he came back from Colorado. We went to dinner with Nick at a steakhouse downtown the day he flew back. I thought he was stressed because of his hair. He shaved it completely off to match Ashley's. He thinks he looks like an alien. I think he looks sexy as hell. When we went back to my place after dinner, he tried to get out of spending the night. He only agreed to stay if Nick slept on the couch. It was very strange and totally awkward because Nick actually stayed.

That was nearly three weeks ago. Nick has also been distant. He flaked on a lunch we were supposed to have with Mariann last week. A reporter from The Guardian was going to join us to discuss the new division of JM Developers that Mariann just started. It's a trade school program that offers job training to high school graduates interested in construction, electrical, and plumbing. Nick is the CEO; the exposure would've been great for the foundation and our lie.

I try not to take it personally. Matt and Nick have other things in their lives that don't concern me. As long as I'm there for them, that's all that matters. It's a support system, not a co-dependency.

After my train ride home from Berkeley to San Francisco, I take Arnie for a walk, then start to pack. I'm getting a baggy for my toothbrush when the house phone rings. Heather is still at school, so I run to the hall and answer it.

"Hello," I say.

"Hi, may I speak to Ms. Danielle Batista?"

As soon as I hear my full name, I know this call is gonna suck. "This is Danielle."

"I'm Special Agent John Freeman from the Internal Revenue Service," he pauses. "How are you today?"

I hate when they ask how I'm doing. Like they give a shit. "Not good now," I answer.

"Well, I'll make this brief. I was calling about your relationship with Nick Marino."

Oh, fuck. "What about it?"

"How long have you and Mr. Marino been dating?"

I know for sure I shouldn't answer his question, but this one seems so simple. If I don't, it will seem more suspicious, like I'm hiding something. "About a year," I say. Technically, it would've been if we were still together.

"It was our understanding that you became uninvolved with Mr. Marino after the attempt on your life by Will Walker."

"Nick and I were never broken up." That's the lie Mariann's lawyer told me to say in case anyone ever questioned me. Even though I'm not supposed to speak to anyone, he still prepped me for moments like this.

"Who is Matthew Augustine?"

Hearing him say Matt's name makes my stomach knot. "He's just a friend."

"He's not your boyfriend?"

"No, of course not." I sound super offended when really I'm shitting my pants. "What is this call about exactly?"

"We're trying to figure out why Mariann Marino would open a trust for you."

"I'm engaged to her grandson," I tell him. "Being part of the Marino family comes with a lot of public appearances and travel. The trust helps me with expenses." Another lie Mariann told me to say.

"I see," Agent Freeman says. "So, the money in this trust came solely from Mariann Marino."

"Yes."

"Well, thank you for your time. Sorry to disturb—"

"Just a second," I interrupt. "I want an update on my father's case. I've left at least six messages." Mariann told me to always bring this up. Make it look like their investigation is causing me distress

He clears his throat and says, "I don't have that information. Another agent will get back to you."

"I want to sell the house. I need money for school."

"It doesn't look that way to us, Ms. Batista," he says sarcastically. "It looks like you are doing quite well for yourself. Have a good day."

I fucked that up. I have to call Mariann so she can let the lawyer know. I dial Mariann's personal cell, and it goes to voice mail. I call Nick next. He answers on the fourth ring.

"Hey, Dani." He clears his throat. "Are you okay?"

"I got a call from an agent Freeman at the IRS. He was asking about our relationship. Who Matt is and about the trust," I ramble.

"Did you call Mariann?" he asks. His voice raises slightly.

"She didn't answer."

"I'm going to see…I mean, I'll let her know."

"I'll be in Eureka this weekend; I'll see her at the wedding." As if I have to remind him. It's being held on the Marinos' property. Mariann let Lucy use an area in the woods. I've only seen pictures, but it looks perfect for the rustic wedding Lucy and Johnson have been planning.

"Yeah. Okay. I have to go, Dani." He pauses. "I'm driving. Have a great time this weekend."

He's telling me to have a great time like I'm not going to see him at the wedding. Something strange is going on. I can feel it. I hate strange feelings.

Matt is quiet when he arrives. He tells me he has a paper due on Tuesday, and he's hoping we get back early Monday so he can finish it. I don't tell him about the IRS call because he's been stressed enough lately.

"Well, I'm ready to go, unless you want to hang out for a little while." I wrap my arms around his waist. "Heather isn't home."

"No, I want to beat the traffic." He removes my hands and grabs my bag. "We still have to drop Arnie at the dogsitter's." He pulls the leash off the hook next to the door and clips it onto Arnie's collar. "Come on, dumbass."

I take my dress out of the hall closet and follow him down the stairs. I watch him lead my dog to a nearby fire hydrant. He looks worried. I want to ask him why, but honestly, I'm afraid of what his answer might be. We're starting to revert back to the couple we hated. The people we were before we took thizz. Matt says we don't need it. I really want him to be right.

The five-hour drive has been a quiet one. Matt updated me on Ashley's progress, then he talked about how much he likes Colorado, again. I told him about shopping with Zack and Antonio over spring break. Once the conversation fades out, we listen to the radio most of the drive. The tension in the car is thick, and I wonder if it's self-inflicted. I didn't tell him about the IRS call, and I should have. I need to come clean.

We're only a few miles outside of Eureka; it's now or never. I don't want to tell Lucy or Johnson. I'm sure they're stressed enough with wedding stuff. At some point I have to talk about it with Mariann, so Matt will find out anyway.

I turn down the radio and give him the short version of my call with the CI agent. I tell him they asked about Nick and my trust. When I mention their interest in our relationship, he freaks out.

"The lawyer said you don't have to answer their questions."

"They caught me off guard. I didn't tell them anything incriminating," I assure him.

"Did you talk to Mariann yet?" Matt asks as we exit the highway.

"No, she didn't answer. So I called Nick."

Matt hmm hmmm's me.

"He was weird," I say.

"Nick's been busy," Matt snaps. "He's got a lot going on."

"Okay," I huff. "But it was like he didn't want to talk at all. He said 'have a nice weekend' like he wouldn't see me. I thought he was going to the wedding."

"I don't know, maybe he changed his mind." Matt shrugs as we pull to a stop in front of Lucy's.

I put this conversation on hold and center myself before I go inside. I unhook my seatbelt. Matt doesn't move. The car is still running.

"You're not coming in?"

"No. I have to run some errands. I'll be back in an hour." Matt kisses my palm then folds my fingers around his kiss. "I love you so much, Dani."

"Geez, you said you'll only be gone an hour." I can't see his eyes; he's wearing sunglasses. But I know he's stressed, and telling him about the IRS just added to his pile.

"I'm just excited, I guess. About the weekend."

"You're excited about Lucy and Johnson's wedding?" Okay, now I know something is wrong.

He runs his hand over his head, just like Nick does. Best friends mirror each other in so many ways. Something I didn't realize until I started hanging out with Heather. I catch myself rolling my eyes way more than did before we moved in together. I even whine like her. Which is why I'm not going to push Matt any further.

"You know what. Go. Run your errands. Just be back before the rehearsal." I lean over and kiss his cheek. He grabs my shoulder and pulls me to him. He buries his face in my neck for a few seconds and then lets me go. "You're scaring me now."

He sits up and stares straight ahead. "There is something I want to tell you." He exhales then says, "It's Nick. I'm going to see him." He takes his sunglasses off. "I didn't want to tell you because I didn't want you to come with me."

"Wow, okay. You don't have to lie about going to see your best friend. I get it." Hiding the tension in my voice is difficult. "If you need boy time, just tell me." I try to make light of the situation.

Matt nods, and I see his jaw clench. "Yeah, okay." He looks as if he might say something, add to this conversation, but he doesn't.

"Unless there is some other reason you don't want me to see Nick," I push. "Is this why Nick canceled lunch last week? Was it you?"

Matt rubs his hand down his face. "Sort of."

"Sort of?"

"Yeah. I might have said something to him."

"That lunch was important to Nick's foundation and he skipped it for you." I can tell he doesn't want to have this conversation. Not now. Not sitting in front of Lucy's. "You know what, forget it." I grab my bag from the backseat and swing it onto my lap, just missing Matt's head. "I gotta go play pretty fucking bridesmaid right now. And you have to go do whatever…" I leave the sentence hanging in the air. "Tell Nick I said hi."

I open the door and get out. Matt pops the trunk so I can get my dress. I lift it by the hanger, then slam the trunk shut. I'm not even to the porch when Matt peels away.

He doesn't show for the rehearsal dinner. I'm too consumed with Lucy's pre-wedding to-do list to care. This weekend isn't about me, it's about Lucy. She is the only real family I have left. This is her weekend, and I won't let my drama fuck it up.

Matt

I leave Dani a voicemail saying I can't make it to the rehearsal dinner. I don't even give her a reason. I can't come up with anything even remotely convincing, and I don't want to try.

I fall back on the bed and close my eyes, wishing for sleep. I haven't slept in weeks. I doubt I'll get any tonight. I've thought about how I should tell her a thousand times. I've rehearsed exactly what I'm going to say. Anticipated her response. This is the best thing for all of us. Once I'm gone, everyone will be safe.

I'm the only weak spot in this whole fucked-up plan. I realized this after my two-hour conversation with those agents. They logged every visit to her house and a few to my place in Santa Clara. Of course, the days she came to visit, Nick wasn't home. Every piece of evidence they had to prove Nick and Dani's relationship was fake was because of me. When I went to Colorado to see my family, I realized what I had to do. It's what I should've done a long time ago. I couldn't make this choice when I thought it was just benefiting me. Now that I know it is the best thing for Dani, it makes my decision marginally easier.

"Knock, knock," Nick says as the door opens. "You jerkin' off?"

"Fuck you," I say and throw a pillow at the door. He ducks, and it flies over his head into the hallway.

I couldn't have done any of this without Nick. He's been nothing but supportive. At first, I thought he just wanted me out of the picture, but it's Nick. He's loyal to a fault. He's never given me a reason to doubt him; I'm the one who can't be trusted.

When I asked him not to hang out or schedule any fake engagement photo shoots with Dani for a few weeks, he didn't even ask why. I couldn't see her, so I asked him not to either. All of that will change after the wedding. The wedding I asked him not to attend.

Nick sits on the end of the bed. "What's up? You want to go to the cottage and smoke?"

"Sure." I stand up and slip my shoes back on. I need to get out of my head for a little while.

"Did you talk to Dani?" he asks as I plug my phone into the charger.

"I just left her a voicemail."

"Punk." Nick stands and walks to the door. He's disappointed in how I'm handling my relationship. She deserves better, and Nick knows it. "You can still change your mind."

"No, I can't." I follow Nick to the door, leaving my cell phone behind.

It's nearly four in the morning, and we're still on his couch, smoking weed and drinking.

"Maybe I should just stay awake all night," I slur.

"Good luck with that." Nick takes a pull off the whiskey bottle.

"Come to the wedding with me. I'll just be sitting there by myself, looking like a dumbass."

"I thought you didn't want me to go?"

Hearing Nick say that out loud makes me cringe. I had no right to void his invite to Lucy's wedding. That just proves how weak I am. "Why do you care what I want?"

"Cause, you know why." Nick places the bottle on the table and lights another joint. "I'll go if you want me to." He takes a hit, then passes it to me.

"Okay, you're going. And for the record, don't listen to me anymore. Do what you want."

"Yes, sir." Nick salutes me.

I inhale and laugh at the same time, and then I start to cough. Nick pretends to pat my back. We look like a couple of idiots. "We gotta go to sleep, man." I pass the joint back to Nick.

He takes a huge hit, then blows it out. A puff of white smoke floats above our head. "I'm gonna go see Haley." Nick stands and walks to the front door.

"Is that for real or what?" I watch Nick fix his fucked-up hair in the reflection of the window. Mine is still so short I don't even have to comb it.

"I don't know. I mean, technically we can't date because Mariann will murder me if I screw things up and she loses another assistant. But I like her. She's cool to hang out with." Nick walks to the bathroom.

He's right, Haley is cool. Aside from Dani, she's the only girl I ever talked to. Haley has always been my friend.

"Go to bed," Nick says and kicks my foot. My left eye opens, and I see his outstretched hand. I reach towards him and he hoists me up.

"I could've fucked Haley," I confess. "Back in the day."

Nick laughs as he walks me to the bedroom. "I know. She told me she used to like you. That she kissed you once."

I recall the kiss on the porch the first time I took thizz. The night Nick and Dani became Nick and Dani. "She said I was hot."

Nick tosses me on the bed then pulls off my shoes. "Too bad you got no game. You could've had her too."

This bed isn't as soft as the one in the main house, but it pulls me towards sleep. "I didn't want Haley. I wanted Dani," I mumble.

Nick pulls the covers over me. "You have Dani," he says quietly. "And you're blowing it."

The light turns off, and Nick closes the door.

Luckily, this is an outdoor wedding, so half the guests are sporting sunglasses. I'm not the only one still drunk. Nick told me he kept Haley up until seven o'clock this morning. Her alarm went off at nine. He's going to get her fired.

"I now pronounce you husband and wife," the preacher says.

Lucy and Johnson kiss, and the crowd cheers. Dani looks back at me with a small smile. We've talked about marriage a few times when we were high. You talk about everything when you're high. Nothing is off limits. She must be thinking about that conversation right now. I smile at her so she doesn't think I'm a total prick. It helps; her face brightens as she turns back to Lucy and gives her a hug.

We let the wedding party exit first, then file out behind them. I get lost in the crowd as we head to the reception area. Nick flags down Haley, and she points us in the direction of our seats.

"Where is Dani sitting?" I ask.

Nick looks over Haley's shoulder and steals a kiss on her cheek.

Haley backs away with a disapproving grin and Nick winks at her. Their banter is natural, their attraction obvious. Maybe a little too obvious. I step between them so Nick will stop flirting with her.

"After pictures, she will join the wedding party at that table." She points to the table behind ours. The seating is just two long farm tables. Mariann had them custom built to hold all the guests. Haley consults her clipboard again, then says, "Dani is sitting right behind you, Matt. She made me triple check that you'd be close to her."

Nick tells her she's killing it at her job. Haley has a huge grin on her face as she heads off to make sure the first course is on time.

Nick watches her walk away, and I realize this may be more than just sex.

"Dude, you're feelin' her."

"Nah, she's just good people." Nick seems to shake Haley from his head. "You ready to hit the bar?" Nick changes the subject or ignores it. Either way, I'm in.

"Yeah, I need a shot."

By the time we sit down to eat, Nick and I have a pretty decent buzz going. We're laughing at something stupid when Dani's head pops between us.

"I'm glad you guys are having fun," she says. I can't tell if she's being sarcastic. I'm too buzzed to care. I wrap my arm around her waist and pull her into my lap. When she laughs I know I'm in the clear. She lingers for a few seconds, then she stands and moves closer to Nick's chair.

"You look hot," Nick tells her.

Her dress is a light-blue flowy thing with yellow flowers embroidered on the edges. Even though it's loose fitting, you can see the outline of Dani's perfect hourglass body beneath. Her hair is down, and a crown of daisies sits on top of her head. She looks like a goddess.

"You guys look like a hot gay couple." She straightens my tie, the tie she made me wear. Nick and I are both wearing light-blue button-down shirts with khaki pants. The only difference is he gets to wear a dark blue tie and his shirt has white around the cuffs and collar.

Nick smiles at me and says, "I'm the dude."

"Why do you get to be the dude?" I protest.

"Because you have on the yellow tie."

I sigh in defeat and hold up my beer. Nick holds up his Jack and Coke, and we toast to our gayness.

Dani laughs and kisses my cheek, and then Nick's. "I love you guys," she says. As she walks away, I recognize the harsh fragrance on her breath.

"Have you been drinking tequila?" I ask, just out of curiosity.

"I might have had a shot or three with Lucy to calm her nerves." She bites her lower lip. "Does it turn you on?"

I slide my hand up the back of her thigh. "As a matter of fact, it does." I want to drag her to the bathroom and rip her dress off. I also know her inebriated state comes with a price. She isn't day drinking in celebration, she was probably still pissed at me for missing the rehearsal dinner and not calling. Drunk Dani is a forgiving Dani.

"I gotta go. Nick will take care of you while I'm gone." She winks at Nick and steps away from the table with a sexy smile.

"I've got him covered." Nick rubs the back of my head. I swat his hand away. That's when I see someone out of place. He's wearing a navy suit; a white wire runs from his ear down the back of his shirt. Once Dani is back in her seat, I turn to Nick.

"Who is that?" I nod to the guy standing on the fringe of the reception area. The clearing is encircled with twinkling lights and lanterns strung from tree to tree. This guy is standing partly in the shadows.

Nick doesn't even turn around; he already knows who I'm referring to. "The security team is making sure nobody sneaks in that doesn't belong."

After the IRS picked me up last month, Mariann hired a team to watch Dani and make sure nobody is following me. The lawyer said if they're making contact, they most likely have all the evidence they need to start investigating Dani's trust. I consulted with Jim Jameson, and he said removing myself from the situation would be best for everyone.

Toasts have been made, the cake cut, and dances are done. There is no use putting off the inevitable. Dani plops down in the chair beside me and places her bare feet on my lap. "What time is it?"

"Ten-thirty," Nick tells her. He waves Haley over and asks what time she's going to be finished.

"At least another two hours. I have to wait until all the vendors are off the premises before I can turn in. Will you wait for me?" Haley gives Nick a flirty look.

Dani kicks my leg. I look at her and realize she has no idea Nick and Haley are sort of a thing. I doubt she remembers anything from New Year's. I can't tell if this news upsets her.

Haley catches Dani's reaction and jumps back into work mode. "Can I get you guys anything?" She rests her hand on the back of Dani's chair and smiles down at her. "Do you want a glass of wine before they start packing up the bar? You like white, right?"

Dani looks perplexed by Haley's sincere gesture. Everything about Haley is genuine, especially her smile.

"No, thank you. I'm going to say bye to Lucy and Johnson." She steps around Haley and places her hand on my shoulder as she slips back into her sandals. "They're staying in the main house tonight with Marguerite. I want to catch them before the honeymoon begins."

Nick and I make gag sounds as Dani and Haley head off in separate directions.

"One more shot for the road?" Nick asks.

"Hell yeah."

Dani decided she should drive my Mustang back to Lucy's. It's the first time she has ever driven my car; she doesn't do that bad. We make it to Lucy's without any incidents. We have the house to ourselves tonight, and I'm about to ruin it.

I'm spinning slightly as I climb the stairs to the attic. Once we're inside Dani's bedroom, thoughts start to swirl in my head. More like images of her and Nick. It shouldn't bother me, but it does.

"Are you okay?" Dani asks as she slips off her dress. She pulls a t-shirt from her overnight bag and puts it on, then offers me a bottle of water. "Are you gonna puke?"

I'm not going to vomit, but I realize I can use this to my advantage. "I don't feel too good." I take the water and grip my forehead. "I think I need some air. Let's go downstairs."

"Oh. Okay," Dani says softly. She's disappointed. I'm a fucking disappointment. To her and myself.

We walk into the living room, and I make sure the blinds are closed. Nobody followed us here. I made sure to watch for cars trailing us, the way T showed me. We're all on high alert. Well, not everyone. We decided not to tell Dani about the CI agents. If she knew how close she is to being busted, she might do something drastic. She wouldn't turn herself in, she can't do that without implicating Nick and Mariann. She would never put any of us in danger. She'd do something really stupid. She would give up the trust, the money, everything to make sure we were safe. Her insurance money will only last another month, maybe two, then she'll have to get a job. Her life will be turned upside down, and none of us are willing to let that happen.

"Come here," Dani says. She's sitting on the sofa with a throw blanket.

I sit down, resting my head on the back of the couch. She rubs my hand, coaxing me to look at her. I keep my eyes closed. The things I want to say are a jumbled mess in my inebriated mind. Anything I try to say won't come out properly. Silence is all I have to offer tonight. I kiss her forehead then pull her into my arms and close my eyes. I just want one more night before of all this ends.

Dani

I wake up alone on the sofa. I hear Matt talking on the phone in the kitchen. It's probably his mom. She calls every morning with updates on Ashley. Matt was doing really well before he went to see them for his birthday. We were the happiest we've ever been. When he came home, something was off, and it wasn't just his shaved head. He misses them more than he lets on. I try to make his life here as pleasant as possible. I'm failing miserably.

I go upstairs to use the bathroom and shower. I'm still in wedding hair and makeup. Yesterday was beautiful. I've never seen Lucy so happy. Even the baby behaved. She didn't cry once during the ceremony. I realized something as I watched Lucy and Johnson exchange vows. I was witnessing unconditional love. Seeing it in the flesh was an enlightening experience. I've only felt that kind of love when I'm high. I wonder if I can be that happy sober. From the way things have been in the last month, I'd say the answer to that question is no.

I get out of the shower and head to my room to get dressed. It's past nine, so Lucy could be home any minute. Mariann said she's having breakfast prepared for them, but I know my aunt. She likes the comfort of her own home. At least I won't have to lie to Johnson. Matt didn't touch me. He was pretty drunk, but maybe part of him was being respectful to Johnson. It makes my insides smile to think of Matt being so thoughtful. I won't allow myself to entertain another reason why we slept on the couch and not in my room. Nick didn't offer us any pills, or maybe Matt declined them. The fact is, we weren't high and we barely touched each other. So many things point to me and Matt being perfect for each other, but how real can it be if the points are tainted with ecstasy? I tell myself they don't have to be. We can be happy and in love without it, but we are so much more when we're high. We love stronger, feel better, our world is one. Is it wrong to want the most out of love? If ecstasy can give us the extra boost we need, shouldn't we take it?

I put on a pair of jeans and my old Eureka Coffee t-shirt. I grab my cell phone and head downstairs. I don't hear Matt talking on the phone. I walk into the kitchen, and I find that it's empty. Suddenly, my phone buzzes in my hand. It's a text from Matt.

We need to talk. I'll call you later. I love you.

His text is even more ambiguous than the first message he sent me on Myspace.

My text back to Matt is even shorter.

Come back.

I stare at the text, and four words stand out.

We need to talk.

Those four words, in that particular order—suck.

When Matt finally replies, I'm sitting inside Eureka Coffee with Mary, talking about how beautiful the wedding was and gossiping about how Haley landed her job.

My phone vibrates on the table, and I pick it up before Mary has a chance to see the caller ID.

"What does it say?"

I move the screen out of her view. "He's coming to pick me up." I shut my phone and take a sip of my lukewarm latte. "I don't see how he can do that when he doesn't even know where I am." My heart starts to race in anticipation.

"He thinks you're just sitting around the house waiting for his call." Mary stands and takes my mug with her. "I knew he was too good to be true."

I don't reply to Mary's snide comment. Part of me thinks she's right. That part can kiss my ass. I stand and head to the counter.

"Tell Patti I said bye."

"Seriously?" Mary spins around with her hands on her hips. "You're going to run home and wait for him? That's pretty pathetic."

"I'm not rushing home," I say. "I want to see Lucy and the baby before I head back to the city." It's a lie. I'm rushing home for Matt because sometimes it's okay to be a stupid girl.

"Keep telling yourself that." Mary comes around the counter and gives me a hug. "Let's do lunch next week." She kisses my cheeks then goes back to the dishes. I notice she is wearing a lot more makeup than she used to. College has really brought her out of her shell.

"Okay. I choose this time," I demand. The last place Mary took me to lunch cost more than my electric bill, and electricity in San Francisco isn't cheap.

"Yeah, whatever," she yells as I walk out the door.

I take my old route home and make it back to Lucy's as soon as Matt pulls up. He stops in front of the house and rolls the window down.

"Hi," I say. I'm excited to see him, even if he pisses me off. I open the door and get in.

He kisses my cheek and asks if I want to go to the beach.

I tell him the beach sounds great. It doesn't. The beach reminds me of Nick. We spent countless hours high out of our minds, rolling around in the sand. Matt knows, he was there. Going to the beach isn't something Matt and I have ever done.

It's a sunny day, so the parking lot is nearly full. Matt parks facing the horizon. He turns off the car and clicks out of his seatbelt. He adjusts the radio and settles into his side of the car. I realize we aren't here to enjoy the view or the weather. Matt obviously wants to talk.

"Are you okay?" I finally ask.

Matt sighs. Then he does something I wasn't prepared for. He shakes his head no.

"Is it me?" I choke back the lump in my throat.

"No. It's my family," he says. His eyes are focused on the Mustang logo in the center of his steering wheel. "I want to be near them."

I rub his shoulder. "You will be; you're going to visit in a couple of weeks."

"What if I decide to stay?" Matt clears his throat in that nervous way he does. "I'm really considering the internship."

He can't mean the internship in Fort Collins. The one he said was a waste of time because it won't benefit his résumé.

"I thought you said it wasn't a good fit." I try not to sound like I'm going to vomit my heart all over the car.

"It's almost unheard of for someone like me to get an internship in an actual law firm. They usually hire first-year law students. This is a chance for me to build my skill set. It's an opportunity I can't pass up." He looks at me, and I can tell that he's already made up his mind.

"I'll go with you. I have nothing going on this summer. I can hang out with Ashley." It's a desperate plea. I know. I suck.

Matt shakes his head again. "You have to stay." He swallows hard. "With Nick."

"Come on, Matt." I sigh. "You know none of that is real."

"You're supposed to be engaged to Nick. You can't give anyone a reason to doubt it. Do you understand how many people's lives are at risk if the IRS finds out it's a lie?"

I know what Matt is saying, but I only hear him rejecting me. "We have it under control."

"No," he yells. "You don't. You have no idea how out of control this whole thing is!" Matt's fury is making the windows fog. He cracks his window to cool the car down. It doesn't work.

"What are you trying to say?" I turn in my seat so I'm looking directly at him.

He sighs and lifts his eyes to meet mine. "I'm moving to Colorado. I want to be near my family." His tone is absolute.

I want to yell bullshit. I want to scream and cry. I don't. Not in front of him. I know he misses his family. He wants to be with Ashley. They have huge plans for the summer. Road trips, theme parks, she's even convinced her parents to let her get a tattoo. Matt wants to be there for all of it. I get it. I just don't know why he's icing me out. Using my fake engagement to Nick is a low blow.

There has to be a reasonable explanation.

"Did someone from the IRS contact you?"

"No," he says. His eyes give me a different reply.

"Matt, they can't come after you," I assure him, even though I'm not sure if it's true. "They want me. As long as Nick and I keep up appearances, it's all good."

"It's not all good, Dani. You and Nick aren't keeping up anything. A blind person could see the truth. It's only a matter of time before they come for you." Matt places his arm across the seat. It's the closest thing to a hug he's given me all day. "If they suspect your engagement is fake, they will investigate your trust. That means Mariann, Nick, and JM Developers. A lot of people are at risk. I can't have that riding on me."

I realize in this moment how selfish I really am. I never looked at this from an outside perspective. So many people are risking their lives, their businesses, for me.

"When things settle down, I'll come back," Matt promises. "You have to know that I didn't come to this decision easily."

I look out the window and watch the waves crash against the shore. How many days have I spent on that sand, waiting for thizz to overtake my body? I want that now. I want to be wrapped in a fluffy cloud of ecstasy where everything is warm and soft. I need to feel something other than this.

"So, it's done then," I confirm. "You did it all behind my back." Anger fills my chest. "Why did you wait until now to tell me? You've had to know for what two, three weeks?"

Matt moves back to his side of the car. "I didn't want to tell you until my transfer went through."

He isn't just leaving me; he's giving up Stanford too. It should make me feel better but it doesn't. I jab the button to roll down my window. The cold air makes me shiver. The smell of salt water awakens my sense memory and the need I have to get high.

"So, we'll do the long-distance thing?" I ask, even though that doesn't sound like what he's offering. "I understand how much you miss Ashley. I miss her too. We can make it work."

"Dani." He sighs. "It wouldn't be fair to either of us, and we don't need the added pressure. It's best for us to just focus on school right now."

I start to laugh. At him. At me. At this whole ridiculous thing. No matter how Matt sugarcoats it, he is dumping me.

"You don't have to explain anything else," I say. "I get it. We're over."

Matt places his arm across the seat so his hand rests on my shoulder. He starts to say the things people say when they're breaking up with someone.

You're still my best friend.

I care about you.

Let's just see how things go.

I look up at Matt; his eyes falter slightly. I see the pain this is causing him. If I didn't know him as well as I do, I'd think he meant all the words he's spilled from his mouth. I might actually believe that he doesn't love me. It can't be true because the Matt that gave me his heart wouldn't throw mine away. All the promises he made me, all the kisses and hugs, all the moments we shared that made our love special and unique. Am I to believe none of it was real? I look towards the horizon; the sun slips ever so slightly towards the ocean. I recall a moment when I stood not far from here and watched that same sun disappear as a familiar rush of pleasure filled my body. Maybe our feelings were a drug-induced hallucination. Nothing more than a side effect. What do I know about love anyway? I've never been in love. Not truly. Love for me is laced with ecstasy.

Nick

June 2007

I look up from my textbook and check the caller ID on my phone. It's Dani. I haven't seen her since we drove home from Eureka the weekend of Lucy's wedding. She called me after Matt told her he was moving to Colorado.

I still can't believe he's gone.

When I found out Matt took the internship in our Denver office, I made sure they set him up in one of our corporate apartments. I thought he'd be gone for the summer. Then he told me he was transferring from Stanford to the University of Colorado. Hearing that floored me. I mean shit, it's Stanford. You don't just walk away from that kind of education. And he sure as hell shouldn't be walking away from Dani.

I called him a dumbass and told him we'd figure something out. It was too late. He was spooked by the IRS agents. He blamed himself for the case they were building against Dani, against all of us. He was adamant about leaving to keep us safe, but I think part of him was relieved. This was the perfect excuse to be near his family. Being away from Ashley really tore him up inside. Can you imagine having to choose between your sister and the girl you love? I can't. Nobody should. Those IRS dicks did Matt a huge favor. They made the decision for him. Ashely needs her big brother, and Dani needs someone she can count on. Someone who will always put her first. Matt can't be both.

I can't really judge Matt. I put my business before Dani. I thought being a player in the dope game was a greater accomplishment than being Dani's boyfriend. If shit didn't get twisted, if Will wasn't the guy who pulled the trigger on her parents, I know I would've left her too. That little piece of truth is what keeps me away. I'm no better than Matt, maybe even worse. Dani needs a man who can be there for her emotionally and physically. Right now, that isn't me or Matt.

Let's be real, I never was that guy. I wanted Dani for purely selfish reasons. I wanted her because she didn't seem like she wanted me.

The first time I saw her at school, she walked past me in the hall, her eyes focused on the ground. She didn't even notice me. Not to be an asshole, but everyone notices me. People stare, gawk, drool, whatever. I don't mind the attention sometimes, but it gets old. When I tried to smile at her, she didn't acknowledge me. I was intrigued. Over the next couple of weeks, I watched her eyes move from the ground to my face. She only looked when she was far away and didn't think it was obvious. She wouldn't just look at me, she watched Matt too. Matt mostly. That day in the parking lot, when she walked up to my car, I have to admit I was hoping she was coming over to talk to me. I wasn't that lucky. I couldn't have been happier for Matt, or more jealous.

Matt being my boy didn't stop me from throwing out some feelers to see if she was interested. I made her blush a few times. We had a little vibe going. But I'm not a total asshole. I made sure Matt wasn't going to make a move. I always look out for my boys. When we'd go to parties and Arnie would stake his claim on the hottest girls there, I let him take his shot and fail. Then I waited for them come to me.

Arnie didn't have feelings for any of those chicks. Unlike Matt. He gets sprung on a girl and suddenly he has tunnel vision. Dani was the first girl he's dated since tenth grade. That chick was a phony. I never told Matt, but she used to flirt with me all the time. She'd rub my back or try to hold my hand when he wasn't looking. It was horrible. Luckily, Matt dumped her after a couple of months.

Dani was different in all the right ways, and I fell for her, hard. I know she loved me too. We had something really nice. But it wasn't strong enough to crush her feelings for Matt. That's why I let her go.

The day Matt left for Colorado, he didn't ask me to stay away from Dani. I can't at this point. We have to make sure there are no more fuck-ups. Mariann said as long as they have no hard evidence to prove our engagement is fake, and they never find out about the cash, we're good. My grandma is sort of a gangster. It was Mariann's idea to keep Dani in the dark about the CI agents and the evidence they collected on her and Matt. She didn't think Dani could handle the pressure. I agree. It's important for Dani to feel self-sufficient, even if we all know she's not.

I accept the call and brace for whatever is about to happen.

"Hey Dani, what's up." I give my voice a little more enthusiasm than the greeting probably calls for. I'm nervous.

"Hey, are you busy?" she asks. She's speaking in a high falsetto, which tells me she's nervous too.

"I'm just studying." I'm taking summer classes. The sooner I'm out of school, the better. Mariann started a new sector of JM Developers that she wants me to head up. I can't do that from a classroom.

"Do you want some company?"

The first thought in my head is hell yeah. So, what I'm about to say goes against every sensation in my body.

"I wish I could, but I'm slammed all weekend. I'm taking a bunch of classes this summer since I'm going to Europe at the end of the year."

"Oh," she says. "Tell me about the trip again. Mariann mentioned it, but she didn't go into details."

"JMD is buying an international company based in Denmark. It's more of a partnership really. But the owner wants me to come out and learn about their business before the merger goes through. I leave the first week of December."

"That sounds like a really amazing opportunity. I'm happy for you," she says.

There's a quiet pause like she's waiting for me to say something. My mind goes blank. I have so many things in my head that I'm not supposed to tell her. I'm afraid to speak.

I can't tell her the real reason Matt left.

I won't tell her how much I miss her.

I don't tell her my roommates are having a party.

I usually just lock my door, put on my headphones, and chill. Been there. Done that. I only got this house for Matt. Housing costs are high in Santa Clara. Anyway I could help him, I would. Now that

Matt's gone, I don't even want to be here. I can't kick the guys out; they're counting on the cheap rent. Yes, I charge them. Mariann said it's the principle. If they live for free, they won't respect the house. She was right. I have a cleaning service come in twice a week just to keep the place habitable.

"Is everything okay?" I finally ask. After all, she did call me.

"Yeah," she sighs. "I've just been stressed, and I was just wondering if you had any pills."

I know it hurt her to ask me that. Almost as much as it kills me to tell her no.

"I'm all out." That's a lie. I have sixty-two left. I counted them the night before Matt left. I was going to give him a few for the road. When we saw the stash had dwindled down to almost nothing over the past six months, we decided to save the rest. We made this stupid pact to meet once a year and take a pill. Like a yearly fishing or camping trip, we're taking a thizz trip. We have enough to continue the tradition for the next thirty years.

"Really?" she asks in a somewhat skeptical tone.

"Yep. I gave a bunch to my knucklehead roommates." Another lie. I'd never give those jackasses drugs. They have no problem scoring on their own. The house smells like a marijuana dispensary.

"Well, that sucks." She tries to sound lighthearted, but I can tell she's disappointed. "Okay, well let's hang out sometime. Other than at a public appearance or some boring dinner."

"Yeah, I'd love to, but right now things are hectic." That's not a lie. Mariann wants me to be the face of this foundation, which means meetings, appearances, and fundraisers. "I'll make some time just for us, I promise."

"Tell me about the foundation. Can I help?" She sounds desperate for something to do.

"It's called American Dream Foundation, or ADF for short. Our focus is to help rebuild communities after natural disasters. We also have an internship for engineers, and a vocational school for plumbing, electrical, and masonry. I'm excited about it."

This new arm of JMD is something that will help so many people. Change lives. I like that. The partnership with the European developers means we can eventually expand to other parts of the world.

"Sounds great, Nick. If there is ever anything I can do to help, just let me know," she says.

"I will," I tell her. Then silence again.

"I don't want to keep you from your homework."

Her voice breaks my heart. I want to jump in my truck and drive to her place. I want to hold her and kiss her and do crazy hot things with her. Neither of us needs that right now. I have to stay on course.

"You can call me whenever you feel like talking. I'll always be here for you, Dani. Always."

"Thanks, Nick," she says, and the phone goes dead.

I shut my phone and jump out of my chair. This is so fucking hard. I look at my keys. She's home alone. She wants me to come over. What the fuck am I still doing here?

What would I accomplish by going to Dani's place tonight?

We could take a picture for social media. We haven't posted a new one in a while, and we need to keep up appearances. I pick up my keys and look at the calendar on the wall. I see the fundraiser marked two weeks from now. Mariann wants us there to pose for pictures.

Come on, Marino, you can think of something better than that.

I could bring her dinner or coffee. A donut. Fuck. I have no reason to see Dani. No legitimate reason. If I drive to San Francisco right now, it's for one thing. If she gives it to me, there is no turning back. I'll spend every second I can with her. Everything I'm working for will be out the window. Just a taste, and I can't walk away. She is my high. She is the best thing that ever happened to me. I'm the worst decision of her life.

It isn't just my future or Dani's feelings I'm worried about.

There's Haley. We aren't a thing, but I care about her. Haley is a great girl. In another life, we might have been something. Right now we're both focused on our careers. Neither of us wants anything more than just good company. If I go see Dani, it will hurt Haley. I don't want to be that guy.

For once I listen to the big brain and sit my ass back in my chair. I open my textbook, pick up a yellow highlighter, and run it across the page.

Dani

I called Nick last night. It was humiliating, but I'm that desperate not to be alone. I've never really been by myself.

Working at Eureka Coffee helped keep me busy in the first few months after my parents were killed. It seemed like a crazy idea at the time. But it was the best therapy I could ever ask for. Focusing on work kept me from feeling sorry for myself. I just lost my family, but I never once felt as alone as I do now.

Losing Matt shouldn't be harder than losing my parents, but for some reason, it feels so much worse. They were taken from me against their will. Matt had a choice, and he chose not to be with me.

I thought about applying at one of the coffee shops on Columbus Avenue, but it feels wrong to take a job when I don't need the money. I wonder if they would let me work for free?

"Dani, I'm leaving," Heather yells from the hall.

I roll out of bed and open the door. I've been in the same sweats and t-shirt for three days. Heather notices and wrinkles her nose at me. "Don't start," I warn her.

"Whatever." She rolls her eyes. "I'm working a double. It's all hands on deck for the next three days. Traffic coming into the city is going to be a nightmare." Heather is a toll taker on the Bay Bridge. It's only part time, mostly weekends. It works well with her schedule, and she loves it.

"Okay, be safe," I tell her as I pick something off my shirt and smell it. "Just chocolate."

She rolls her eyes again and says, "Take a fucking shower, you're starting to smell."

I flip her off as she walks out the door. It shuts hard, and Arnie's leash bangs against the wall. His head pops up from his doggy bed. He looks at me with hopeful eyes. I don't want to go out. North Beach is crazy packed with all the tourists in town for Pride weekend. It's only Wednesday, but the madness is already starting.

Arnie stands and does a doggy stretch then walks over to me. I sit on the cold, dusty floor, and he waddles into my lap.

"You're my best friend now, buddy." I kiss him between the ears and hug his fat head.

The last thing I want to do is go outside. Everything reminds me of Matt. The stupid bench in the park where we used to sit for hours and talk. The spot under the tree where we made out on Valentine's Day. Even my favorite coffee shop is ruined by Matt memories.

I stand up and walk towards my room. Arnie begins to whine. He's another person in my life I'm disappointing. Even if he is a dog. I slip on my Vans and grab the leash. Arnie spins in a circle with his tongue hanging from the side of his mouth. "Let's go, boy."

I take him through our normal route and end in Washington Square Park so he can socialize with other dogs. Lots of people are sitting around day drinking. I see one of my neighbors, and he waves. I walk over to say hi because I could use a little socializing myself.

"Hey, Dani." Trey smiles as Arnie investigates his pizza box.

"Sorry." I pull the leash, but Arnie doesn't budge. I realize I haven't fed him today. "Arnie, get out of there!"

"It's all good, we're done anyway." Trey pulls out the last slice and lets Arnie go to town. "This is my boo, Stone." He gestures to the shirtless Magic-Mike-looking hottie sitting next to him.

"Hi." I wave and check to see if Arnie is done inhaling the pizza.

"Dani is my *upstairs* neighbor," Trey says. The way he emphasizes the location of my flat makes me curious.

Stone smiles and then says, "Oh, that neighbor. The one with the boyfriend that goes all night." He hi-fives Trey.

I roll my eyes and sigh. "He wasn't that great," I tell them. My body tenses at the memory of Matt in my bed.

"That's not what it sounded like to me," Trey says. He starts to make moaning sounds, my sounds.

"He had help." I raise my eyebrow. I can say whatever I want about Matt. I'll lie and tell everyone that he sucks in bed. I'll say he snores and farts in his sleep. I don't care. He's gone.

"The little blue pill?" Trey inquires.

"We were on ecstasy." I look at Arnie; he's lying on the blanket now, his belly full and ready for a nap.

Stone whispers to Trey, and then he asks if I can score some pills.

"Sorry. My source dried up." I think of Nick studying in his room. If this were another time, he'd be in the city this weekend, selling pills and partying. He would've loved all of this. If I tell him just how huge this weekend is, he might change his mind and drive up. Even if he doesn't have pills, it would be nice to hang out. But I won't.

I can't put myself through that humiliation again. Nick has another plan for his life. One that doesn't include getting high with me.

Trey gives a little pout for like two seconds, then scratches Arnie's belly. "Speaking of dried up, I haven't heard your man around lately."

"He moved to Colorado." I like telling people Matt moved out of state. There are no follow-up questions. They assume the break-up was amicable or at least unpreventable.

"I'm sorry, boo." Trey rubs my leg. "Do you want to hang with us this weekend? We're hitting all the clubs. Stone has VIP, he's a dancer." Trey winks at me. Of course he is.

"Thanks, but I'm in hibernation mode."

"You look like you've been hibernating all winter with that hair." Trey shakes his head in disapproval of my messy bun. That's what I'm calling it. The thing has taken on a life of its own.

"I have nobody to impress." I shrug and look around the park. None of these people give a shit about the status of my hair.

Trey stands up and takes me by the shoulders. "This is the time you should care. Fuck your ex, fuck everyone. You need to look good for you. When you look good, you feel good." He leans down to look into my eyes. "You hear me?"

I barely know Trey, other than the occasional hi and bye, so his sincere advice throws me off. I wasn't ready for someone who only knows my name to have that much effect on how I'm feeling.

"Yes," I choke out. "I think I needed to hear that."

"Oh, I know you needed it," Trey says as he sits back down. "You also need a shower."

I laugh and pull Arnie off the blanket. "I gotta go. You guys have fun this weekend. It was nice to meet you, Stone."

As I'm walking up Columbus towards Union, I see a sign for a twenty-dollar haircut in the window next to the deli. I take Arnie home, change my shirt, then head back down.

Thirty minutes later, I'm in the chair.

"So, what can I do for you today?" A middle-aged Italian woman with red lipstick and a cheetah print sweater stands behind me, assessing the mop on my head.

I took the bun out and sprayed some Febreze in my hair before I tried to brush it. I didn't want to show up smelling like I haven't showered for three days. From the look on the hairdresser's face; I'd say I failed.

"I don't know, what do you think?"

She turns my head this way and that then spins me around to face the mirror. "With your cheekbones and this chin." She points to my chin with a comb. "Your sweet spot is about here." She places her hand about two inches below my ear.

"Really?" I choke out. "That short?"

"Yes," she says with no further explanation.

I've never had short hair. I wouldn't even know what to do with it. Lucy will freak out. Heather will think I've lost my mind. Nobody will recognize me.

"Let's do it. I want highlights too. Red ones."

"Now you're talkin'," she exclaims and starts pumping up my chair.

Two hours later, I walk into my flat and catch my reflection in the mirror. It's not me I see. I don't know the girl staring back, but I can't wait to find out what she's all about.

The next day I'm shopping on Market Street when I see Zack and Antonio on the sidewalk ahead of me. I weave through the crowd and catch up with them in front of the Powell Street BART station. A street musician playing the bongos smiles at me as I move in front of my favorite gay couple and twirl.

"Holy shit, is that Dani?" Antonio says. "You look hot, mamma."

"Thank you," I say and flip my hair with my hand. Confidence and compliments are great mood enhancers.

"What inspired this new you?" Zack adjusts the shopping bags in his hand then gives me a hug.

"I just wanted a change." I silently thank Trey.

"You look too good to stay home this weekend. You're coming to Candy with us tonight. It's dyke night. They're going to fucking love you!" Zack drapes his arm across my shoulders the way Matt or Nick might do. The way a friend would do.

"I'm not twenty-one," I inform him.

"Oh please, honey. Everyone is twenty-one on Pride weekend."

Last week Zack invited me to go out with him and Antonio for Pride, and I told him no way. But now, with this hair, I have totally changed my mind. Or lost it. Either way, I'm in. "Okay, fuck it. Let's go."

We plan to meet up in two hours. I go straight home, walk Arnie, then change into a white tank top and a black San Francisco Forty Niners hoodie. I put on a little bit of lip gloss and a lot of mascara. I'm not sure what to do with my hair, so I put on a black beanie. The red highlights peek from the bottom, making me look sort of badass. I look like someone I would hang out with. Isn't that the point? Be someone you can stand to be around?

It takes a bus and a train to get to the Castro. As soon as I emerge from the station, I spot Zack waiting for me. We hug and he yells to Antonio, who is talking to a couple of girls nearby. He hands them something, then catches up with us as we head down the street.

"Who are they?" I ask. If I didn't know Antonio and Zack were a couple, I'd think he was flirting with those chicks. They certainly looked interested in him.

"A couple of gay-for-a-day bitches from Marin. I gave them my card in case they need to get ahold of me later." Antonio winks then walks a few steps ahead of us. He's wearing a black t-shirt with an image of Tupac painted on the front. Zack is in baggy jeans and a white wife-beater. He's got a silver chain around his neck with a large Z dangling in the center of his chest. They are the least gay-looking dudes on the street.

The line for Candy is long, but the boys walk up to the bouncer and he lets us right in. We pass through a black curtain into a dark hall. The light at the end of the tunnel is blocked by a man in a fairy costume. His electric blue spandex shorts look about two sizes too small, and he's covered in body glitter. His white wings glow under the black light above his head.

"Hey Norman," Zack greets him. They air kiss.

"Hey, sexy." Antonio holds out his hand, and I see him slide something into Norman's palm.

"This is Dani," Zack says. "This is her first Pride."

Norman regards me for a moment. He didn't ask the guys for ID, but he's looking like he may be considering my age. "Where you from, Dani?" he finally asks.

"Here. I grew up in North Beach," I tell him.

"A local girl. Well, in that case, have a good time." He steps aside and allows me to enter my very first bar.

"That was easy," I say to Zack as we maneuver our way through the dance floor.

"It pays to be local." He kisses my cheek then grabs me by the waist and starts dancing to the whistle song.

Antonio appears with a blue drink in his hand for me. He goes back to the bar for two more then joins us on the dance floor. I have a feeling this is going to be a great night.

"Are you drunk yet?" Zack yells over the third T-Pain song I've heard in the last two hours.

I slam the shot and nod. "I think so." If I could hear myself over the music, I'm almost certain I'd be slurring. I pick up my blue drink. It's called an Adios. Not quite sure why.

Zack loops his arm with mine and says the show is about to start.

"What show?" I blink up at him. Suddenly three men appear in the empty perches on the back wall. "Holy shit! Is this a strip club?"

He laughs and says, "No, they're just teasing for tips."

I sigh in relief. I'm not ready to check strip club off my list of firsts tonight. When Akon's "I Wanna Love You" comes on, the place goes off. Even I'm cheering as the guys start to remove their top layer of clothing. I'm not sure if I should close my eyes or take notes.

As we watch the show, I notice Zack is especially interested in the guy on the far right. He's facing the wall, so I can't tell if he's good-looking. Not that it matters, the crowd isn't interested in his eye color.

Faded Levi's sit low on his waist. His red-and-black-checkered boxers slip down a millimeter, and Zack yells so loudly, I think he's going to pop an artery. The mystery dancer flips his snapback around so it sits backward on his head. The word LOCAL glows under the black light, and now I cheer. The guy turns around and rips his white t-shirt off, and I'm probably the only person here looking at his face.

"Oh shit!" I yell. "I know him!"

"Bullshit," Zack says.

"It's my neighbor's boo," I laugh.

"I knew there was a reason I liked you." Zack gives me sweaty hug. "I want to meet him." He dance-drags me to Stone's perch. We wait about thirty seconds before he gives me a signal to make contact. I guess he doesn't want to look obvious. Like he didn't just drag me across the bar.

I tap Stone's leg, and he looks down, all serious. I wonder if there is a no-touching rule. Once my face registers in his mind, he smiles. Then he notices Zack. A look passes between them. It's part what's-up-dude, part I-want-to-lick-you.

He kneels down on one knee. "Hey, Dani." He kisses my cheek. I think it's very aggressive behavior for someone I barely know, but it feels kind of good. All the dudes around me look crestfallen like he's one of mine and not one of theirs.

"This is my friend, Zack," I introduce him.

They say hi, shake hands, then Stone goes back to dancing.

"He has a boyfriend," I tell Zack before he gets too attached.

"Everyone is single on Pride weekend." Zack finishes his drink and places the cup on a table. I wonder if he's annoyed that Antonio left to meet some friends at another bar over an hour ago and hasn't come back. Antonio works the crowd in a familiar fashion, sort of like

Arnie did back when he was selling pills for Nick. I want to ask Zack if Antonio is selling ecstasy. What if I'm wrong and he's offended? Or worse, what if he is?

"Go get more drinks." Zack places a twenty in my hand.

"I still have a drink." I hold up my half-full cup.

"The bartender is feeling you, she'll give you a discount." He pushes me towards the bar.

Wait, what? How does he know the bartender is feeling me? I look at the bartender; her name is Cheri. That much I know. She's got a pixie cut, large brown eyes, and big hoop earrings. She's wearing a white tank top with the word PRIDE across the front in rainbow lettering. I took off my hoodie hours ago, so I'm in my white tank top. We're like twins, but not.

I walk to the end of the bar and wait for her to notice me. It only takes about fifteen seconds.

"What can I get you, sweetie?" She leans over and listens intently.

"Um, two more of these." I hold up my drink.

She nods and winks, then leaves to fill my order. Zack is crazy. Cheri doesn't like me. She's just doing her job. She finishes the drinks off with a cherry and slides them in front of me. I suck down what's left of the one in my hand. I can't hold three. I unfold the twenty and lay it on the bar.

Cheri shakes her head. "It's on me." She winks again.

Goddamn, Zack was right.

I thank her and walk back to Zack. I look around the dance floor with the drinks in my hand. The crowd erupts in cheers, and I turn towards the excitement. Zack and Stone are sharing his perch.

The space is small; they are big. So, you can imagine the position they're in to keep from falling off the side.

I walk back to the bar and set the drinks down. A few minutes later, Cheri comes back.

"What happened to your boy?" She gestures to the untouched Adios.

I point to the wall. Cheri follows my finger. "Oh shit!" She whistles and cheers with the rest of the bar. "You want a shot?" Cheri winks. She's a winker.

I don't think I can stomach another shot, but I can't say no. It's a gift. I wonder if Cheri thinks I'm flirting. I wonder if she thinks I'm gay? Cheri fills two shot glasses with clear liquid.

"Cheers." She holds up one of the shots. I take the other. We clink them together, and I pour the poison into my mouth. I take a quick sip of my Adios to keep the tequila down.

"Love your hair," she yells. "The red is badass."

My hand goes to my head. It still feels weird to touch my short hair. I'm sure it looks jacked since I took my beanie off.

Cheri grabs my hand. "You look good." She winks as her hand slides off mine.

That was weird. Not bad weird. New weird. Unfamiliar weird. This whole night has been a new experience. One I'm having without thizz. I'm drunk, but hey, that's better than being high, isn't it? Is alcohol any better just because it's legal? Yes. I vote yes.

I chill at the end of the bar for the next hour. If bar groupies were a thing, I'd be one. Zack and Stone went to "talk" after Stone's set was over. I finally see him walking in at the same time the crowd cheers on the other side of the dance floor. A girl in a Rainbow Brite costume is leaning over the bar, kissing Cheri. They break away, and the girl starts walking in my direction. I'd know that face anywhere. She walks past me towards the bathroom, and I finally find my voice.

"Mary?" I yell.

She turns and does a double take. I realize she doesn't recognize me. My hair. This bar. I'm the last person she expected to see. The feeling is mutual.

"Dani?" She walks towards me, her pigtails swaying against the sides of her head. "What the fuck did you do to your hair?"

She's asking about my hair when she's standing in front of me dressed like an eighties cartoon character. The costume and white thigh-high boots are a far cry from the Banana Republic sweater set she was wearing the last time I saw her.

"My hair? Pigtails, Mary. Seriously?" I flip one of her tails up, and it slaps against her face.

"You guys know each other?" Cheri places her arm around Mary and kisses her neck.

"Yeah, we used to work together," Mary tells her. "Back in Eureka."

"I thought you were from the city?" Cheri looks at me like I'm a liar.

"It's a long story," Mary tells her. "Come on, boo. You owe me a dance." Mary kisses Cheri on the mouth.

What. The. Fuck.

I leave the club at one in the morning with Mary and Zack. Both have been ditched. Cheri has to close up, and Antonio is missing in action. We share a cab back to my place. Heather is asleep when we creep in. We go to my room while Zack heads to the bathroom.

"I need to get out of this," Mary says as she unzips her boots.

I throw Mary a pair of sweats and a Eureka Coffee t-shirt. She laughs as she takes the costume off and pulls the shirt on.

I lie on the bed and watch her change. She still looks and sounds like annoying Mary. She is definitely not the person I knew in Eureka.

"Just ask me already," she says.

"Ask what?" I pretend like I'm not dying to know how, why, when. Mary throws her bra at me. I duck and say, "Okay, when, how?"

"I've always known I liked girls more than boys. Going to an all-girl's school just confused the situation. I didn't realize the things I was feeling towards girls would be classified as gay. I thought it was, like, female bonding or something. I didn't really accept that it was real until my final year in high school. It was you, actually."

My mouth falls open. "You liked me?"

"More like I didn't like that you liked boys. I was mad that you were with Nick. I hated Matt just for being your friend."

"I thought you liked Nick."

"That's just it. I should've liked him, and I liked you more." She smiles and winks.

I throw my pillow at her. "Does your family know?" I ask, remembering her very strict parents.

"I told them the night before I left for college." She laughs. "It was a long night."

"Were they pissed?"

"Shocked, mostly. Patty thinks it's a phase. Maybe it is. I'm just happy to finally be living the life I want."

Mary's statement makes me think about how I'm living my life. Am I the person I want to be? The old Dani wouldn't have gone to the bar with Zack. I've already outdone myself, and all I did was

129

change my hair. If I keep doing things that make me cringe, things the old Dani would be absolutely against, maybe I'll find the person I'm looking for.

Dani

December 2007

I pop open the bottle of chardonnay Nick brought for me. We don't have wine glasses so I grab two juice glasses from the cabinet.

"Fancy," Heather teases. "Since when are you a wine drinker?" She sets the bottle down and opens the refrigerator for a beer. She twists the top off and takes a swig.

I grab her beer and gulp it down. "I'm more sophisticated than you think." A burp bubbles to the surface and escapes my lips.

"Yeah, sure." Heather snatches her beer and leaves. I hear her stop in the living room and say hi to Nick.

He asks how she's been, they bullshit back and forth, then she retreats to her room. Heather has a lot of animosity towards Nick. She blames him for Arnie. There is nothing anyone can say to change her mind about Nick. I don't try.

I take the wine to the living room and pour us each a glass.

Nick stands and holds his glass towards me. "To new beginnings."

I smile and clink my glass to his. The wine is just as good as the last time I had it as the Marino's. I down mine and pour myself more.

"When does your plane leave?" I sit on the couch and kick off my flip flops.

"Midnight. I wanted to come by and see you before I left." He sits beside me and sips from his glass. He isn't the same slouchy, comfortable guy I used to hang with in his cottage. This is an entirely different person.

"That was nice of you." My attitude is at a ten.

Other than the occasional event with Mariann, I haven't seen Nick in months. At the events, we usually just smile for the cameras then leave with very few words spoken. He was always the one running away to a meeting or back home claiming he had an early class.

"Things have been really intense with school and getting this foundation off the ground." He sits on the edge of the couch like he's about to stand and leave. As much as I want to hate him. I really don't want him to go.

"It's okay, Nick. I'm glad you came by." The wine must be working because my bitch-meter just went down a few notches.

Nick sets his glass down and exhales like he's about to say something really important.

I drain my wine glass in preparation.

"A year is a long time be away and even though we don't see much of each other, I take comfort in knowing you're close by. Now that I'll be on the other side of the world, I guess I'm feeling a little nostalgic. That's not the right word. Maybe, it's a little bit of fear." He rakes his fingers through his hair.

"What are you afraid of?" I have no clue what he's trying to tell me. "We can still text and email each other."

"I know. Let's do a better job than we have in the last year. I know most of that was me. There's a good reason behind it." He blows out a long breath. "I really was busy and overwhelmed with school. My responsibilities have tripled in the last six months, you know that."

I nod. Nick has been preparing for this trip since the summer. His success in Denmark is crucial for the future of his foundation.

"I guess what I'm trying to say is. You are still really important to me and you might be the reason I'm trying to fast track my life. I want to be someone you deserve."

I wasn't expecting that.

"I'm in love with you, Dani." He pauses and runs his hand through his hair. "I also know being with you isn't realistic at this point. Not just because I'm moving to Denmark. There's Matt."

"Matt is a non-issue," I say. "He isn't the reason we aren't together." I'm not with Nick because I don't love him the way he thinks he loves me.

"You may not care about Matt right now, but his feelings played a huge part in why I didn't call you. Why I didn't see you."

"I have no communication with him at all." I try to emphasize the at all. Matt cut me off when he left. I don't even message or email Ashley anymore. It's like the Augustine family has been wiped from the earth.

"Matt doesn't want me and he sure as shit, doesn't love me."

"That isn't entirely true."

Nick launches into a story about Matt and CI agents, and pictures of us together.

"They picked him up in March, right before his birthday. That's when he decided to move to Colorado," Nick explains.

The story Nick delivers seems to work in Matt's favor. What he doesn't understand is, Matt had a choice and he chose not to be with me. All the reasoning in the world doesn't change that.

He totally cut me out of his life; he doesn't get a free pass because his motives may have been honorable.

"I don't see why any of this matters now." I pour myself the rest of the wine. "Why are you telling me this?"

"I needed you to know there's still a chance for you and Matt to be together if you want it."

"Really, Nick?" I stand and move to the window. "We're done. Forever."

"Mariann is pushing to have the IRS investigation closed and I just wanted you to know the truth." Nick stands and puts on his jacket. "I should go."

I realize that Nick's intentions were not as selfish as I want to believe. He's telling me this so I can move on. Or go back. He gave me all the facts so I can make my decision. I appreciate that.

"Thank you, Nick."

"For what?" he scoffs. "I ruined our last night together."

"No, you didn't." I walk to him and wrap my arms around his torso. "You have always respected my feelings. I really appreciate that. It's one of the reasons I love you."

Nick holds me for a long time. It feels good in his arms.

"I'm gonna miss you," I whisper into his chest.

"Not as much as I'll miss you." He kisses the top of my head. "Text me all the time. Just to say hi or a random boobie pic. Whatever."

I slap his chest and back away from him. "Don't be gross."

"I won't make it through the next year without you, promise you'll keep in touch?"

"Pinky promise." I hold my finger and he loops his around mine.

I walk Nick to his SUV. I let him hold my hand as we walk down the hill.

He unlocks the door then turns around and holds opens his black wool coat. I slide my arms around him and he locks me in his arms.

"I love you, Dani."

I tell him I love him, kiss him on the cheek, then I let him go.

I watch his taillights disappear down Columbus Avenue and find myself feeling relieved that he's gone.

Matt

May 2008

I close my laptop and place it in my backpack. The girl in front of me turns around and smiles. She always does this at the end of class. I smile because I don't want to be rude. I shake my leg in anticipation and check the clock. It's a race to the door once the hour is up. I don't think she realizes that I'm running away from her. If she did, she wouldn't keep sitting by me.

Our professor finally checks his watch. "Looks like that's it."

I shoot out of my seat and head up the stairs to the door. Samantha follows me. I step into the hall, and I don't hear the door close behind me. Great.

"Do you have any plans for the summer?" Her winded voice calls to me. It takes some effort to scale the stairs at my speed. She does it. Every time.

"Yeah, I'm going to California," I lie. I tell her I'm late for something, then speed walk to the parking lot. When I think it's safe, I slow down and make sure Samantha isn't behind me. She's relentless. At first, I thought she was just being friendly. Smiling at me in the hall before class. When we merged into study groups, she made sure to be in mine. She even baked me cookies. Chocolate chip ones. I see right through her cookies. And I'm not interested.

I drive to my apartment, the one Nick set me up with. It's decent and close to school. I would live with my parents, but it doesn't make sense to commute. I see them at least three times a week. I haven't missed a Sunday dinner since I moved here. I can't believe it's been almost a year.

In all this time, I haven't spoken to Dani once. I hate myself for hurting her, but I don't regret leaving. The time I've spent with Ashley, the relationship I've repaired with my parents, it makes all the pain worth it.

I still ask about her every time I talk to Nick. He always says the same thing. She's good, but different. I'm not one hundred percent certain he means that in a good way. She blocked me from her social media accounts. Her profile picture is a girl with short red hair in a black beanie. The face in the picture is hidden from the camera; I can't tell if it's her or not. Ashley thinks it is. Yes, I enlisted my little sister to help me stalk Dani.

There's only so much I can ask Nick. If he knew how much I missed her, how badly I still want her, he'd kick my ass. Then he'd probably tie me up and drive me back to San Francisco. I can't do that. Not now. Not until the IRS closes the case on her father and they break off their fake engagement.

The last time I spoke to Nick, he said the case had stalled. They can't hold it open much longer without cause. That was six months ago. Nick came to visit right before he left for Europe. He looked different. I don't know, older somehow. He's been so focused on school and his foundation, it changed him. I can't imagine what he's going to be like after a year in Europe. He enrolled at the university in Copenhagen to keep up with his classes. He's in full-on beast mode.

I get home and check my voicemail, no messages. I set my laptop on the desk and plug it in. Facebook is my new obsession and quenches my stalking urges. I look up Heather's account, nothing new. Then Mary's.

Let's talk about Mary. She likes girls. Who knew? She has several pics of her latest conquest. Not only does Mary like girls, the girls that like Mary are Nick-Marino-level hot, back when Nick was getting chicks. For all I know, he's conquered half of Europe by now. Unlike Dani, he doesn't have the IRS watching his every move. She still posts random tweets about her and Nick on Twitter. Since he's on the other side of the planet, there are no new pictures, just fake I-miss-you and I-love-you tweets. They still hurt. I know I have no right. Tell my heart that. The fucking thing won't let her go.

I check my notifications. Samantha liked one of my posts about study habits of pre-law students. Nick posted a picture of himself on the roof of a house in Japan. And Dani sent me a friend request.

Wait.

I click back. Dani Batista sent me a friend request. I click accept and my heart starts thumping against my chest. What am I, a girl now? Thumping hearts and shit.

The first thing I do is click her photos. She is the girl with short hair. And a nose piercing. And a tongue piercing. And a boyfriend. I can't stop looking at the picture of her lips locked with some dude in a pair of lime green sunglasses. The picture was taken in a club at night, so the fact that he's wearing sunglasses makes him a douchebag. Dani is kissing a douchebag.

I slam my laptop shut and push away from the desk. I walk to the sink and close my eyes. What did I expect? She would just crawl into a fucking hole and become a nun?

Yeah. That's exactly what I was hoping. I haven't even looked at another woman since I left Dani. Why would I? She's the only one I want.

Worst case scenario, I thought her and Nick would get back together. I could stomach that. Not this. Not even fucking close. She obviously friended me on purpose. She wanted me to see.

I go to bed feeling like shit and dream about her. It's not my Dani. Not the shy girl I met in computer class. I dream about the vibrant redhead who posts pictures on social media of her kissing douchebags that wear the letter Z around their necks.

I left because I thought I was putting her in danger with the IRS. What changed? Nick would've told me if the investigation was over. He only checks in a few times a week. They could have sent notice that the case was closed, and he hasn't gotten around to telling me yet.

I guess it really doesn't matter now. She's got someone new.

We both lose.

I get up, shower, drink two beers, and text Nick to see what he knows. It's one in the morning in Denmark; he won't get back to me for a while. I pace the living room of my small apartment with a million things running through my mind. Good things, illegal things, really fucked up things about a girl I loved more than anyone in the world. A girl who just obliterated my heart.

I sit at the desk and open my email. I type out a message to the person I've been avoiding for months. This self-imposed celibacy was my punishment for leaving Dani. I also didn't think I was ready to let somebody in. I didn't think I had anything to give. All of that changed when I saw Z-boy kissing Dani.

Before you start hating me more than I hate myself, I'll admit that this is my fault. I left her. I let her go. Cutting off communication in those first few months was crucial for me. I knew if we kept in contact, I would cave. It was selfish, I know. Don't think I wasn't aware of the risks. I was. I even hoped Dani would find someone who deserved her. Who would love and care for her in a way I couldn't. I can't tell you the type of man I imagined Dani would fall for, but it sure as fuck isn't the dude she is kissing on Facebook.

Dani

"Holy shit!" I yell. "Mary, he accepted my friend request!"

She comes running into my room with a towel wrapped around her naked body. Water runs down her legs and puddles on the floor.

I sit up on my knees with my laptop in front of me on the bed. "What should I say?"

Excitement bubbles up inside of me. I've waited so long to make contact with him. It's been nearly a year since I heard his voice.

I know why he moved to Colorado. He was trying to protect everyone. I was pissed for a long time. Just because he was trying to do the right thing doesn't mean he executed his plan properly. He asked me not to call or email him. He said it would be easier. Maybe for him. But it killed me.

Just when I thought I was over it, I received a letter in the mail stating the investigation on my father has been concluded. No evidence of tax evasion or fraud was found. Last week, Will Walker was sentenced to forty-five years in jail. There is nothing holding me back. I can finally move on with my life. Matt was the first thing on my list.

"Tell him you're horny," Mary suggests. She's serious, and she's right. I haven't had sex with anyone since Matt. She sits on my bed and looks at his profile picture. "Ugh, he's still adorable."

She's right again. I click through his pictures; there aren't very many. Mostly just ones that Ashley tagged him in. He hasn't changed at all. His hair has grown out since the last time I saw him, but his blue eyes are the same color as the tiny crystal sitting on the table beside my bed.

He looks good. Ashley looks thin and pale beside him. I regret not keeping in touch with Ashley. I check her Facebook almost every day to make sure she's okay, alive. Occasionally, she posts a picture of Matt. Since I blocked him, I don't have access to his page. Heather lets me stalk him from her account. I didn't block Matt to be a bitch. Matt cut me out of his life first, long before I even had a Facebook.

Mary leaves to get dressed, and I stare at Matt's picture for a full twenty minutes. When she comes back, she looks at the screen and sighs. "It's starting all over again, isn't it?"

"What?"

"The Matt-Dani drama. Does he love me? Do I love him? Do we love each other? Should we fuck?" Mary opens my closet and pulls out one of my hoodies.

"You have become a serious potty mouth, you know that?"

She pulls my favorite Ecko sweater over her head and says, "At least I know what I want."

"Yeah, my clothes." I gesture to her outfit. "Don't you have a closet somewhere?"

Mary always crashes at my place when we go out. Heather is working full time during summer break, so Mary will probably be here pretty often. I like that.

"Don't hate because I rock your clothes better than you." She flips her hair and walks out of my room like she's stomping down a runway.

Thirty minutes later, Mary leaves to meet Cheri for brunch, and I decide to post something on Matt's wall.

~~What's up, Matty? How's Colorado? Why did you leave me?~~

~~Hey you, sorry I haven't written. Or called. Or cared. Fuck you for leaving.~~

~~Hi, Matt. How's Colorado? Sorry, I haven't written or called but you left me. Fuck you.~~

~~I miss you.~~

Hi, Matt.

I refresh my screen every three seconds for the next hour before I give up. He's probably sleeping. Or maybe he's working. I don't know what Matt does with his time or who he spends it with. I start to wonder if he's still single. I check his profile for a relationship status. He doesn't have one. That's good I guess.

I haven't dated anyone since he left. It doesn't feel right. The only feels I get come from the pills I score from Antonio. I was right about him being a drug dealer. I can spot one a mile away, especially when they're selling my favorite thing in the world. Mollies don't even come close to blue dolphins, but after a few shots, they do the trick. Right now, good enough is enough.

I take a shower, drink two cups of coffee, walk Arnie, then check Facebook. Nothing from Matt, but Zack posted about the party at Candy tonight. I tell him I'll meet him at nine, then log off. I refuse to torture myself. Not when I can just call him. He has the same number.

I pull my cell phone from the charger and text Nick. He's ten hours ahead of me, so I won't hear back for a while. We text a few times a month just to say hi and check in with each other. I always feel like I'm intruding. Nick is creating a new life for himself, one I'm no longer a part of. Especially now that our fake engagement if off. Nick and I are officially over.

It's the longest day of my life. Waiting for Nick to reply. Waiting for Matt to acknowledge me. I start drinking early. By the time I meet Zack and Antonio, I'm already tipsy.

"You smell blue collar," Zack says when I kiss him hello.

He's referring to the beers I drank while I was getting dressed and putting on my makeup. The guy Heather is dating left a six-pack in our refrigerator. I owe him some beers.

"Shut up." I push him away and continue dancing to T-Pain's "Bartender."

Zack slides behind me and wraps his arms around my waist. He likes to pretend he's straight sometimes. He says it makes him more appealing to the gay dudes and less threatening to the curious ones. The only action I get is fake affection from Zack. Even though he doesn't want me, being held by him is good enough.

He's trying to get me to bend over in front of him when I feel my phone vibrate. I stop shaking my ass and pull it out of my pocket. When I see the text is from Nick, I run outside to read it.

What's up D. I can't be in the middle of this right now. You and Matt need to talk. Call him.

In the middle of what? I just wanted to say hi. Jerk. I open my Facebook app and check to see if Matt replied to my post or commented on any of my pictures. Something. Anything. The last notification from him is when he accepted my friend request.

I click on his page, and the first thing that pops up makes my stomach turn. I reach into my pocket and pull out the capsule Antonio gave me earlier. I didn't take it because I was hoping to talk to Matt. I didn't want to do that when I was high.

Fuck him. Fuck Nick. Fuck everything.

Nick

I wake up to texts from Dani and Matt. This isn't the first time they've tag-teamed me for information. Most days I'm happy to feed their addiction. This isn't most days.

I volunteered with a group of builders who are helping the Southeast Asian country of Myanmar. It was hit by a cyclone last week. Close to one hundred thousand people lost their homes. Today I have more important things to worry about than Matt and Dani.

I close my phone and get up. I have a long day ahead of me. Bed is a thin cushion on the floor of what used to be a hotel. Water damage from flooding ruined most of the building. The second and third floors are safe and will be our home for the next three to six months. I stretch my back and do a quick set of jumping jacks to get my blood flowing. It's something I picked up while I was in Japan.

I slip on my work boots and walk downstairs to the back of the building where the makeshift bathroom has been set up. It's a garden hose and a hole in the ground shielded by a moldy shower curtain. There are no working toilets or running water yet. More than two hundred men are working on fixing pipes. Disease is the main issue at this point. Preventing an outbreak means we need running water and proper drainage. So, yeah, Matt and Dani's drama can take a backseat to the literal shit I'll be digging today.

The area around the hotel has been cleared for mobile medical units and trucks carrying fresh water. I spot my group filtering out of the hotel with empty water containers. I grab one and get in line. This is the last access to clean water we'll have today.

As I stand in line, I listen to the conversations around me; none of them are in English. The guys on my team are Dutch and Danish, and although they speak English, they drop into their native languages in casual conversation.

I miss the companionship of people that speak my language. I don't just mean in the literal sense. The last five months have shown me there is so much more to the world than the one I created. Outside Humboldt County, the name Nick Marino doesn't mean shit.

I feel something tug at my leg and look down. A little boy with a toy car sits at my feet. He runs the car up my leg then over my hand. He makes a car sound and slides it up to my arm.

"Hey, I used to have a car just like that," I tell him, even though he doesn't understand English. "Can I see it?" I hold out my hand, and he places it in my palm.

I wonder how a child on the other side of the world got his hands on a Hot Wheel. Let alone a replica of the same car I used to own. The one my best friend died in. It's funny how things come full circle. A car that brings pain to me, gives joy to this little boy.

I kneel down and make the car pull a wheelie. The kid laughs, and two more join us. I don't know how long I play with them; when I look up, my group is loading the van with supplies.

"I gotta go." I hand the car back to the boy. He puts his hands together, the car held between his palms, and bows to me. The gesture

147

chokes me up. I don't know, just something about the innocence in his eyes. His country is in ruin; his chance of living a long, healthy life is literally in our hands. I bow to him and get back in line to fill my container.

"Marino, let's go," Nils, my sort-of boss, yells. Technically, I own Nils's company. But nobody here cares. They treat me like the ignorant kid I am.

I fill my container with water and run inside for my hat and gloves. As I walk towards the van I wave to the boys playing on the sidewalk. An old woman carrying a basket stops in front of me and offers what looks like a giant green pinecone. I refuse it at first, then remember the lesson we were given on local culture, and I don't want to be rude.

These people have lost their homes, their businesses, and their families, and yet they greet us with smiles and blessings. I've never felt more inspired. We are tasked with planning the rebuild of homes and a school. Even though I only planned to be gone a year, I'll stay as long as it takes.

"Damn, Marino, you scored," Valter says and takes the weird-looking fruit out of my hand. "Trade you for three protein bars?" Protein bars are the only thing we're living on until tomorrow when our supplies get here.

"Don't do it, kid." Nils takes the fruit from Valter and gives it back to me. "That thing is delicious." Nils turns to the driver and gives him the go. "It'll taste really good after all the shit you're gonna smell today." The guys laugh as the van takes off down the bumpy road.

"Great," I sigh. I don't really care about the shit or surviving on crappy protein bars and supplements. Or that I haven't actually showered in a week. I'm just happy to be part of something that will make a difference. I thought selling drugs was the key to unlocking my potential. What a fucking joke.

I place the fruit on the seat beside me and put my hat on. It's a black fitted hat with the Forty Niners logo on the front. Matt gave it to me for my sixteenth birthday. It's my favorite. I'd be lying if I said I didn't miss him. I really want to call and tell him about everything I've seen and the things I'm going to do. But I can't be here and in the middle of the Matt-and-Dani soap opera at the same time.

Matt moving to Colorado was a good thing. CI had nothing once Matt was out of the picture. They believed the bullshit Dani and I posted on Twitter. Before I left, went to all of Mariann's events together. We even pretended to look at wedding venues. I let Dani bring one of her new friends along, the gay one that wears that stupid Z on a chain. He pretended to be our wedding planner. Even though she laughed through most of the day, I could tell it was killing her. I don't know if it was the lies or the fact that she was hungover. She's different in so many ways. I almost feel like I don't know her anymore. Now that the investigation is over, hopefully, she can return to the person she used to be. And I don't just mean her hair color.

Mariann sent word the investigation was over in her last email. I kind of hoped Dani would reach out to Matt, but if he's asking me for updates, apparently she hasn't told him. He doesn't know it's safe to go back. They can finally be together without me or the United States government standing in their way. I say that like it doesn't rip my heart out. It does. Right now, he's the better man. The closer man.

I haven't completely ruled out being with Dani. If Matt fucks up somehow, if she's single when I return home, then nothing will keep me from her.

Matt

I'm on my date with Samantha when Nick finally gets back to me. The message is short. It says, "Go home." The investigation must be over.

"Is everything okay?" Samantha asks from across the small table. We're at an Italian restaurant near campus. I let Samantha choose the place since I have no clue where to take a girl on a date in Colorado. She was born and raised in a small town outside of Denver.

At first glance, she seems like a dainty dancer type, but she's really outdoorsy. I've let her do most of the talking so far, and I learned that she loves hiking, skiing, and white water rafting.

I close my phone and shove it in my pocket. "Yeah, it's fine. Just a friend of mine volunteering in Myanmar."

Samantha looks impressed. If she only knew the Nick I grew up with. There was nothing impressive about that guy. He's come so far since those days. He's done everything right since we left Eureka.

"So, you were telling me about your brother," I say to Samantha as I shove lettuce around my plate. I'm sure she thinks I'm a freak for ordering a salad at a place famous for its pizza.

"He was four years older than me."

I catch the word was, and I look up from my plate.

Samantha takes a sip of her red wine. She drinks red, not white. I'm grateful for that.

"He died when I was twelve. Leukemia." She wipes her mouth with her napkin and exhales.

"I'm sorry." I debate on whether I should tell her about Ashely, only I don't want to rub my sister's remission in her face.

"Part of the reason I sort of stalked you is because I know about your sister. I saw you leaving her chemo treatment last year." Her cheeks turn a soft shade of pink. "I recognized you when classes started. I wanted to say something, but I felt weird."

I'm in a tiny bit of shock when Samantha admits this. I probably wouldn't have dodged her all semester if I'd known we had something like this in common.

"How is she?" she asks timidly, unsure if the question is going to cause me pain. I really appreciate the fact that she knows exactly what that pain feels like.

I reach across the table and pat her hand. She looks up, surprised. I'm just as shocked that I'm touching her. It just feels right. "She's doing okay right now."

"I know how it is. In and out of the hospital. Never knowing if the treatment is working."

She picks up her utensils and cuts her pizza with a knife and fork. She places a small bite in her mouth and chews. She doesn't speak again until after she swallows. "The worst part is, I used to hate it. I hated holidays in his hospital room. Eating dinner from a vending machine. I was the biggest brat." She covers her mouth when she laughs. "Then after he was gone, I would've given anything for a cold turkey sandwich on Thanksgiving."

I listen as Samantha tells me about her life before and after her brother's death. It's so familiar. Not a lot of people understand what it's like to watch someone you love die. The guilt you carry for being healthy. One minute you're praying she gets better, the next day you're hoping it all ends. All the while you hate yourself for being so selfish.

I used Ashley's condition as an excuse for every shitty thing I've ever done. From staying out late to ditching school, to selling drugs. Even though she's better now, I have to live with that guilt forever.

"I was at camp when he died," Samantha continues. "My parents knew he was close to the end. They already stopped treatment. I didn't want to be around when he finally passed. It's the biggest regret of my life." She takes another sip of her wine.

"That's why I'm here," I tell her. It's the first time I've ever admitted that to another person.

She nods knowingly. "Good. Don't leave her."

"I won't."

It is in this moment that I decide not to return to California. It is also the first time since I moved here that I no longer feel guilty for wanting to stay.

The waitress stops by and asks if we need anything.

"Actually." Samantha hands her cell phone to the waitress. "Can you take our picture?"

Dani

February 2009

Today is my twenty-first birthday, and I'm spending it with a toddler. I missed the holidays with my family, so they kind of guilt-tripped me into coming to Eureka for my birthday.

Johnson and Lucy went to Lake Tahoe for Christmas with Johnson's family. I was invited, but being stuck in a cabin with a bunch of strangers was the last place I wanted to be. I spent Christmas Eve and most of Christmas Day at a rave. I don't think I fully recovered from all the partying until a week after New Year's.

When Lucy called to invite me up for my birthday weekend, I couldn't say no. Plus, Zack is out of town, Heather is working, and Mary is doing a year abroad.

One weekend we rented a foreign film on Netflix about a guy who spends a year in Spain, and three months later, she tells me she's leaving. It must be nice to know what you want and have the balls to go for it.

Everyone in my life has their shit together. Heather loves her job. Zack is in Los Angeles for the opening of a club he might help manage over the summer. Nick is saving the world, and I'm back in Eureka because I literally have no place else to be.

"Daaani," my birthday date squeals as I walk back to the booth.

"Yes, Miss Marguerite?"

"Sit by me." She scoots closer to the window so I can slide in beside her.

"Yes, ma'am." I sit down and scan the menu. Now that all the molly is out of my system, I'm starving. "Looks like this menu hasn't changed."

"Why fix it if it ain't broke," Johnson says and waves the waitress over.

She says hello to Marguerite and asks if she wants her usual. I smile in spite of my shitty mood. This diner holds a lot of memories. For one, I used to come here with Lucy and my parents when I was Marguerite's age. I ordered the same thing, no matter what time of day. Chocolate chip pancakes and milk, which is exactly what Marguerite orders.

"And what about you, hon?" She waits with her pen poised to her notepad.

I consider a salad, but Lucy already made a comment about my weight. Lucy is working, so it's only Johnson, but I'm sure he'll have something to say about me eating rabbit food.

"I'll have a chicken salad sandwich on wheat with fries." I close the menu and hand it to her. As soon as she walks away, Johnson starts to grill me.

"So, tell me about school," he says as he opens the little box of crayons that comes with the kids' menu. "You gonna pass or what?"

I smirk and say, "Or what."

"Don't be a smartass."

Marguerite looks at Johnson with a shocked expression. "Daddy, you said ass."

"I'm sorry, baby." He pushes the pile of crayons towards her. "Draw me a picture and pretend you can't hear anything me and Dani are saying."

"Okay." She shrugs.

I love watching them together. She's turned Johnson into a bigger softy than he already was.

"School?" he urges.

"School is school. I'm doing okay this semester, and that's it. What else do you want me to say?" I try to downplay the situation.

Zack went through a rough patch when he and Antonio broke up. They're friends now, but it was bad for a few months. Of course, I totally capitalized on his heartbreak. I convinced Zack that popping molly was the cure to getting over Antonio. Our grades suffered, but Zack has really started to make a name for himself as a promoter. He has three regular nights at clubs all over the city.

The waitress comes back with the drinks and tells us our order should be out soon. The interruption stops Johnson's inquisition long enough for me to change the subject.

"I want to hear about the shop. Any good weekend warrior stories?" I sip my diet soda and sneak a look at Marguerite's drawing. "Lucy said the new location is doing really great." I look up at Johnson and realize he isn't paying attention to me. I follow his line of sight to the parking lot.

I see him first, then her. They're walking towards the diner, and my first instinct is to bolt for the door. He pauses when a truck pulls in. It isn't just any black truck, it's Nick. Fuck.

"Are you gonna be okay?" Johnson asks. His jaw tightens, and the veins in his neck bulge.

"Are you?" I look at Marguerite, then back to Johnson. "Just take a deep breath. You don't need to kill anyone for me today." I play calm to diffuse Johnson's anger. Honestly, it makes me happy. I like that he cares. Even if he is overreacting. Matt left me a year and a half ago, I'm over it. As far as Nick is concerned, he's just an old friend. One I barely speak to anymore.

I look down and ask Marguerite how her drawing is going. Johnson plays along. We both ignore the gust of wind that rustles our hair when the door opens. When a server stops at the table with our food, I refuse to look up. I pretend the picture in front of me is so fucking amazing, I can't rip my eyes away. Just because I'm pretending he isn't here, doesn't make it real. I can't duck or hide. As soon as he looks up, he'll see me sitting in this booth and there isn't a damn thing I can do about it.

"Dani."

I look up like I'm surprised to hear my name.

"Oh hey, Nick." I slide out of the booth and give him a hug. I make sure to keep my head below his shoulder so I can't see who he is with. "When did you get back?"

Nick wraps me in his arms. Even though this is about to be really awkward, his embrace feels like home. I inhale him and allow myself a few seconds of remembrance.

"I've been home a few weeks." He steps back so he can look at me. Then he pulls me against his chest again. "I missed you." He holds me tighter this time, uncaring that Johnson is inches away, ready to rip his arm off.

I finally pull away and sit back down. Nick reluctantly lets go of my hand so I can pretend to eat.

"Johnson, how are you?" They shake hands.

Johnson tells him he's doing fine and doesn't seem as hostile towards Nick as he has been in the past.

"Hi, Nicky." Marguerite stands on the bench and leans over to give him a high-five. Not just any high-five. They do a low, a side, then a high. After they're done, Marguerite sits down and goes back to coloring.

"How do you guys know each other?" I look from Nick to Marguerite.

"JMD sold me the building for the second location," Johnson explains. His face flushes slightly like he's embarrassed. "Nick came back last week to see how things are going."

"That building is on the first piece of land my grandfather ever purchased. Mariann didn't want to let it go for sentimental reasons, but when she found out it was for your uncle," Nick pauses and looks at me. His eyes dance with joy. "Well, he's family now."

Johnson makes an uncomfortable throat sound and picks up his burger. I can tell he feels like the Marino's did him a favor. Johnson hates owing people.

"I don't want to keep you from your lunch." Nick motions over his shoulder where Matt is sitting with the blonde from his Facebook page.

"Do you want to join us?" I play it off like I didn't see who he walked in with.

Nick runs his hand over his head and looks back. "Uh, I'm here with—" He stops speaking when Matt appears beside him.

"Hey, Dani." He gives me a weird little head nod.

His voice sends shivers down my back. I don't look up. I can't look at his face. I don't even acknowledge his greeting. Marguerite does.

"Hi," she says. "Are you Dani's friend?"

"Uh, yeah. I'm Matt," he tells her. "Me and Dani went to school together."

I snort and glare at Matt. That's it? We're just old high school buddies? He has the nerve to stand there and lie to a little girl.

Nick makes a motion for them to leave, and I find my voice.

"Who's the blonde?" I snap.

"Oh, she's ah, her name is Sam. Samantha."

He's nervous. Good. He should be. One look from me and Johnson will have him face down in my chicken salad.

"Cut my pancakes, Daddy."

Marguerite's innocent request snaps everyone back to reality. Johnson reaches for the plate and starts slicing her food.

"We'll let you guys enjoy your lunch. How long are you in town?" Nick asks while Matt scurries back to his blonde.

"It's Dani's birfday!" Marguerite blabs. "We're having a party with cake and balloons. Pink ones!" She throws her hands in the air and jumps up and down on the bench beside me.

"Sit down, darling,'" Johnson says. "Eat your lunch."

"Oh man." Nick runs his hand through his hair again. I see some things never change. "Damn, I forgot. I'm sorry, Dani."

"It's no big deal." I wave it off and shove a fry in my mouth. "I'll text you when I get back to the city." The last thing I want to do is double date with him and Matt.

"Well, if you have any time this weekend, call me. I'd really like to take you out to celebrate."

"I don't think so, we're doing family stuff." I nod towards Johnson. For once, his rudeness comes in handy. If Lucy were here, she'd invite Nick to dinner tomorrow at the house.

"Okay, well, another time then. It was really good to see you." Nick leans down and kisses my cheek. Then he whispers something that makes my heart tingle in spite of the utterly fucked-up few minutes I just endured.

"Bye, Nick." I pretend his words don't make my insides melt.

He smiles at me, then says bye to Johnson and Marguerite.

"Air high-five," he says to Marguerite and holds up his palm. She does the same then giggles as he walks away.

I force myself to eat, just so we can get the hell out of the diner. Johnson inhales his food, and most of Marguerite's ends up on the floor. I offer to wash her hands in the bathroom while Johnson gets the check.

As Marguerite rubs soap between her chubby little hands, she looks up at me and says, "Mommy said you and Nick used to be in love."

"What? Why did she tell you that?" I turn off the water and rip a paper towel from the machine on the wall.

"I saw your picture at Mariann's big house. You look really pretty then."

"I don't look pretty now?"

Marguerite tilts her hand back and forth, "You had a pretty dress in the picture." She tosses the paper towels in the trash and walks to the door. "And your hair was long."

I smile at her honesty.

I lead Marguerite out of the bathroom and find Johnson waiting at the front door. Marguerite runs ahead of me, and I pretend to chase her. She keeps me from looking back.

Fuck. Fuck. Fuck.

"Matt, did you hear me?" Sam asks.

I look at her oblivious face. "Uh?"

"I said do you want to share a side salad?" She looks at the waitress and then back to me.

"Yeah, sure."

"Is that all you want?" Jody, the waitress that never ages, asks.

"No." I pick up the menu. "I'll have a cheeseburger and fries." I hand the menu back. Then I remember Nick. "Oh, and Nick will have the same." He'll need it, because we're drinking tonight.

Jody leaves, and I realize that I'm tapping my finger on the table. I pull my hand into my lap. If Sam suspects something is wrong, she doesn't show it. I love that about her. She's drama free. I was too, until about eight minutes ago.

Why did I go to her table? Why is Nick still over there? I can't turn around. I can't look at her again. What are the odds that she is even in Eureka this weekend?

"Dude, you're in my seat." Nick stands at the end of the bench and I just slide over. I don't want to move to the other side of the table.

If I do, I'll have a clear view of her. "Did you order for me, too?" Nick laughs and sits down.

"Yeah, ordered you a burger and fries, same as me," I tell him.

He looks at Sam and smiles his charming Nick Marino smile. "We've always loved the same things." He leans back and places his arm over the back of the bench, and I choke on my water.

"So, who's the girl?" Sam finally catches on. "She looked like someone special to you."

"Oh, she is." Nick leans forward and sips his iced tea. "That's Dani. She's the one that got away."

Sam looks at me, and I regret our open-book policy on our past.

"Is that the same Dani that Matt dated before he moved to Colorado?"

For the first time since I've known Sam, she looks skeptical.

Nick has an oh-shit look on his face when he looks at me. "Uh, yeah."

"I told her about everything." I pretend it isn't a big deal when really I want to gouge my heart out with a dull fork. "She knows me and Dani dated for like six months after high school."

A wicked smile slices across his face. I use the word everything very loosely. Sam knows Dani is my ex, she doesn't know about her and Nick, or anything about Will and thizz. I honestly never thought Sam would meet Dani. We've been together eight months; I still consider us casual. When I told her I was coming to California, she invited herself. Not in a pushy way. She's never been to California. She wanted to see Humboldt County and meet Nick. I thought it was safe.

"So, Dani was your girlfriend first?" Sam connects the dots.

"Yeah, but we only went out for three months," Nick says. "We've been good friends ever since. All of us."

I finish off my water and wish to God it was something stronger. This was supposed to be our thizz weekend, but I fucked it up when I let Sam tag along. Nick didn't seem to care. He has a big paper due next week; he can't afford to slack off.

Honestly, I didn't want to do it. It feels too soon, if that makes sense. Bringing Sam was my excuse to get out of it, and even though seeing Dani was one of the worst moments of my life, I have to admit it was probably better than running into her while on thizz.

"You still love her?" Sam questions Nick.

"I do."

My eyes flit to Nick. This is the first time he's openly admitted this to me. Maybe it's because I have a girlfriend. My feelings are longer an issue. His feelings for Dani shouldn't make me feel sick. They do.

"Today's her birthday," Nick says when Jody returns with our food.

A mental calendar flips through my head. "She's twenty-one."

"I know."

We look back at her table just as she gets up with Marguerite and goes to the bathroom. "Dude, we have to do something," Nick says.

Dani was never big on birthdays. The last one I spent with her was like any other day, except I stuck a candle in a chocolate croissant and forced her to make a wish. Then we popped four pills. I want to say it was a good day, but I really wouldn't know. When you have that much MDMA in your system, nothing is real. That's what I like about being with Sam. Everything about her is genuine. Her smile, her laugh, everything.

"Dani hates when you make a big deal about her birthday," I tell him. Then I pick up my burger and shove it down my throat.

"Does she have plans?" Sam asks in her concerned voice.

"Yeah, she's doing stuff with her family," Nick says.

"See, she's good," I mumble with a mouth full of food. "Plus, we have plans." I nudge Nick under the table.

"We do?" Nick looks at me like I'm crazy.

"Yeah, we're drinking," I inform him. "Sam, you're good with that, right?"

"Absolutely. I know this was supposed to be a boys' weekend." She takes a small bite of her salad. When she finishes chewing, she wipes her mouth and sips her water. "Mariann is going to show me her art collection."

"Sounds like a blast," Nick deadpans with a mouth full of food.

"Sam's an art major." I nudge him with my elbow. "I bet you didn't know your house is full of artsy shit." I think of the only piece of art I ever cared about. The portrait of Dani and the Marinos. I asked him to take it down for the weekend. He said Mariann didn't even ask why. She just replaced it with a piece she bought from an artist in England.

Johnson walks by on his way to the door and looks at our table. "Take care, boys," he says and gives us a little wave.

Nick and I nod respectfully to him. That guy is still scary as shit. We watch Dani walk out of the bathroom and beeline to the door. Any desire to talk to her diminishes. This encounter was painful. It's killing me, and she was just here with her family. I can't imagine what this day would've felt like if she were with one of the douchebags from her Facebook page.

This wasn't how I expected our first encounter to be. Not by chance, and certainly not with a girlfriend. If either of us ever wanted closure, we just got it.

Dani

I wake up to a toddler jumping on my bed.

"Wake up. Wake up!" She lands on the pillow, millimeters from my face.

Johnson treated me to my first bottle of whiskey last night. It was awful in the beginning. After a couple of shots, I learned to appreciate it. After Marguerite went to bed, Lucy joined us. I don't remember much. I have a vague memory of Johnson doing the "Cupid Shuffle."

"It's time to get up!" Marguerite announces as she prances around my bed.

"Do you know how to tell time?" I ask her.

"No, silly. I can't read."

"Then how do you know it's time to wake up?"

"Cause my eyes are open."

Fuck, she's a genius.

I get up and take a shower; it's the only way to escape Marguerite's wrath. After my shower, I get dressed and pack. I head downstairs with my bag and drop it at the front door. Lucy comes around the corner with a cup of coffee.

"Here." She hands me the mug. "I had Patty grind some of your favorite so I could make you a cup." She looks super proud of herself.

I take a sip and tell her it's great.

"I think I'll catch the early bus." I still don't have a car, so I took the Greyhound.

"Really?" Lucy pouts.

"Yeah, the earlier I get home, the better. And I have to pick up Arnie from the sitter." I can't bring my dog to Eureka because Marguerite is allergic. The one time they came to visit me, the poor kid couldn't stop sneezing.

"Okay." Lucy sighs and heads upstairs to tell Johnson I'm leaving. I sit on the couch and pretend the throw blanket doesn't remind me of Matt. It does, only now I don't care. Seeing him with the blonde made me realize that I've been wasting my time. He was never coming back for me. Hell, I wasn't even really waiting for him.

Lucy drives me to the bus station, and I tell her she doesn't have to wait. I don't feel like pretending anymore. It's exhausting. After she leaves, I find an empty chair inside and take out my phone. I'm scrolling through Facebook when a pair of shoes stop in front of me. My eyes travel up his blue jeans, past his black t-shirt, to his blue eyes.

"Hi," Matt says.

"How did you know I was here?"

"I followed you." He shrugs. "I was headed to see you at Lucy's, and I saw you leaving, so I just—"

"So, you're a stalker now?"

"Yep, and I'm pretty awesome at it." He sits in the empty seat beside me.

I close my phone and look at the panel on the wall. As soon as my bus status switches to boarding, I'm out of here. "What do you want?"

"Let me drive you back to the city."

"Are you serious?" I look past him, towards the door. "Don't you have a girlfriend around here somewhere?"

"Mariann took her to some antique thing. They'll be gone all day. I can drive you there and be back before dinner. Nick will cover me. I just really want to talk."

Wow, he hasn't changed. Still running around behind people's backs. "Go home, Matt." I look him in the eyes. "Wherever that is."

"I want a chance to explain. I owe you that much."

"You don't owe me a goddamn thing." I stand up and lift my backpack to my shoulder. "I'm good, Matt. I don't need anything from you."

"Please, just sit and talk to me." He takes my hand. We both look at the point where we're touching. I can't wrap my head around the fact that Matt Augustine is holding my hand. "I'm so sorry I hurt you, Dani. I never should've left the way I did."

I absorb every single word out of his mouth. I can use the pain I feel right now to fuel my anger later.

"I really wanted to be with Ashley." He drops my hand. "I thought it would be easier for both us if we just broke it off. I told Nick I would bow out if I couldn't be the man you deserved. So, that's what I did."

"You guys still don't get it, do you?" I snap. "There is a great big world of people out there." I point to the window. "Where is it written that I have to end up with you or Nick?"

Matt is silent. He knows I'm right, and that I'm fed up with this triangle.

"I don't hold any grudges. If I had a family, I'd want to be near them, too. But I loved you, Matt, and I thought we would be together forever. It hurt when you left. Not just because I was losing my boyfriend. I lost my best friend, too."

The dispatcher announces my bus is boarding. Some of the people sitting around us stand and move towards the door. A couple of them steal glances our way.

"Dani, wait."

I shake my head to let him know there is nothing left to say. "Goodbye, Matt." I walk away. This time I don't want to look back.

The bus ride is long. It takes nearly ten hours because of all the stops. I finished my book, and my iPod died, so I'm stuck looking through my backpack. I find a bunch of old receipts and a couple of assignments I never turned in. In the bottom of the side pocket, I find a dirty, partly smashed capsule. The one thing I can always count on to make me smile.

I wait until I'm close to home to take it. I stop for a soda at the corner store a few blocks from my apartment. Molly and diet Coke. It's just what I need after this cluster-fuck of a weekend.

I pick up Arnie, then let him lead the way home. He stops to sniff and pee three times. We turn onto Union Street and start up the hill. I notice a black truck parked in front of my building. Just when I thought this day was over.

Nick jumps out as if he's surprising me.

"Happy Birthday!"

"My birthday was yesterday," I tell him unenthusiastically as I pull out my keys. "Remember, I saw you at the diner with Matt and Blondie."

"Her name is Sam," Nick informs me with a sly grin.

"That's a stupid name," I snap.

I open the door and Arnie runs up the stairs. His leash bouncing behind him. I lift it up so I don't trip over it. When we reach the top, I unhook him and hang the leash on its hook. I look down the hall towards Heather's room. The light is off.

Nick is laughing as he climbs the stairs behind me. I drop my backpack on the floor in the hall, kick off my shoes, then head to the kitchen to fill Arnie's food and water bowls.

"This weekend was fucked up. So, I'm here to offer you a proper celebration," Nick announces. "Is Heather home?"

I pull two beers from the refrigerator and walk into the living room. "No. She's probably working or at her boyfriend's place." I sit on the sofa and sip my beer. He walks over and sits beside me. "What are you doing here, Nick?"

I wonder if he knows Matt accosted me at the train station this morning. I doubt he'd be here if he did. Nick and Matt have a strange understanding when it comes to winning my affection. Do they ever stop and think that maybe I don't want either one of them?

"I'm sorry you had to see that yesterday. On your birthday."

"I don't care. Really. Matt can do what he wants." I take a huge gulp of my beer and resist the urge to burp.

"I want to take you out." Nick sits up and places his beer on the coffee table. "Come on. I'll take you to a club and get bottle service in VIP. We'll get wasted, and I'll hold your hair when you puke." He makes a gag face, and I laugh. "Or we can hop on a flight to Vegas." Nick lowers his eyes at me, and I can't help but smile. "I'll teach you how to play craps."

I stand up and walk to the window. All of those things sound amazing, but none of them can actually happen. When I turn around, Nick is standing right behind me.

"We can't go to Vegas," I start.

He steps closer. "Why?"

"First of all, you aren't twenty-one yet." I push his chest with my finger.

"Damn, you're right," he says in a tone that sounds like it really doesn't matter. He places his hands on my waist, and I stop breathing. "And second?"

Second, what is second? My body temperature starts to get manic. "It's hot." I choke out. My throat feels dry and itchy all of a sudden.

"It's hot." Nick repeats. "In Vegas or this room?"

I sound and feel like an idiot. "Yes, it's hot in Vegas." My voice is just a whisper or a whimper.

Nick pulls me closer, and my heart throws a flying kick at my chest.

"I don't trust—" I start to say something then stop when Nick hooks his fingers into the belt loops on my jeans and pulls me closer.

"You don't trust, what, the weather?" His voice is low and seductive, just the way I like it.

"Us. I don't trust us in Vegas." I clear my throat and pretend his hands aren't causing waves of electricity to course through my body. "We're friends."

I move backward until I'm up against the wall between my two front windows.

"Friends can't go to Vegas?"

He's so close I can taste the beer on his breath. It tastes so much better coming from Nick's mouth.

"Are you afraid we'll do something stupid, like get drunk and end up married?"

"Wh-what?" I stutter. I'm stuttering. My heart is stuttering; my brain just paused and restarted.

"Are you afraid we'll get drunk, have mind-blowing sex, then end up in a drive through marriage chapel?" Nick moves his hands from around my waist and holds my face. "Not necessarily in that order."

Being in Nick's personal space feels really fucking good. Him entertaining the idea that we would have drunk sex and get married makes my body tingle.

"Is that like a fantasy of yours?"

"As a matter of fact, it is." He leans in and kisses me softly. No tongue. No pressure. Just our lips softly brushing against each other.

How easy would it be for me to let Nick take control of my body and my heart all over again? No more decisions. No more worries. Money will never be an issue. Getting a degree won't really matter, since I never have to work.

Life goals—only one, to make him happy.

We'll travel the world. See all the places he's helping to rebuild. The people whose lives are made better by him.

Everything would be about him.

"Nick," I whisper. For a split second, I'm not sure which way I'm going to go.

"Dani," he whispers and pushes his body closer to mine. Every part of him is touching me. Every part.

Suddenly, a familiar surge flows through my body.

This isn't real.

I took a molly. Everything I'm experiencing right now is altered. Even if I wanted to make a choice about me and Nick right now, I can't. It wouldn't be me.

"Nick, stop." As soon as the words leave my lips, space grows between us.

He takes a step back, then another. I try to regain my composure and peel myself away from the wall. I can't let him know I'm high. I've hidden it before. I can do it again.

"I'm sorry I pushed too far." He runs his hand over his head and clears his throat. "Should I go?" He thumbs towards the hall.

I want so badly to say no. Right now, the way I feel, I want his fantasy. I want him. Isn't this how it started last time? With a pill? It may be a different color, a different recipe altogether, but it still gives me the same high. Some people call it vitamin e, or vitamin x because that's how they see it. A supplement. One that provides a feeling of emotional bliss. Something inexplicably missing in our lives. My life.

Nick is handing me his heart. No pill required. I don't think I've ever been as vulnerable as he is right now. I can't take advantage of him. He deserves better.

"You have school and your foundation," I reason. "We can't just run away together. I'll just complicate things."

A grin breaks across his face. "You're right. Fuck." He seems to snap out of whatever daze he was in. I start to wonder if he's on something too.

I move back to the couch and pick up my beer. "Yesterday wasn't your fault. I was at the wrong place at the wrong time." I wrap my tingly hands around the bottle and try to steady my nerves.

"It was a bad coincidence," he says.

"More like fate. It can go either way. Good or bad," I say. "You just gotta roll with it and remember everything happens for a reason."

"Did we happen for a reason?" Nick steps forward and takes my hand.

"We ended for a reason." I pull free and keep my eyes on the floor. They're a dead giveaway to my condition. I'm not sure what Nick will think if he realizes I'm high. I don't want to find out.

I walk Nick to his truck and give him a hug goodbye. I'm fully rolling and getting really smiley. If he stays even a moment longer, I'll blab that I'm high. Call Antonio for more molly and spend the next two days in bed with Nick.

"Promise you'll let me buy you a birthday drink this summer when school's out and I'm legal?"

I close my eyes and inhale him. "Promise."

"And Dani," he pauses and kisses the top of my head. "One day, fate will bring us back together. And there isn't a damn thing you or I can do about it."

I nod my head against his chest. I want Nick's fantasy to come true. I want all of his dreams to come true.

Dani

August 2009

Mariann was supposed to meet me for lunch today. She had an emergency to take care of and sent her mini-me instead. Haley is sitting across from me in a burgundy wrap dress. She looks nothing like the girl I knew in high school. Her wavy hair is pulled to the side and held in place with a diamond-encrusted clip.

We were supposed to discuss my trust. This should be my last year of school, but I haven't earned enough credits to graduate. Money Mark says I don't have anything to worry about financially. We just have to extend the agreement another year. As long as I keep my shit together, another year should be all it takes.

Haley knows my engagement to Nick was fake, but she doesn't know how my trust was funded. She thinks it was another generous act by the Marino's, so the topic of my trust is put on hold, at least for today. Rather than cancel, Mariann thought it would be nice for Haley and me to have lunch together. I feel like I've been set up on a play-date.

We order our food and fall into a comfortable conversation. She lets me ramble about Zack and the most recent party we went to. I listen to her stories about traveling with Mariann and all the cool hotels she gets to stay at.

"When was the last time you spoke to Nick?" Haley asks after the waiter clears our plates.

"About six months ago," I say as I pour myself the last of the wine.

I stopped returning Nick's texts, calls, and emails right after my birthday. I guess Matt was right, it's way easier to break contact with someone you don't want. Only I didn't do it because I don't love Nick. I stayed away because I don't want to bring him down. He is focused on his career. I would've been a distraction.

"Where is he this summer?"

"Macedonia."

Haley tells me about their efforts to provide housing to the region and how much impact his foundation is having on people's lives. Haley's face glows when she talks about Nick.

"He's doing truly amazing things."

"Do you guys talk often?"

I know they hooked up in the past, but I didn't think they were into each other beyond that. From the dreamy way Haley says Nick's name, I'd say she would love the chance for more.

"We text every day. Mostly business stuff," she adds. "There's nothing else going on." She tries to make that sound like it's a good thing.

I grip my wine glass and wave at the air. "Hey, it's none of my business. It's no big deal if you guys, whatever."

"You know Nick still has feelings for you." Haley's eyes bounce from me to the table and back. "He was pretty upset after your birthday."

I can't believe he told her about that.

"What did he say?"

"Just that you wouldn't run away to marry him in Vegas."

I choke on my wine. "What?"

"I'm joking, Dani." She pats my hand. "He drunk-texted me about your conversation and said you were right. He wasn't in a place to have a relationship."

"I'm glad he finally saw things my way. I don't know why he's so hell-bent on being my boyfriend."

"There are worse things in the world than having Nick Marino chasing after you." Haley blushes at her brash remark, and I realize that she cares for Nick. Like really cares for him.

I find myself feeling a little jealous. Not because she wants Nick. I envy the fact that she has those feelings for him. That she has feelings period. There were nights I lay in bed wishing I loved Nick. Wanting him to be the one I dreamt about. His smell that I missed. When I close my eyes, his face isn't the one that haunts me. Nick isn't the man of my dreams.

The waiter drops off the check, and Haley places her hand over the top of the little tray. "It's on Mariann."

"Of course it is." I finish my wine and place my napkin on the table. "This was, uh, fun."

"Yeah, it kind of was," Haley agrees. "There's no rule saying we can't be friends." She places a credit card on the tray and slides it to the end of the table. Our waiter comes right back to retrieve it. "And if you ever just want to talk, I'm a pretty good listener."

177

Haley asks questions in the right places. She looks you in the eye when she speaks. She really is easy to talk to and always has something interesting to say. I wonder if this is something Mariann taught her, or if she just evolved into this socially acceptable person over the last three years.

The waiter comes back with the check and tells us to have a nice afternoon. Haley is very gracious. I marvel at her confidence and maturity.

"You really like working for Mariann." It's more a statement than a question, but Haley answers anyway.

"It's the best thing that ever happened to me, and I owe it all to Nick."

"How so?" I ask, thinking this girl would give Nick credit for the sun rising.

"I was on my way to a job interview and my car broke down. While I was waiting for my cousin to come get me, Nick pulled up. He offered me a ride, and when I told him where I was going, he turned the car around. He said his grandmother was interviewing assistants, and that I should apply." She pulls out a little mirror and checks her makeup. She doesn't add lip gloss or make any adjustments before closing the compact and placing it back in her stylish black purse. "I was freaking out the entire drive to his house. I was dressed properly, and I knew I wasn't qualified. But Nick kept saying everything was going to be fine. He went in and talked to Mariann while I waited in the hall. When he came out, he hugged me and said to just be myself. I had nothing to lose, and Mariann wasn't as scary as I thought she was going to be. You know." She looks at me and I nod. "We talked for over an hour, then she offered me the job."

I'm not surprised by her story. Mariann and Nick are two of the most generous people on the planet.

"It's really great how everything worked out."

"Lucky for me my car was a piece of crap," she whispers as we walk to the door. "I always think, if my cousin was just around the corner, Nick wouldn't have found me. I wouldn't be here today." She looks around the five-star restaurant and smiles. "It was destiny."

"No, it was fate. If your car didn't break down, you might have gotten the other job." I open the door and walk onto the sidewalk. A cool breeze flows through the busy downtown street, and I wrap my sweater around my body.

Haley buttons her navy coat. "What's that saying about summer in San Francisco being colder than winter?" She's referring to a Mark Twain quote. I remind her then to start walking towards the curb to get a cab.

"I have a car waiting," she says. "I'll give you a ride." She pulls out her cell phone and texts the driver. He pulls up two minutes later, and we climb into the back of a black town car.

"Where to, Haley?" the driver asks.

She looks at me.

"Union and Columbus," I tell him and he pulls into traffic.

Haley checks her phone, then looks up and catches me watching her. "What?"

"It must be really nice doing something you love." Everyone around me seems to have life figured out. I can't even manage to feed my dog on a daily basis.

"I do love my job, and compared to what I could've been doing..." she shivers. "I don't take a single day for granted."

"What was that other job, the one you were on your way to apply for?" I imagine her waiting tables or working at a grocery store.

Haley sighs and looks out the window as we drive through the Tenderloin. It's filled with seedy bars and strip clubs.

"That was my future." She points to a billboard advertising live nude girls. "I was on my way to Lady's. You know that strip club in Arcata?"

I know the place. They have a huge billboard on the side of the freeway that advertises free hot wings on Sunday.

"That's the job interview you were going to when your car broke down?"

"Yes, so you know why I say Nick saved me. They both did."

I think about my choices, the roads I've chosen, and the dreams I've bailed on. Before my parents were killed, I had it all figured out. I knew who I was, where I was going, and what I wanted to be. Now I can't find the motivation to care about anything.

"I envy you, Haley."

I feel her look at me. "That's funny because I envy you."

I make a snorting noise and turn towards her. The seat is big, so I can sit sideways and look at her crazy face. "My life is a train wreck."

Haley's cheeks flush and I figure it out. Nick.

When we pull in front of my building, I thank her for lunch.

"Nick will be back next week; we're going to have a welcome-home dinner. You should come," Haley suggests.

I really want to hate her, but there is nothing about her tone or facial expressions that make me believe she is being insincere. I do think it's odd that she says things like we're having a dinner. She has fully integrated herself into this household. Even though I'm standing beside Nick in a portrait hanging in the foyer, I'm no longer part of his family, and I don't necessarily want to be.

One week after my lunch with Haley, she texts me at nine in the morning to let me know Nick is home and to remind me about dinner. I tell her that classes have started and I'm too busy to make it. She texts back a sad face and asks when I'm available for lunch. I don't reply.

Unlike Haley, I don't want to see Nick. He confuses me. Knowing he's just a phone call away. That he would jump in his truck and drive here at the drop of a hat to see me; make me feel fucked up on so many levels. He has played an important role in my life. I'll always care for him. But being with him in the way he wants me—that I can't do. Nick is an amazing human. He just isn't the human I'm supposed to love forever. And that makes me feel defective. If I can't love someone as amazing as Nick, I can't love anyone.

Matt

August 2009

Today was the last day of my internship. The managing partner, Dan Glasser, came downstairs to personally invite me to lunch. We went to a steakhouse downtown and talked about my future. I explained that I was putting off law school for now.

When he asked me if I was staying in Colorado, I froze.

This is my last year of college. Ashley is starting her senior year. She was determined to finish high school at an actual school after being homeschooled most of her life. You can't stop that kid once she sets her mind to something. Mom let it slip that she's going to apply to college in California. I think she was feeling me out. As much as they love Colorado, I know they miss home.

California is our home, but I'm building a life here. All of my work experience has been in local firms. My contacts are here. And then there's Samantha. She's everything a guy could want in a girlfriend. We never fight, and on the rare occasion that we disagree over something, she always tries to find a middle ground. Sam thinks life is too short to waste it being hostile. I really like that about her. Samantha uncomplicated my life. She showed me how to stop worrying and start living. I have a new appreciation for my family, my sister, my education. I look back at my time with Dani; it was nothing but stress and worry. We didn't know how to be together.

When I saw her in the diner, every part of me wanted to run to her. I didn't think I was still that connected, that hooked. Following her to the bus station was a disaster. I thought it was slick or romantic. It was wrong. I never told anyone about that day. Not even Nick.

I think it was a wake-up call for both of us. Dani doesn't exist in the world to satisfy some need in me or Nick. She's just a girl I knew in high school. We dated a few months and broke up; it doesn't have to be anything more than that.

Okay, I'll stop bullshitting myself now. Dani will never be some girl from my past; that's my problem.

Do I love Samantha? I don't really know. It's complicated.

Did I love Dani? Without a doubt, but guess what? It was really fucking complicated. Not my feelings, just our relationship in general. We couldn't make it work. You can blame age or timing or Nick. When it comes down to it, we weren't ready. I don't know if I can ever love someone like I loved Dani. To be honest, I don't think I want to.

If love were measured in fireworks, Dani would be a bottle rocket and Samantha would be a sparkler. Dani is a ball of fire that, once uncorked, will explode into something dangerous and beautiful. Or she can malfunction and blow off your hand. Samantha burns slower and safer. Little kids can play with Samantha. Dani is the kind of girlfriend that should come with a warning label.

At the end of our lunch, I shook Mr. Glasser's hand and thanked him for the support and experience I gained while interning at the firm. He said he was glad to have me and to make sure I sent him a résumé after I graduated, giving me another reason to stay.

I moved to Colorado with a promise to myself that I would eventually go back to California. Now I have nothing to go back to and every reason to stay.

Dani

November 2009

I walk out of my advisor's office and into the hall. The last thing I need is a pill, but it's the first thing I think about. The two rolling around in my pocket are just begging to be swallowed.

My phone vibrates in my hand.

"Hey, Zack."

"How bad is it, boo?"

I hear the wind through the receiver. He's already in the city, prepping for his event.

"So bad that I shouldn't go out tonight."

"Maybe you shouldn't," he says.

"Please don't start on me. I already heard an earful last night from Heather."

"Okay, okay. Just promise to get some work done before you meet me."

I don't know how the hell Zack manages to keep his grades floating in the three point five area and party as much as I do. Sometimes more.

I hang up and head to the train station to go home. I don't have class for the next seven days; it gives me a week to catch up on the papers and homework that are due.

While the rest of the world is enjoying turkey and pumpkin pie, I'll be home alone with a stack of books and a pot of coffee. Something miraculous needs to happen in the next seven days to keep my ass from flunking out of school.

At least I wasn't lying when I told Lucy I was too slammed to come up for Thanksgiving. I hate lying to them. That's all I seem to be doing lately. I lie to Heather when she asks me if I want her to stay home and hang out. I do, but I don't like her boyfriend. Her being home means his creepy ass stays too. There isn't anything specific I don't like; he just stares a lot. Once I was changing and didn't close my door all the way. When I opened it, he was standing right outside in the hall. He claims he was retrieving Arnie's ball, but it just felt weird.

I lied to Mariann when she asked if I would be graduating in the spring. There is no possible way that is going to happen.

I lie to myself about being happy, safe, in control. The most honest thing about me is my dishonesty. You can always count on me being full of shit.

I wake up and try not to think about the fact that I'm alone on Thanksgiving.

It's just Thursday.

I roll out of bed and start my non-holiday with a quick shower, followed by a load of laundry. I pick up my dirty jeans to toss them into the basket, and a plastic bag falls to the floor. I pick up the baggy and roll the two pills between my fingers before shoving the bag in a bathroom drawer. I have no plans to get high, but seeing them comforts me.

I eat a peanut butter and banana sandwich, then I start a pot of coffee. I have a paper due on social stratification. It's as bad as it sounds. I pull out my notes, then check my phone. No messages. I position myself in front of my laptop and write:

In all stratified societies, there are two major social groups: a ruling class and a subject class...

I get one line typed and my phone rings.

"Hello?"

I answer without checking the caller ID. I don't really give a shit who it is at this point. I'm just happy that someone thought of me and dialed my number.

"Hey, Dani. It's Haley."

She is the last voice I thought I would hear today.

"I'm downstairs. Can you let me in?"

She is also the last face I thought I would see today.

I go downstairs and open the door. Haley follows me upstairs into the living room and looks around. I can tell she thinks it's cute. It is, thanks to Heather.

"What brings you to the city today?" I'm positive she isn't on an errand for Mariann. Not on Thanksgiving.

"I ran into Lucy at the market a couple of days ago, and she told me you were going to stay home for the holidays." She gestures to my laptop on the coffee table. "She also said you would be studying."

For once in my life I'm glad I was doing exactly what I said I would do.

"Anyway, I thought I would stop by and say hi."

"Thanks," I say, and it comes out very skeptical. That's because I am skeptical. "Why aren't you having dinner with the Marinos?"

"I decided to volunteer this year. There's a shelter in the city that offers free meals on holidays. We served dinner yesterday for single men, and we'll do another service today for families."

"That's amazing," I tell her. "I guess Nick is rubbing off on you."

Haley laughs at my choice of words. When I realize how it sounds, I laugh too.

"My family wasn't exactly the turkey and stuffing type." She fidgets with the bottom of her gray wool sweater. "The Thanksgiving when we were at the Marinos together, that was the first real dinner I'd ever had."

I don't know what to say. It's heartbreaking, and it makes me feel like shit. I didn't appreciate a single second of that meal. It was just another turkey dinner.

"That's really sad," I tell her.

"It's fine." She shrugs. "I never really cared about it before. I would tell myself it's just another Thursday."

My right eye tears up.

"When I was fourteen, I started volunteering, and it made the day a little more special."

Haley keeps blowing me away. I can see why Matt used to say she was cool and why Nick likes her company.

"I think what you're doing is amazing, and I'm so glad you came to say hi." I step forward and give her a hug. She smells really expensive.

"Well, I didn't stop by just to say hi. I was sort of hoping you might want to come with me." She pulls back and bites her lower lip. "I mean, no pressure. But it's a great way to get out of your head. Focusing on others really gives me clarity. I thought maybe you could use a little right now."

I have no idea how Haley could've known about my failing grades or overall destructive behavior over the last few months. I haven't had contact with anyone in Eureka, and I don't think Mariann is still having me tailed. So, I have to chalk it up to good timing.

I was sitting at my computer writing a paper, but my mind was on the pills in my bathroom. I don't know how long I would've held out before bailing on work. If I stay home, I will cave. The only way for me to stay sober this week is to stay busy.

"I'd love to go."

Dani

January 2010

Heather comes back from carrying the last box to the moving truck. She knocks on my door and says, "I'm out of here."

I climb over the bed and give her a hug.

"I'm not going to miss you."

"Oh my God, I'm so not going to miss you."

Her boyfriend, Rod, clears his throat from the hall, and I look at him. He gives me a tight-lipped smile. I throw him the same back, and he walks down the stairs.

"Are you sure he's like, the one?" I ask her again.

"Yes," she says with absolute certainty.

I pull back with a scowl on my face. "You seem like you hesitated that time."

She sighs and picks up her backpack. "I love him. My parents love him. You are the only one who doesn't love him," she reminds me. She's right. I still think he's a creeper.

"I feel like I'm never going to see you again." I lean against the wall and watch her pet Arnie goodbye.

"I'm only moving to the other side of the city." She stands up and gives me another hug. "We're still in the same area code." She starts down the stairs, and I lean over the rail to watch her.

"What day is your housewarming party? I want to make sure I already have plans."

She flips me off and says, "Goodbye, Danielle." The door slams shut.

Goodbye, Heather.

Heather was hardly ever here, but it was nice to know I wasn't completely alone. Arnie scampers down the hall, and I smile. He's best friend now.

I'm lying on my bed, staring at the ceiling, when the phone rings.

"Dani!" Zack yells into the receiver. "I'm coming for you."

I sigh like I don't want to go out, and I sort of don't. "Where?"

"There's a pop-up rave in the Mission. Get dressed. I'll be there in five minutes!" He hangs up, and I drag myself off the bed.

I walk to the closet and look in the full-length mirror Mary hung on the door. She'll be back next month from her year abroad. I can tell she's changed by the words she uses in her emails. She's less focused on the hot girls and more into the art and the culture of Spain.

I've changed too. I wonder if she'll think I'm better or worse? My hair has grown out and the red is gone. When I take the makeup off and put my hair in a ponytail, I can almost recognize the reflection staring back at me. There was a time when I thought that girl had it all. Good grades. The perfect boyfriend. A future. It was just an illusion. I had no clue what I was doing. I still don't.

I sit at my computer and pull up an email from Haley. It's a list of places that need volunteers. It's my new vice. I've helped at shelters, food banks, a free clinic on Haight Street, and sometimes I walk dogs at the animal shelter. Anything to keep moving. Haley was right, helping others is the best way to get out of my head. When I'm tasked with making two hundred peanut butter and jelly sandwiches, or stocking canned foods, I don't think about my grades, my love life, or getting high. For those few hours, I can breathe.

I sit across from my advisor, biting the end of my pen. His face isn't as red as it was the last time I was in here. "So, have I improved?"

He removes his glasses and lays a sheet of paper on the desk. "Considerably. I think we can lift the probation."

I exhale and relax into the chair.

"You've done a great job getting back on track this semester. Have you given any thought to your career path?"

I tense again. Everyone is always asking what I plan to do after I graduate. I still have no clue. "Not really. I'm still trying to find something I connect to."

"Oftentimes we don't find our dream job until we've tested the waters in other fields. You're not going to knock it out of the park on your first at-bat." He is reciting a quote from a framed picture on the wall. His office is filled with baseball analogies, which leads me to believe sitting in this office wasn't the homerun he was hoping for. "You've done a great job, but you still have another semester to go. Keep your eye on the ball."

I leave his office and get a text from Zack. It's a picture of four capsules in the palm of his hand. Under the picture it says, "Good news or bad news, we're getting fucked up tonight." I see that theoretical ball go flying past my head.

Zack is the kind of person who can go hard for a weekend. Drinking, smoking, popping pills, and then wake up Monday morning and go to class. He can flip a switch from party mode to real life. When someone like me has a friend like Zack, it's really hard to say no. I tell myself I'll ruin his night. Or worse, he'll stop being my friend. I cannot lose another friend.

I know I shouldn't get high. Sometimes I even tell myself I'm not going to do it as I'm removing the pill from my pocket. I say this as I fill a glass with water. I'm convinced that I won't take the pill even as I place it on my tongue. I can say I don't want it or I don't need it. The truth is, I don't want to want it. I don't want to need it.

Dani

February 2010

I don't hear my phone ring.

I don't hear the doorbell.

I don't open my eyes until I feel cold water on my face.

I look past Mary and see Heather and Rod standing at the end of my bed.

"What are you guys doing here?" My voice is hoarse and my tongue feels like sandpaper. I look to my nightstand and pick up the cup. I sniff it to make sure it's just water.

Mary throws a towel in my face and asks me what day it is.

"Um." I take another gulp of water and look at the clock. It's four in the afternoon. I went to Candy with Zack last night. No, that was two days ago. Last night we went to a bar here, in North Beach. They had karaoke. That's why my voice is gone. "Friday," I finally say.

The somewhat frustrated, mostly worried faces peer back at me. Mary, in her baby-soft voice, says, "It's Sunday. You missed my welcome-home dinner on Saturday and didn't answer any of my calls. So I called Heather. She still has a key."

"Okay." I drag myself out of bed and notice I'm still wearing my jeans. I move past my uninvited houseguests to the bathroom.

I turn on the water and jump in the shower, hoping they'll be gone when I get out. I close my eyes and let the water run over my face. I really wish I could remember what happened. Where I've been for the last twenty-four hours. I've heard the term black-out before, I just never thought it was a real thing. Sure, I forget things I've done or said on occasion. I've never lost an entire day.

I get out of the shower and find Mary sitting on my bed. Her long hair is pulled into a topknot, and she's dressed in a pair of jeans with brown knee-high boots and a simple white t-shirt. She looks very mature, classy.

"Did Heather and Rod leave?" I ask before I start to get dressed.

"Yeah, she had to work. She gave me her key." Mary holds up the My Little Pony keychain that used to belong to Heather. "She said I'm in charge now."

"What's that's supposed to mean?"

"You really have to ask?"

I don't feel like having another conversation about my social life, so I change the subject.

"How was the welcome-home party?"

I slide a pair of underwear up my legs before letting my towel fall to the ground. Mary rolls her eyes.

"That great, huh?"

I pull on a pair of gray sweatpants and my favorite Eureka Coffee t-shirt. Then I bend over and towel dry my hair.

"Dani, I'm worried about you."

I knew this was coming. Whenever friends have to break into your apartment to make sure you aren't dead, a lecture usually follows.

"Cheri told me you're at Candy four to five times a week with Zack. And you're popping molly." Mary pauses to see if I'm going to speak. I don't. "I thought you were over that."

"Why would you think that?" I ask as I continue to squeeze water out of my hair.

"Let me rephrase; I thought you had more control over it." The bed squeaks when Mary stands up. I feel her behind me. "I care about you, and I won't watch you fuck your life up."

I face Mary. It's really hard to look her in the eye and lie. This is a girl I shared secrets with when we were high. She told me about the girls she kissed, and I admitted to her that Nick was a better lover than Matt. There was a short period of time before she left for Spain that Mary was the most important person in my life. Then she left like everyone does. I want to remind her she's been gone a year; she hasn't watched me do a damn thing.

"I have everything under control." I smile, then give her a hug so she can't see how fake it is. "Come on, it was the end of my birthday week."

I feel her relax in my arms. "That's kind of what I thought," she admits and squeezes me back. "You scared me when I didn't hear from you."

"I'm sorry." I pull away and pick the towel up off the floor. "Come on, I'll buy you a welcome-home pizza at Golden Boy."

"How generous of you," she scoffs. "There is something else you can do for me." Mary sits on my bed and watches me brush my hair.

"Sure, anything." I pull the brush through my hair, and water flies onto the mirror.

"Do you think I can stay here for a few months?" She bites her thumbnail. "I lost my apartment, and my parents are trying to force me to stay with my aunt and her six cats."

I stop brushing and stand up. "Yes, hell yes!" I rush the bed and knock Mary over with my embrace. I need someone here. Someone to keep me on track. Mary is the perfect solution.

Dani

May 2010

I sit at the gate, waiting for my plane to board. Mary caught a stomach flu and had to stay home. It sucks because we've looked forward to this trip for months, and now I have to go alone.

This was going to be our last hoorah. Mary and most of my other friends graduated a week ago. Mary is moving to Los Angeles in a month. She landed a great job at an art gallery. Heather graduated with a degree in marketing but decided to keep her job with the state. She loves working on the bridge. I haven't seen much of her since she moved. She and Rod are busy playing house.

When Mary suggested we volunteer for this build, she waited until everything was confirmed to tell me it was Nick's foundation. Not that it makes a difference. It's not like he's going to be there. He's probably off saving the world again. I can't keep track of all the places he's been. He isn't very active on social media, and sometimes he's in remote places without cellular service. My Nick updates usually come from Haley. She's always throwing out little tidbits about his latest projects. I can't imagine the number of lives he's changed. Including mine.

"Danielle," one of the volunteers calls my name.

"Call me Dani," I tell him. "I'm sorry, I forgot your name."

"Daryl." He extends his hand. "I'm an apprentice. Electrical."

Daryl looks like he's mid-thirties, probably an ex-addict I assume by the discoloration of his teeth. The more I volunteer at the shelters, the easier it is to recognize the signs of addiction. I can tell who's using and who is crashing just by the look in their eyes. Right now, Daryl's are clear and full of excitement.

I shake his hand from my chair. "Cool. I'm just doing it for the experience."

That's the answer I give whenever someone asks why I'm volunteering. My motives for being here aren't like the others. I'm not trying to gain job experience or even build my résumé. I'm here to keep myself from getting high.

"We're going to the bar for a pre-flight drink. You wanna join us?" He gestures to the group, waiting a few feet away.

I could really use a shot, but the last thing I need is to get drunk in front of a bunch of strangers. I also promised Mary I'd be a good girl, meaning no booze and no boys. "This is a dry run for me."

"Righteous," he says and gives me a double thumbs-up as he walks away.

The flight is bumpy. I almost break my promise and have a Bloody Mary. By the time I make it to baggage claim, my nerves are back to normal. I'm taking off my hoodie when I spot my suitcase coming down the belt. Mariann bought it for me when we spent a weekend in Santa Barbara. She took one look at my beat-up carry-on and took me straight to some fancy luggage store at SFO. Nick chose the bright blue color; he said it would make it easy to find.

My airport blue suitcase is a bright spot in a sea of black. I step up to the carousel, then suddenly someone moves in front of me and takes it off the belt. I'm about to yell for security when the man with my bag turns around.

"Nick?"

He smiles his Nick Marino smile, and I leap into his arms. We hold each other for a long time. Long enough for me to silent cry into his neck and recover. If I didn't know Nick, I would swear he was crying too. When we finally break apart, the group lets out a long "aww."

"Show's over," Courtney, the group coordinator, announces. "We have one more volunteer joining us." She points to Nick. "Everyone, this is Nick. He's part of the apprentice program." The group welcomes him, and he winks at me.

As we walk to the van, I ask him what's going on.

"I asked Courtney not to tell them who I was. I want to experience the program like the rest of the volunteers."

"Like an undercover boss situation?"

"Something like that."

We walk into the humid Louisiana air and into a large van. Nick sits beside me during the drive to the church. He makes sure to choose the cot next to mine in the large basement we're calling home for the next six days. After a short orientation, where we meet Father Blanco, the director of the church, we gather in a common area for dinner.

I sit at the cafeteria table with my tray and prepare for my very first Cajun dinner.

"Have you ever had shrimp and grits?" Father Blanco asks as he places a bottle of water in front of me.

"Nope. It's my first grit-eating experience," I tell him with forced enthusiasm.

"Yum," Nick says and sits across from me.

Father Blanco hands a bottle of water to Nick and says, "You're in for a treat."

"Looks delicious," Nick says sincerely as Father Blanco moves to the next table.

"Does he know who you are?" I ask.

"No. Just you and Courtney." Nick cracks open his water and takes a drink. "You look good." His eyes smile the same way they did when we were kids. Nick's demeanor has changed. He carries himself with a new confidence. More worldly and mature than the cocky kid I met in the parking lot at Eureka High. But his eyes hold the same playful expression.

"You look happy," I tell him.

"I am." He sets the water down and picks up his fork. He takes a bite of his dinner and gives an approving nod. Suddenly it hits me that Nick is here. He's really here. I reach out and touch his free hand.

He squeezes my fingers and smiles. "I missed you."

"I know. Me too." I pull back. "So, tell me about Myanmar. What was it like?"

He tells me about the village he helped rebuild and the school they're naming after the foundation. The tenor of his voice has changed. He no longer speaks in that lazy slang he used in high school. He sounds like an adult.

"You'd think Samoa would've been an easier clean-up. They had a lot more help in some ways, but it was worse in others. Red tape

201

and politics. Boring stuff." He pauses and takes a huge bite of his dinner without flinching. I can't tell if he likes it. I can't read him at all. He isn't the same Nick Marino I met four years ago. He isn't dropping f-bombs or selling drugs. He's a respectful member of the human race. A very good-looking member. He smiles when he catches me staring.

"What?" I say, feeling totally naked in front of him. Nobody can look at me the way he does. There is something about being in the company of a person who knows your secrets and your lies. Someone who connects with you on a totally unspoken level. I don't even think Matt can look at me the way Nick just did. One wordless expression and he knows exactly who I am.

"I'm really happy to see you, Dani. Tell me about you. How's school?"

"Ugh, I don't want to talk about school." I drop my fork and lean on my elbows. "I hate all my professors. I have no clue what I'm going to do when I graduate." It's sort of embarrassing to be in school this long and still be undecided.

"You'll figure it out," he says. "You still have time." He shrugs like he's not worried about me.

I like that.

"These last two years flew by. It feels like we were just partying in your cottage." I swallow the lump in my throat when I realize how much time has passed.

"I know." Nick reaches across the table and pats my hand.

When you recall a moment or a memory of being on ecstasy, you don't think about laughing at a joke, or dancing to a song. It isn't even the people you miss. It's the pill. Thizz gets all the credit. All the glory.

The truth is, I don't want to go back to that cottage with Matt and Nick. I want to go back to the feeling that nothing else in the world mattered other than the three people in that cottage. Knowing a pill can bring you that level of joy is a scary feeling. It awakens urges I haven't had in months.

"Life doesn't have a pause button, but if it did, that would've been a great time." Nick smiles, and I feel like I want to cry. The old Nick would pull a baggy from the pocket his jeans and hand me a pill. I wonder if there's still a little of that Nick hidden in the responsible adult sitting before me.

"You really are a grown-up." It's more of an observation than a compliment.

He contemplates his statement like he's recalling the moments that shaped him into the man he is today.

"I've been all over the world. I've seen and done things people only dream about. I wouldn't change a single second because it showed me the kind of man I want to be." He pauses and reaches for my hand. "It also helped me figure out exactly what I want out of life." He doesn't have to elaborate, because everything I need to know is apparent in his eyes, the way his lips curl into a smile. A familiar tingle awakens my senses.

After dinner, we head to the basement for bed. We have an early wake-up call, and with the time change, we need the extra sleep. There are only two bathrooms for fifteen of us. Father Blanco gives us a lecture about time management and being respectful of our bunkmates. Short showers, use air-freshener, replace paper products. After he leaves, we take turns in the bathroom. I brush my teeth, wash my face, and pee in record time.

When Nick comes back from his five minutes in the bathroom, I'm inspecting the bed. I pretend I'm doing recon for Nick so he can report back the sleeping conditions to the board, but really I'm just checking for spiders.

"This isn't Marino-level accommodations," I tease.

Nick smirks and lies on the cot next to mine. He makes some adjustments to his pillow then turns to face me. "I slept on a floor in Myanmar for three months. It still wasn't as bad as these wood slabs they used for beds in a village in Japan. It killed my back."

"You went to Japan?" I sit crossed-leg on my cot. "What was the food like?"

"We went for a week so I could see an actual build. The food was interesting."

Nick runs his hand through his hair. The muscles in his arm bulge. The manual labor he's been doing shows.

"Look I just want to tell you I'm sorry about your birthday. I know I freaked you out. I really wish you didn't cut me off."

I lie on my cot and face the ceiling. I should've realized he would bring this up. I don't really know how to explain what happened after he left my apartment that day. I stopped caring. About school, my grades, my liver. Seeing Matt and the blonde, Nick trying to whisk me off to Vegas—it was too much, and the only way I knew how to deal with it was by not dealing at all.

"Lights out," Daryl announces and hits a switch.

The basement is dark for half a second, then night lights illuminate the exit doors. This place is way more rustic than I thought it would be. The fact that we're all sharing the same sleeping space kind of weirds me out. I'm grateful to have Nick here.

"Goodnight, Dani," Nick says when he realizes I'm not going to reply to his apology.

"Goodnight, Nick." I turn over and face the wall.

"Goodnight, Ed," Darryl says from the other side of the room.

"Goodnight, Daryl," Ed says.

Everyone follows Daryl's lead and says goodnight. Nick and I laugh each time someone new speaks. Eventually, the room quiets down, and by some miracle, I fall asleep in a room full of strangers, in a cot beside the first person I ever loved.

We work from seven to seven. Every. Single. Day.

The good news is—the cot feels like a feather bed after the second day. The bad news is—the food still sucks.

Nick and I have been too busy to continue our conversation from the first night. More like Nick's been busy. I've spent the first two days of this build not building a damn thing. I've moved wood, bricks, from one area to the next, and I've dumped a lot of garbage. I got to use a nail gun today, so that was kind of cool. Plus, I was the first one in, so I got to take a hot shower. It's the little things.

I shove my dirty clothes in a plastic bag hanging on the corner of my bed. Courtney said we'll have time to do laundry tomorrow. I need it. I've gone through half my socks.

"Hey Dani," Darryl says as he walks in. We're the only people in the room. "How goes it?"

"It goes good," I say as I sit on my cot, waiting for something interesting to happen. "What's up for tonight? There was talk of heading down to the Quarter." I'd love to get away for a few hours and have a drink. Or at the very least, a cheeseburger.

Darryl takes his boot off and sniffs it. He takes the other one off, then walks to the door and sets them outside.

"That's very courteous of you," I tell him.

"This humidity is doing bad things to my feet." He pulls his socks off and shoves them in a plastic bag, then rolls them up the same way Lucy does with the baby's smelly diapers.

"Are you and your feet up for a little fun? A daiquiri sounds really good right now."

"I thought this was a dry run for you?" He gives me a concerned look, like I'm falling off the wagon or something.

It takes a beat to realize he's referring to our conversation at the airport. "No, it's not like that. I'm not in rehab or anything."

Darryl looks at me like he's not convinced just as Nick walks into the basement.

"S'up Darryl." Nick nods to him, then falls onto his cot. His arms are tan and his face is dirty. I get tingles at the sight of his sweaty body lying inches away from me.

Being around Nick has stirred some feelings. Old feelings. Ones that remind me of endless nights on the beach and afternoons in my room. I chalked it up to nostalgia, but it could have something to do with watching him work shirtless in the Louisiana heat.

"You feel like hitting the Quarter tonight, Nick?" Darryl asks as he pulls a clean set of clothes out of his duffel bag. "Dani's itchin' for some fun." He winks at me as he walks to the door and says, "Y'all should go out. You make a cute couple."

I probably shouldn't have brought up her birthday our first night here, but I had to clear the air. If I had known she was going to shut me out, I wouldn't have shown up at her place. I don't always make the right choices when it comes to my feelings for Dani. I plan to fix everything between us; starting tonight.

She takes out a shirt, folds it, and shoves it back into the bag. She does this three times with the same shirt. It's obvious she's avoiding me; I know she can feel me watching her, yet she won't turn around. If this is going to happen, I have to make the first move.

"Do you want to go out tonight?" I ask her.

She zips her bag and turns around. "Do you want to go out?" She bites the corner of her mouth like she's nervous. It turns me on.

"Yeah, sure. We can get dinner," I suggest. "Someone told me about a great steakhouse."

"Oh my God, yes!" She turns back to her bag and opens it. This time she pulls out a pair of jeans and a black tank top. "Let's keep it casual though." She holds up her outfit for my approval.

"Perfect," I tell her. She's fucking perfect.

I take a quick shower and skip shaving. I put on a white t-shirt and a pair of jeans, then go to the common room to find Dani. She looks happy to see me and makes a comment about my scruff.

"Love this." She runs her hand down my left cheek, and it affects other parts of my body. I can't wait for this night to begin.

"Let's roll," Daryl announces and opens the door.

I look at Dani, and she tells me Courtney and Daryl have decided to tag along. I sense a bit of disappointment in her voice. That also does things to my body.

I don't think Daryl can afford the steakhouse. I don't want to seem like a rich douchebag and offer to pay for his dinner, so I let him choose the restaurant. Dani doesn't seem disappointed after she finds out they have cheeseburgers. It's a little hole in the wall, but the barbecue is pretty stellar. After dinner, Courtney lets us hit one bar. I don't know if she's just putting on the responsible act for me, or if she's really this boring. Drinking on builds isn't permitted, but we're pretty lax. We want our volunteers to have a good overall experience. Keeping them locked in the basement of a church doesn't fill that criteria. If the NBA finals weren't on tonight, I'm sure more of the volunteers would've joined us.

"We've never been to a bar together, not since we've been old enough to drink," Dani says as she sips a strawberry daiquiri.

I hold up my drink and toast. "Another Nick-and-Dani first." She laughs and touches her glass to mine. I take my shot just as the band starts playing. It's an eighties rock cover band called The Fritters. "Come on, let's dance." I pull her towards the dance floor.

She hesitates and makes a face likes she's embarrassed.

"For real? I've seen your Facebook. I know you dance." I look at her hand in mine and resist the urge to kiss it. Just touching her feels good. I don't want to push too far. I can't lose her again.

Now that I'm finished with school and the foundation is up and running, I can put some effort into winning her back. The timing needs to be perfect.

"I'm too sober to dance." She sucks on her straw, and I see the liquid level in her glass lower. "One more round?"

I agree, because its Dani. I do whatever she asks. I lean over the bar and order our drinks. Out of the corner of my eye I see Courtney approach us.

"Is everything okay over here?" Courtney asks.

"Yeah, it's great," Dani tells her as she slides off her bar stool. "I'll be right back."

We watch her walk in the direction of the bathroom. When she's out of earshot, Courtney turns to me.

"Nick, I think it would be best to leave now." She clears her throat and leans in towards me. "Daryl mentioned that Dani might have had a substance abuse issue."

I stumble back in shock. "What are you talking about?" My words come out in a not-so-friendly manner. "She doesn't have any issues. I know her."

The bartender sets my shot on the bar beside Dani's daiquiri. I toss him a hundred and tell him to keep the change.

"You guys head back; I'll take care of her." I suddenly feel very protective of Dani. It isn't a new feeling. Keeping Dani safe has always come naturally to me. It's something I failed to do in the past. That won't happen again.

I watch Courtney and Daryl say goodbye to Dani on the other side of the bar and worry that she'll want to leave with them. Maybe we should leave. I never make good decisions when it comes to this girl.

"Looks like it's just me and you." She smiles and lifts her drink from the bar. I watch her drain half the glass in one breath.

I hide my concern at her ability to down two drinks in under ten minutes with a lie.

"I'm impressed."

"I'm in college," she yells over a really bad rendition of a Bon Jovi song. "Come on, we're halfway there!" She takes my hand and drags me to the dance floor.

We're standing in front of the stage watching the band when Dani suggests we get one more round. I tell her no.

"We can't get wasted; tomorrow is another long day."

She agrees with a somewhat disappointed look on her face. Even though I'm sure she can handle another daiquiri, Courtney's comment makes me wonder if there is some truth to what she said. I haven't seen Dani in a long time. What I do know about her comes from Facebook. It's filled with pictures and posts of her partying. She is in college. It's not abnormal for her to drink. I wonder if that's all she's doing.

The band starts a slow song, and I put my concerns aside when Dani threads her hand with mine. I close my eyes and concentrate on all the areas of our bodies that are touching. Her hand, my shoulder. I lean over and smell her hair. I know without a doubt that come Friday, I won't be able to walk away. I can't say goodbye to her again.

"Should we go?" she asks as the song ends.

I snap from my daze and nod my head. We turn to leave when a familiar chord rings through the bar.

"No way," she yells. "It's our song!"

I let her pull me back to the stage because I've just lost all rational thought. She doesn't watch the band like before. Her arms wrap around my neck, and she sways in front of me. I keep her at arm's length just so I can look at her. Her eyes close, her lips move. She sings this song with more emotion than any other that played tonight. My arms slide around her waist. I pull her to my chest and hold her against my heart.

We've been separated a long time. I've seen and done a lot. Even when we were miles apart, she was never far from my mind. She never will be. She lives inside of me; she is a part of my soul. I wasn't complete until I met Dani. She taught me to love, to forgive, to strive for more. I thought, for a brief moment, that we weren't supposed to be together. Crazy, I know. With all that was stacked against us, who I am, who she was, it didn't seem like we'd ever overcome our past. Letting her go was the best decision I ever made. I wasn't ready. I wasn't mature enough to love her the way she deserves. I am now. And nothing is going to stop me.

Dani

We're quiet in the taxi back to the church. I stare out the window, watching signs for fancy hotels fly by, and I wonder if Nick wants me as badly as I want him. It isn't love I'm after right now. I just want to be held. I want to feel good. Nick Marino can definitely make me feel good.

His hands are folded in his lap. He watches me reach across his thigh before he turns his palm up and wraps his hand around mine.

"I'm glad you're here," I say.

"Me too."

The taxi pulls to a stop, and Nick reaches for his wallet. I'm suddenly nervous about what happens next. It isn't like we have anyplace private we can go. This is the most awkward date I've ever been on.

I step out of the taxi and wait on the sidewalk. Nick closes the door and turns towards the church.

"Can you believe how warm it is? The weather here is crazy."

"Do you want to go for a walk?" I ask, hoping we can extend this night just a little longer. My buzz is still strong, therefore I'm still brave.

"Sure, just let me tell Courtney we're back." Just as Nick reaches for the door, it swings open, and Father Blanco appears.

"There you are," he says to Nick. "I was hoping we could meet after dinner. I didn't know you had plans. I am pretty busy for the next two days." He looks at me with a smile. "I have time now, if you still want to talk."

Nick clears his throat. "Uh, yeah. Now would be great." He looks back at me with a sad smile. "Goodnight, Dani."

I didn't think Nick and I would hook up. Not really. Unless we snuck into the bathroom or something. Not that I have given any thought to good hook-up spots in the church. It doesn't matter now. He just ditched me for a priest.

The alarm on my phone goes off at six, and I spring from sleep. Those two strawberry daiquiris didn't seem like much last night, but I'm sure feeling them now. I turn over to retrieve my phone and see that Nick's cot is already empty. He didn't come down to the basement until after I fell asleep. I tried to wait up for him, but I dozed off. When Daryl's snoring woke me up at three in the morning, Nick was sleeping soundly. Part of me wanted to wake him up. The dirty little voice that never makes the right choices wanted me to climb out of my bed and kiss him. His hand was hanging off the cot, and I debated for a full five minutes on whether or not I should touch him. Then I remembered why I'm here. I didn't volunteer for this trip to hook up with Nick.

I'm the last one up and dressed. By the time I make it to the kitchen, breakfast has already been cleaned up. I grab a bagel, then head outside. I find Courtney handing out work assignments on the side of the church.

"Daryl, you're going to help with framing the arch for the doorway." She hands him a tool belt and a hard hat.

"I'm in electrical," he protests.

"We have no electrical work today; it's either this or the food bank," Courtney tells him as she hands out tools and instruction sheets to the rest of the team. "We really need help on the arch. They're reframing the front of the church. You'll learn a lot." She looks up with a pleading smile. "What do you say?"

Daryl accepts his assignment and turns to leave. He walks past me, then stops and smiles. "How did it go last night?" His grin turns wicked.

"I got cock-blocked by a priest," I tell him and shove a piece of bagel in my mouth.

Daryl laughs as he walks away. I don't think he actually believes me, which makes the situation even funnier.

"Dani, we're going to the food bank today," Courtney says. "It's actually run by the church, so it's part of the build." She's ready to state her case.

"You don't have to convince me," I assure her. "Anything to get out of this heat."

Her shoulders relax when I don't protest. "Good, then let's go."

The food bank is around the corner, but we drive anyway. I don't understand why until Courtney opens the back of the van. It's stacked with crates filled with canned goods. They are heavy. Really heavy. Me, Courtney, and another volunteer unload them from the van.

214

"Another group will stack them on the shelves, we're just here to drop off," Courtney tells us. "Grab those empty crates and load them up." She points to a pile in the corner. "Then we can take a little break." She winks and walks towards an office in the front of the building.

As I'm loading the crates, I think about Nick, about all the old feelings that surface when he's around. Every moment we have spent together was laced with ecstasy. So, what is it exactly that I miss? Little jolts of adrenaline surge through me when Nick touches my hand or smiles in that way he does. We have too much history to have a random fling. If something happens between us on this trip, I don't think either of us could just walk away.

On the way back to the church, Courtney stops at a café. Me and the other volunteer, Eliza, follow her inside. Courtney orders three coffees and an assortment of pastries. We sit at a table near the window and people-watch as we eat.

"So, tell me your story, Dani," Eliza says.

I shrug and shove half a croissant in my mouth. "I don't have a story."

"Everyone on these builds has a story." Eliza insists. "I'm divorced. My kids are spending the summer with my ex, so I decided to do something productive." She looks so proud of herself. Courtney smiles and thanks her for all the help she's given to the team.

I nod and pretend I don't want to gag. Eliza's self-serving smugness makes me want to vomit.

"So, how do you know Nick?" Courtney asks.

I choke on the second half of my croissant. "Um, he's just a guy I know from high school." I give Courtney a what-the-hell look. She isn't supposed to tell anyone that Nick is the head of the foundation. Even speaking about him feels wrong.

"I'd say he was more than just some guy," Eliza adds.

"We all see the way he watches you, and the way you smile at him when he's not looking. There's a story there, I know it."

Courtney sips her coffee. A strand of her short light-brown hair falls in her eyes. When she tucks it behind her ear, I see several piercings lining her left ear.

"How old are you?" I ask Courtney. I can tell she's young enough that the question doesn't offend her.

"Twenty-four. What about you?" She puts her cup down and checks her cell phone.

I tell her I'm twenty-two. Eliza says she's thirty-one.

"When did you starting working for ADF?" Eliza asks her.

Courtney places her cell phone back in her pocket. "Right after college. I'm one of the original employees. You should really think about coming to work for us, Dani."

"No, thanks," I say. I really want to say hell no. Like hell to the no. I'm almost done with the Marino's; I don't want to get sucked back in.

Since my money was laundered into a Marino family trust, I have to wait until I graduate to get it. Because I screwed up, I won't graduate for another semester. It isn't like I need the money. Everything is paid for. It's the freedom. Just being on my own.

Money Mark has taken good care of my account. I still have enough money for a down payment on a house, a car, or a long vacation. I can pay my way through law school, or move to Greece for a few years. I have so many options; too bad I have no clue what I want.

"What exactly is your job, Courtney?" Eliza asks.

Courtney finishes chewing her éclair before she answers. She's refined like that.

"I'm a project coordinator. I act as the onsite liaison between the volunteers, the client, and the foundation. I travel, meet people, help communities, and at the end of the day, I get paid for it. It's a win-win."

"Sounds amazing," Eliza says. "I wish I chose an easier path."

"What do you do?" I ask her because she's dying for someone to ask.

"I'm a teacher." She smiles. "Third grade."

"You think Courtney's job is easier than yours?" I scoff. "You get a paid summer vacation."

Eliza looks at me and I cower. Like I'm in trouble, by a teacher.

"Working with kids is a huge pain in the ass. These kids think they know everything thanks to the internet. They don't want to read about history in a textbook when they can google it."

I listen to Courtney and Eliza discuss their careers, and I begin to feel completely inadequate. Eliza goes on about making ends meet with her kids and her mortgage. Courtney has over a hundred thousand dollars in student loans that she might never be able to pay off. Here I am with a trust fund of laundered drug money paying my rent and tuition. All I do is waste it on booze, pills, and shoes.

We leave the café with two boxes of pastries for the rest of the team. During the drive back, Courtney and Eliza brainstorm places to hide them until breakfast tomorrow. Courtney parks the van, and we walk around back to unload the crates. I scan the side yard and find what I'm looking for.

Nick is working on the arch. His old Forty Niners hat sits backward on his head and a dirty white t-shirt clings to his sweaty body. The Louisiana humidity is my new best friend.

"Ahem," Eliza interrupts. She hands me the crate with the pastry boxes inside, then stacks an empty one on top. "You can't even see it." She steps back to inspect. "Get inside before the chocolate ones melt."

I walk around the side yard where most of the construction is taking place. They built a platform to hold the arch until they finish framing out the front of the church. Nick is painting on a coat of sealer when I walk past; it smells awful.

"Hey Dani," Daryl says. "What do you think?" He puts his hands on his hips and looks above his head. "Isn't she a beauty?"

"Yes, she is," Nick says.

I turn around and find him staring at me. Warmth rushes, well, everywhere. Sweat runs down my arms, causing the crates to slip. I stop to readjust them on my knee, and Nick runs over to help.

"Let me get that for you." He takes the crates and starts towards the door.

"I can't believe that used to be a pile of wood." I gesture to the arch. "It's amazing."

"Woodworking is an art, not a trade." Nick looks into the crate. "Whatever you have stashed in here smells good."

"It's a secret," I tell him. "If you tell anyone about this crate, I have to kill you."

"You know I'll always keep your secrets, Dani."

I lead Nick into the kitchen and tell him to put the crate behind a stack of empty boxes. Nick arranges them so the crates are hidden.

"Make sure you tell Courtney this is back here, otherwise someone might throw it out," Nick suggests.

"I will," I tell him and turn to leave.

Nick grabs my hand and pulls me into his arms. My first instinct is to pull away. Instead I look into Nick's eyes and smile.

"Is this ok? I don't want to push too far."

I grip his bicep to prevent him from moving. I want him in my personal space. Sweat and all.

"Yes. It's fine."

He slides his arm around my waist, and I rest my head against his chest. I'm reminded of our first date. Standing on the beach, the wind rustling my hair, the salty taste of the ocean in my mouth. I try to conjure the feelings I had then. The fear and excitement of being in Nick's arms. I was a kid. With kid feelings. This is real. More intense in some ways, less penetrating in others. Maybe I'm overthinking it. Overanalyzing my reaction to this moment. I want him, but I don't want him.

"Dani," Nick whispers my name.

I slowly lift my head and tilt my face towards his. Our eyes remain open as he kisses me softly, tentatively. The way you take a cautious sip of hot coffee. Three gentle kisses, then he pulls away.

The emotion isn't what I thought it would be. My heart has nothing to do with what I'm feeling in this moment.

"That didn't have to mean anything," Nick says. But his eyes are full of hope and longing. "I just really needed to kiss you." He backs away, allowing me the space I need to process the moment. "It's hard to be close to you sometimes. I don't mean physically. I just mean like

219

this. Friends. Whatever." He sighs and runs his hand through his hair. His nervous tick. "It's hard to see you smile or make you laugh and not take you in my arms. It kills me to look at you across the room and know you aren't mine."

"I'm still your friend, Nick." I know it's a stupid thing to say in this moment. But I say it. Cause, yeah, I'm stupid.

"We're friends," he scoffs. "But that won't stop you from going home with another man." His arms retract from around my waist, and he takes my hands in his. "You're not mine, and I'm not yours."

The pain in his voice crushes my chest. I want to reach in and pull it out. I don't want him to hurt. Not for me.

"I really liked being yours, Dani. I like it so damn much. I can't be anyone else's." He lifts my hand to his lips and kisses my knuckles.

For the first time since I sat on K's bed, the first night we took thizz, I feel something real for Nick. I don't know if it's pain, love, lust, or pity, but holy crap do I have feels.

Eliza bursts into the kitchen, and the top two crates in her stack tumble out of her arms. Nick rushes over to help her.

"Thanks, Nick." She sets the crates on the opposite side of the kitchen. "Dani, there's still a van that needs unloading." Her voice is stern, but a playful grin dances across her face.

"I'm on it," I tell her and rush out of the kitchen before any more feelings spill out of me.

Nick and I sit next to each other at dinner, but we keep our conversation limited to the build and stories of Nick's time abroad. When the group goes to the common room to watch a basketball game, I take a shower. I have to process what is happening. It's been so long since I've felt things. Especially for Nick. There have been other men. They didn't mean anything. They were just entertainment. I learned a lot in the last year. Like three shots and pint of beer gives me the best buzz. How to kiss a cute stranger and not care if he calls. That if I keep moving, keep the music turned up, eventually I'll forget what I'm running from. I also know dealing with feelings this intense is not my strong suit. I want to run now. Or get really wasted.

When I return to the basement, Nick is sitting on his cot. I'm not totally upset to find him waiting for me.

"Hey," I say.

He looks up and smiles. He watches me move around the basement without saying a word.

"I ran out of shampoo, so I had to use the hand soap. I smell like a gas station bathroom." I take out a pair of clean socks and sit down in a chair at the end of my cot to put them on. "Do you want to smell it?"

Nick stands up, walks to my chair, and kneels in front of me. He runs his hand through his hair.

"What?" I ask. Even though I can tell he has something to say. I focus on his lips, wishing he would kiss me instead.

"I could be monitoring this build from a five-star hotel in the Quarter. Or a beach in Bali. Do you know why I'm here?"

"Because you're not a rich douchebag?" I joke. My hands are fidgety. I want to touch Nick, but I don't. I've spent the last two years doing all the wrong things. I don't know if this is right. I can lie to myself about how I feel, what I want; I can't lie to Nick. He can see right through me. To the real me.

He allows himself a half smile. "Because not being here means I don't get to sleep in this dusty basement with you tonight. I won't get to wake up at five in the morning and watch you sleep. Yes, I'd rather watch you sleep in a king size bed at a five-star hotel." He grins at the thought. "But I'll take a shitty cot and a flat pillow in this rundown church as long as I'm lying next to you."

Nick stands and walks to the cabinet on the other side of the basement. He picks up a bottle of water and twists off the top. I watch his head tilt back as he drinks. He just laid his heart at my feet. He's freaking out.

"Nick," I say and walk to him.

He sets the bottle down and drops his hands to his sides. I see my reflection in the metal knob above his head. He's waiting for me to make the next move. He's played all his cards. It's my turn. If this doesn't happen now, it never will. If I don't speak my heart, he'll never know. I don't even know what I'm about to say. I'm going to open my mouth, and my heart, and let words pour out.

"Nick." I place my right hand on his left shoulder. He waits half a second before he moves.

He turns around and slides his hand around my waist in one swift motion. I let him take me in his arms because being in Nick Marino's arms is the closest thing I have to a home. I let him hold me while I breathe him in. He doesn't smell like my Nick. He smells like the cheap soap in the bathroom mixed with the sealer he's been working with all day. I close my eyes, and we hold each other for an infinite amount of time. I can't help but think about the hours we spent holding each other when we were high. It feels the same. I'm confused. Does he get me high? Is it sensory recall, or is this love?

"Dani, I lo—" Nick starts to say the words I've dreaded to hear since I saw him at the airport.

I open my mouth to stop him when suddenly a siren rips through the basement. I clamp my hand over my ears, and Nick pushes me behind him like something sinister is going to come through the door. The white flood lights above the double doors start flashing.

"I think it's a fire alarm," Nick yells over the siren. "Let's go."

He takes my hand and we run towards the exit. We enter the hall and find Daryl coming down the stairs.

"The frame for the archway just went up in flames!" he says with way too much excitement.

Nick asks him what happened as we run through the kitchen and out the back door.

"I don't know, but it's going up fast!"

We run around the side of the church where the archway was standing a few minutes ago.

Two fire trucks stop in front of the church, and suddenly, something ignites. A ball of fire shoots into the sky. Luckily, the fire station is just a few doors down. They must have seen the flames and came straight over.

"Wanna bet that was a can of sealer?"

Daryl nudges Nick with his shoulder, and Nick's face goes white.

"Some dumbass probably forgot to put it away. All it takes is one idiot with a cigarette and poof!"

One of the firemen yells for us to move across the street in case there's another explosion. I spot Courtney with some of the other volunteers. They're doing a head count to make sure everyone made it out. I start towards them, and I feel Nick pull his hand from mine.

"Nick, come on. I want to let everyone know we're okay."

He runs his hands over his head and clutches the back of his neck. Something is wrong.

"Nick." I reach for him, and he jerks back.

"It's my fault. This is my fault." He turns around and starts walking down the street.

I look back at Courtney; she's speaking to Daryl. Good. He'll tell her we're okay. When I turn back to Nick, he's halfway down the street. I have to run to catch up to him.

"Nick, this isn't your fault. It was an accident."

"No!" He whirls around. "It was my job to put the sealer back in the storage unit. I forgot. I helped you carry in those stupid crates." He shakes his head in disgust. "I'll never learn. I'll never fucking learn!"

In all the years I've known Nick, I have never seen him this emotional. He hates himself right now. Or worse, he blames me.

"I know better. I've been around construction my entire life, and I fucked up. I left those cans outside under the arch because I saw you!" He takes two backward steps away from me. "This is a sign, Dani. Holy shit. I can't believe I was doing it again." He laughs, sort of. It's more hysterical than comical.

"What are you doing again?" I feel the threat of tears rising in my throat. His eyes are cold. Just like his uncle Will's.

"This. Us. That fire."

"What does the fire have to do with me and you?" I look back at the inferno and wonder if he's right. Are we cursed?

"Everything happens for a reason." He smirks. "Is that what you said?"

I can't believe this is the same man who was on his knees a few minutes ago.

"What are you trying to say, Nick?"

"That." He points to the flames. "That is one helluva sign that we don't belong together."

We spend the night in a motel that makes the basement look like a five-star hotel. The next day, I get on a plane to head home. The rumor circulating through the group is that the foundation is sending a crew to clean up the damage and finish the build. I am one hundred percent positive Nick shut us down. There wasn't anything we could do anyway. Not in the three days we had left.

Courtney let me know Nick was okay but didn't elaborate on his whereabouts or ask me if I knew what happened. She just told me to have a safe flight home.

Nick said the fire was a sign that we didn't belong together. The fire was an accident. Something out of our control. We didn't belong together before the arch went up in flames. What Nick and I had burnt out a long time ago.

Matt

July 2010

I open the door to my apartment and find Ashley and Samantha packing boxes. Correction, Samantha is packing. Ashley is dancing to a Katy Perry song.

"Hey, Matty." Ashley stops bouncing and gives me hug.

"What are you doing here?" I put down the pizza box in my hand. Samantha has changed so many things in my life. How I look at relationships, the type of beer I drink, and pizza. I eat pizza.

"Can't I stop by and say hi to my brother?" Ashely says in a semi-sweet voice. She's so full of shit. I love it. Ashely got her license a few months ago; she's always coming over just to get out of the house.

When Samantha turns around to lower the volume on the stereo, Ashely gives me a look like something is up. A million things run through my mind. First being, her health.

"Hey Sam, I left my phone charger in the car. Can you run down and get it?" I hand her my keys.

226

"Actually, I need to run some errands. You guys can have some brother-sister time." She kisses my cheek and places my keys on the counter. "See you later, Ashely." She waves and walks out.

"God, I wish I hated her," Ashely says as she falls onto the couch.

"That's a shitty thing to say." I pick up a pillow and hit with it. I sit beside her and tap the back of her head just to piss her off. Messing with Ashley makes her feel normal. "So, what's up?" I watch my sister's playful eyes turn serious. "Are you okay?"

She sighs and moves out of my reach. "I'm fine. It isn't me."

I exhale, and then I realize what she's said. "Is it Mom?" She's been complaining a lot about her back and having headaches.

"Nobody is dying. I'm here for you, dummy." She puts her hand on mine. "You're really screwed up, Matty."

"What are you talking about?" I stand and walk to the kitchen for a beer.

My father ambushed me last week about moving back to California. I told him I wasn't interested. I tell my nosey sister the same thing as I sit at the desk and open up Facebook.

"What are you doing here, Matt?" Ashley leans on the desk, trying to gain my attention. She looks good, healthy. She even thinks she's getting fat, like a normal eighteen-year-old girl. I can't believe she's the same age Dani was when I first met her. If my relationship with Samantha has taught me anything, it's how adults treat each other. I respect Sam on a level I never did with Dani. For one, I never get jealous. We make time for each other when it's convenient. Nobody's feelings ever get hurt.

"What do you mean?" I click on my notifications to see what people are up to.

"You graduated two months ago, your lease is up in August. What are you going to do?"

"I'm pretty sure the firm I interned at last summer is going to make me an offer. I killed it in my second interview."

"Why are you applying for jobs here? Why not in California?"

I don't answer because I don't have an answer.

"I'm not going to die." She places her hand on mine so I stop randomly clicking shit on my computer. "Even if I was, you being here won't stop it."

Ashley is cancer free. They're pretty confident she will remain in remission. She wants to move back home; my parents are even talking about going back to California. I'm the only one trying to find excuses to stay.

I take a pull on my beer to prep for what I'm going to say next. "In case you haven't noticed, I'm moving in with Sam."

"You don't love her."

There is no way my little sister can determine my feelings for Samantha; I don't even know how I feel. It took nearly a year for me to tell her I loved her, and I still don't know if those words are true. I care about her. Isn't that enough?

"You will never love anyone like you love Dani."

"You don't know what you're talking about." I almost call her a kid, but that isn't true anymore. She's as mature as I was when I fell in love with Dani. That's the problem. I look at Ashley's immaturity and wonder if Dani and I were just as naïve. Sure, we did adult things, but mentally, we weren't ready to make choices about who we love. At least that's what I tell myself on the nights I sit at this desk, stalking her social media accounts.

"You don't look at Samantha the same way you did with Dani."

She's right of course, but I don't admit it. There's no point. "Dani moved on, Ash. What do you want me to do?"

"She didn't move on, you left her, and now it's time to go back."

I interned at law firms every summer for the last three years. I'm qualified to work as a legal assistant or even a paralegal. My plan is to work a few years then go to law school. If I'm lucky, my firm will help support my education.

I applied to four firms. Three in Colorado, and one in San Francisco. I didn't tell anyone about that one, it's a long shot anyway. I click off Facebook and check my email. I have one new message, from the San Francisco firm. This is perfect; I'll read the rejection in front of Ashley and shut her up. I open the message and start reading.

Dear Mr. Augustine...we want to offer you a position...

"Holy crap, that's Dad's old firm," Ashely squeals from over my shoulder. "Is it in Eureka?"

"No, the city."

"Oh my God, Matt! This is a sign!" Ashley bounces to the kitchen and pulls her cell phone from her bag on the counter.

"Who are you calling?"

"Dad." Ashley holds the phone to her ear. "He's going to flip out."

"Wait!" I yell. "Just let me figure out what I want to do first. I haven't heard back from the other firms."

Why did I open that email in front of my sister? I wanted to make this decision on my own. Now I'll have my family influencing me. I'm pretty sure I only got this job because of my father. I kind of wanted to do this on my own. I sound like Nick. He was so hell-bent on making his own future, creating his own fate. He did just that, with the help of his grandmother, and there is no shame in it.

All of my contacts are here. And then there's Samantha. She's a nice girl. She loves me. I can't just cut and run. Again.

Ashely looks at me like I'm a freak. "Matt, you have to go back. You and Dani belong together."

"It isn't that easy. This isn't one of your romance novels. This is real life."

"You know why those books are so amazing, Matt?" Ashley sighs as if she's explaining simple math to a child. "Because we wish moments like those existed. You have an opportunity to be that guy. You can be the best book boyfriend in the history of book boyfriends if you go to her now. Sweep her off her feet. Be the man I know you are."

I look at my sister's sweet face. Even if she is wrong, I can't say no to her. What if she's right?

I send Ashely home. Then I text Samantha and tell her we need to talk. She texts me back a sad face. Then a happy face. Then she texts: choose one. She's the sweetest person I've ever known, and the last person on Earth I ever wanted to hurt.

Matt

August 2010

We've been staying at the house in Santa Clara for the last two weeks. The roommates moved out, and the lease isn't up until the end of the month so it's home base for Operation Get Dani Back.

Ashely's plan isn't working. Dani refuses to see me. She won't return my calls or reply to my texts and emails. This is my last-ditch effort to get her attention. She was tagged in a post yesterday about a going-away party for one of her friends. Ashley took that as a sign. Everything is a sign to that girl.

I walk into the bar where she hangs out. She checked in here an hour ago on Facebook. This is it. I pay a five-dollar cover and flash my ID. My heart is jumping as I walk down the hall and land in the main bar. I find her instantly. She's dancing with Zack, the guy I thought was her boyfriend. I learned later, from Nick, that he had his own boyfriend.

The song ends, and he looks up. We make eye contact, and he narrows his gaze. Something clicks, and his expression changes. He recognizes me. I'm scared he's going to say something. Instead, he winks, whispers something to Dani, and walks away. He goes to the bar and grabs another dude, equally as handsome. He points at me, and then to Dani. The guy turns around and tells the bartender. Now I have an audience. The only person clueless to my presences is her.

This wasn't how I wanted our first meeting to happen. I went to her apartment twice, but she wasn't home. The third time Mary was there. She's the one that clued me in on what's been going on. How fucked up she's been since New Orleans. Mary said Dani was doing really well before the trip. She was volunteering with Haley and working hard to keep her grades up. After what went down with Nick, she spent the entire summer partying. Mary is moving at the end of the month, and she doesn't want to leave Dani alone.

Nick explained his side of what happened. He knows the fire was an accident, but still blames his carelessness and his lack of focus on Dani. Not her personally, but his feelings for her. His judgment is clouded when she's concerned. He said it perfectly; she's a drug to him. He went to New Orleans looking for a high.

Nick thinks if I win her back, he'll stop loving her. He's crazy. Loving Dani is part of who he is. He needs to figure out what his feelings mean. I'm not just tossing bullshit advice his way. I'm in the same boat. That's why I'm here now. I'll never be able to love someone completely until I know why I still love Dani. We have this weird connection, something that solidified during the nights we spent together on ecstasy. We're bonded in a way that none of us can explain.

I take a step closer to where Dani is dancing, when suddenly a familiar song comes on. It's the song we danced to in my room. She throws a thumbs-up to the DJ. That's a good sign, I guess. If she hated the song, then that might be an indicator about her feelings for me. I take a cautious step closer and tap her shoulder. She spins around with a huge smile. It fades when she sees me. A dozen emotions cross her face. I know she has a lot of things she probably wants to say.

What are you doing here?

Where's the blonde?

Get out.

"Hi," is what she chooses to say.

"You want to dance?"

She doesn't say no; she doesn't say anything. She just stands there, so I start to dance. I don't give a fuck. I'll make a fool of myself in front of her hipster friends. I grind her ass for a few beats, then I switch positions and shake my ass in front of her. She laughs a little. Her friends start cheering me on from the bar. When the song ends, I yell to the DJ to play it again. The guys at the bar and the bartender join in. He actually replays the song. The rest of the dance floor empties, leaving just me and Dani under the soft pink lights.

She realizes what is happening and starts to sway. I step back and watch her just like I did from my bedroom door. She points at me and waves me over with her finger. Her face is expressionless. No smile, nothing. I chalk it up to surprise, and maybe a tiny bit of anger for busting in on her the way I did. Her lack of emotion doesn't stop me. I move into her personal space.

She reaches up and pulls her hair loose. It falls over her bare shoulders and clings to her sweaty skin. I forgot how sexy she can be.

As the song comes to an end, the DJ mixes it into another track, and suddenly she's gone. I watch her move through the crowd, straight to the bar. Her friends have shots lined up in front of them. She takes a shot, then reaches for another. I hold her hand, preventing the glass from moving to her lips.

"You don't need that," I say.

She shakes my hand off.

"You have no right to tell me what I need. You think you know me." She laughs. It's a sad laugh. "The girl you knew is gone. I killed her."

She opens her mouth to allow the liquid to pass her lips. I slap it out of her hand, and the glass shatters at her feet. Shock registers on the faces of everyone at the bar. I can't believe it either. Zack and the other guy move towards me as the bartender yells to someone for assistance.

This is not going the way I planned. I have to do what I came here for, before I get thrown out. I grab her face. Her eyes widen as I descend on her mouth. She resists for half a second, and then I feel her hands in my hair. We kiss until I no longer taste tequila on her tongue. She finally breaks away when the DJ starts cheering over the mic. Her eyes aren't filled with anger or disgust; they're overflowing with tears.

"I love you," I say. "I want to make it right. I'll do anything."

There were other things I wanted to say. More coherent and rational words. I don't have time for them now.

I watch her closely, so I know immediately that I've made a mistake. I can't hear her over the music. I don't need to. Her face tells me everything I need to know. Her mouth moves again. She says, "Leave."

I walk out of the bar and spot Ashley leaning against a parked car talking to a group of kids dressed in Care Bear costumes. She scrambles past them when she sees me. Her gaze drifts to the doorway of the bar, and her smile fades.

"Let's go," I tell her.

"I'm sorry, Matt. I really thought she'd take you back."

This isn't my sister's fault. It's mine for thinking I could walk in there and get her back. Just because she didn't want Nick doesn't mean she wants me.

We weave through the sidewalk, back to the metro station, and take the train downtown to get my car. I left it in a pay-by-the-hour garage. Ash was so sure she'd take me back; she even had me convinced. Ashley's confidence was so absolute, I thought maybe she had spoken to Dani. That they planned this somehow. I'm such a fool.

"Where are we going?" Ashley asks as we get in my Mustang.

The studio apartment I rented won't be ready for two weeks. I don't feel like going back to Santa Clara. I crank the engine and rev it up. I can still taste the residual tequila in my mouth. I want to bury all memories of today. Squash the feelings I let float back to the surface.

"Anywhere but here."

I look at my little sister, and she smiles.

"I've never been to Disneyland."

I've just had what is possibly the worst experience of my life, and she wants to visit the happiest place on earth. I love this kid.

"Fuck it. Let's go to Disneyland."

Dani

My head is spinning, and my mouth is so dry I can barely swallow. When my eyes adjust to the light, I remember where I am. I let out a low moan.

A loud buzz/beep echoes into the white room, and the door opens. A nurse walks in and checks something on the machine. She checks the line that runs from the machine into my arm, then writes on a sheet of paper. She doesn't speak to me before turning to leave.

"Wait," I choke out. "I'm thirsty."

"I'll get you some water," she says as she washes her hands. "How is your pain?" She gestures to the chart on the wall. It's a series of smiley faces ranging from happy to really fucking pissed.

"I'm a seven."

"Okay. I'll see what I can get you." She walks out, closing the door behind her.

My head falls onto the pillow, and I wince. I have a monster headache, and my arm hurts. I close my eyes and try to remember what the hell happened.

Matt. Matt happened.

He actually thought he could just show up after all this time, and I'd go running back. He has no idea who I am. He also forgets that

I've seen his social media accounts. I know all about the blonde and the pizza. I have no idea who he is anymore.

Her profile picture was the two of them, up until a month ago. He left her and came back to California. His whole family moved back. His parents are living in Napa. Ashley is going to Sonoma State. She reached out to me and I really wanted to see her. So, when she asked me to meet her for lunch, it killed me to say no. Ashley is a hopeless romantic. I wouldn't put it past her to trick me and Matt into seeing each other. I wasn't ready two weeks ago, and I sure as hell wasn't ready last night.

As much as I hate Matt right now, I can't stop thinking about how I melted into him when we kissed. Just because my body is lusting for Matt, doesn't have to mean anything. He turns me on. So what? A lot of people turn me on.

After I told Matt to leave; Zack and I went to a club in the Tenderloin. We saw Antonio with his new boyfriend. So Zack and I went for a shot record. We did six or seven shots of tequila. Every time that stupid song came on, the crowd chanted, *Shots! Shots! Shots!* We listened.

After the club, we took a cab to the Mission to get a burrito, and that's all I remember. The rest comes in flashes, like scenes from a movie. I look at the road rash on my hand and the brace on my wrist. I must have fallen or tripped on the notoriously uneven sidewalk in the Mission District. I put my hand to the side of my head and feel a bandage. The ambulance ride is a blur; I don't remember Zack being there. Where is Zack?

The nurse returns with a pitcher of water and a small white cup. "I can give you Tylenol for the pain." She hands me the pills and a cup of water.

"Thank you," I say and take the medication. "Do I have a concussion?"

"Yes," she says and logs something in the chart on the wall. "And alcohol poisoning." Her words are clipped like she hates speaking to me. "A social worker will be in to talk to you soon."

Before I can protest, she tells me it's procedure. The nurse helps me to the bathroom and then back to bed. She hands me the remote for the television and tells me lunch will arrive in an hour.

Fifteen minutes after she leaves, the social worker knocks. She's a short Asian girl with long black hair. She introduces herself as Brandy. I smirk. Brandy looks like someone who's never been drunk, even though she has a stripper name. She looks at me from behind her Prada glasses, as if they give her some sort of super power. She's just a person, like me. Maybe not as fucked up as me, but she's human.

Brandy asks me a series of questions about my life. Where I live, do I work, how is my home life, am I single. I don't know what that has to do with anything. Are single people more fucked up than non-single ones? When I tell her I don't have a boyfriend, she makes a note of it on her little clipboard.

"Do you have a boyfriend?" I ask. It doesn't seem fair that she gets to ask all the questions.

"I'm engaged." She glances casually at the rock on her ring finger.

Nick gave me a small ruby-and-diamond ring for our fake engagement. Mariann insisted I keep it, but it felt too weird. When our engagement officially ended, Nick was on the other side of the planet. It wasn't a life-changing moment. I didn't cry. I didn't smile either. Handing the ring back to Mariann should've felt like closure. It just made me feel empty and alone.

"I was engaged once, but it didn't work out." I don't know why I'm telling her this. It isn't like I have to keep up the lie.

"Is that when you started drinking?" She adjusts her glasses.

"No," I snap.

She looks down at her clipboard. "How often do you drink?"

I drink almost every day. I won't count the occasional mimosa or Bloody Mary. I'm sure she's referring to the drinking I do at bars and clubs. Not what I consume at home. "A few times a week."

"On days that you drink, how many drinks do you have on average?" She scribbles something on her clipboard.

"Four," I lie. There is no freaking way I'm telling prissy pants my drink number.

"Do you black out often?"

I pass out, is that the same thing? Brandy doesn't have a clue what passing out and blacking out are like. Everything she knows about drinking she probably read in a textbook. How is she even qualified to be here?

"No," I tell her.

"Do you think you have a substance abuse problem?" She finally looks up. I see that she's wearing fake eyelashes. This really pisses me off.

"Absolutely not," I huff. "I'm only here because I fell."

"Yes, out of a moving car." She flips through some pages and says, "The cab driver says you opened the door to vomit and fell out."

Holy shit.

She pulls out a pamphlet and lays it on the tray table in front of me. "If you want help, it's here for you." She gives me a tight-lipped smile and walks out.

I don't get drunk every day. I only smoke weed once or twice a month. I stopped taking pills after New Orleans. Drinking became my go-to vice. Drinking seemed like the lesser of two evils. Vodka never got me in trouble like ecstasy did. I was completely dependent on that high. The illusion I was okay. Even now, as I lie in this bed with a broken head, it beats the shit out of having a broken heart.

My problem isn't drugs or alcohol. It isn't even something I can describe in a sentence or a word. Sad is a poor representation. Hopeless, depressed. I'm all of those things, plus so much more. I'm lost.

If I could just find my place. Figure out where I belong in the world. I pick up the phone and dial the only phone number I remember without checking my contacts. It rings three times before someone answers. When I hear the voice on the other end, I start to cry.

Dani

May 2011

The day after I graduate from CAL, my trust is fully funded. Mariann calls to congratulate me and invite me to dinner. We meet two days later at Top of the Mark. I've been here a few times with Zack. This swanky hotel restaurant let him host parties here on Saturday nights. Once dinner service is completed, the restaurant becomes a nightclub.

Zack freaked out after my accident. That's what we call it. Like I accidentally opened the door of a moving car. He felt responsible because of a conversation we had a few months earlier. I asked him how he was able to go hard on the weekends then turn it off. He can pop eight pills over the course of two days and still make it to class on time.

He said, "I let it take over my night, you let it take over your life."

He feels like that was me asking for help. I wasn't. I was just trying to find out what his secret was.

Zack was offered a job to run one of the largest nightclubs in Las Vegas. Something that started out as a way to meet dudes turned into a career. While he was off starting his new life, I was trying to save mine.

I spent the last half of 2010 with Lucy. Technically, I spent it getting clean. I opted for an outpatient program offered through St. Joseph's Hospital. After a month, I didn't need four meetings a day. I went because I liked talking to the other patients, listening to their stories, learning what they've overcome and lived through to be there.

I can't tell you how many times I lay on my bed at night and thanked God for keeping me safe. To say I'm lucky is an understatement. I've dodged more than just the bullets fired by Will Walker. Falling out of the cab was a huge wake-up call for me. One I couldn't ignore.

I had to change my lifestyle, and I considered staying in Eureka. Lucy wouldn't let me. She said I was running, and she was right. I've been running since the night my parents were shot. It was time to face my demons, not hide behind them with boys, booze, or pills.

I did everything in my power not to feel the loss. I started school in Eureka two weeks after they died. I just kept moving, kept sidestepping the pain. Therapy helped me grieve. Not just losing my parents. I mourned everything I'd lost in my life. Nick, Matt, the years I spent high. Addicts come in every shape and size. One person's addiction isn't the same as another's. We're all unique in our faults.

The weeks I spent at Lucy's, playing with Marguerite, working with Patty again, they were the happiest I've been in a long time. No drug, no drink, and certainly no boy could've given me the clarity I needed. Only time could do that.

Now that my trust is funded, this part of my life has come to an end. I will be forever grateful to Mariann for helping me. This money has kept me afloat and will allow me to move on to the next chapter in my story.

Mariann and I are seated at a table near the window. It's foggy, but I can see all of downtown San Francisco. The waiter is pouring water in our glasses when Mariann looks past me and says, "Look who's here."

I turn around and see Nick walking towards us. The restaurant sits on the top floor of the Mark Hopkins Hotel. There are dedicated elevators that bring you from the lobby to the restaurant. The elevators are slow, so Nick must have already been here when I arrived. I haven't seen him in nearly a year, not since he left me in New Orleans.

I want to strangle him with Mariann's pearls when he sits across from me. She gives him a brief kiss on the cheek and then waves a waiter over. The waiter asks what we want to drink, but I give him my entire order to hurry this horror show along.

"I'll have an iced tea," I tell him. "Just plain tea, not the Long Island variety. And the chicken."

Nick makes note that I'm not having alcohol with a slight head nod. He orders a water, while Mariann goes for red wine. I feel him watching me, but I refuse to look up. I don't want to see his playful hazel eyes. It's bad enough I can smell him. It's a thick, manly smelling cologne that only someone like Nick can pull off. It's the scent you dream of having on your pillow. The smell you want to linger in your hair for days. I hate him for smelling so good.

We keep the conversation light and limited to Nick's foundation. He talks about the work they're doing in Mississippi after the tornado outbreak that devastated the area. Nick speaks to the table, never addressing me directly. I don't ask a single question.

"Danielle, have you given any thought to what you're going to do?" Mariann places her wine glass on the table and dabs the corner of her mouth with a napkin.

"Not really," I lie and steal a glance at Nick.

I feel the table vibrate, and we all look down at our phones.

"It's me," Nick says. "Excuse me."

Nick leaves the table, and Mariann apologizes.

"I wasn't trying to ambush you; I'm just as surprised as you are."

"How did he know we'd be here?" I try not to sound accusatory.

"I told him we were having dinner tonight. He knows he shouldn't show up someplace uninvited." She finishes off her wine, and the waiter walks over.

"Another glass?" he asks.

"No, just the check please." Mariann pulls her wallet from her purse, and I reach for mine. "Don't you dare, Danielle."

I smile when she calls me Danielle. My mom used to use my full name in the same way when I was in trouble.

The waiter comes back, and she just hands him the card without checking the bill.

"Now, tell me your plans?" She focuses her attention on me. "Mark said you were interested in opening some sort of non-profit."

Of course he would only focus on the fact that the career I want doesn't actually make money. "It's a sober living facility to help women transition back into the real world after rehab."

Mariann's eyes turn glossy. "I think it's a wonderful idea. You'll just be helping girls?"

I knew Mariann would have a soft spot for this. After all, she lost her only son to drugs.

"For now. I want to focus on girls between fifteen and twenty-three. Eventually, we can look into expanding."

I tell Mariann about the house I found in a quaint middle-class neighborhood in San Francisco. The West Portal area has access to public transportation, churches, even a mall nearby. It's clean and drug-free. "The house is beautiful, but it needs a lot of work. Mark negotiated a pretty good deal."

"With the housing market still in a decline, the owners were probably happy to sell. And what about your house in North Beach?"

She's referring to my childhood home. "I want to hold onto it until the market improves."

Mariann offers me a small smile. "I understand."

Nick returns to the table and sits down. "T has the car waiting in front," he says to Mariann. That was his subtle way of asking his grandmother to get lost.

"Okay, dear." She kisses Nick on the cheek. "I expect to see you next week at the house. Georgia is making your favorite cake."

"I'll be there." He smiles up at her as she walks around him to my side of the table.

I stand and give her a hug. "Thank you for dinner, for everything." I hold her a few extra seconds since I'm not sure when I'll see her again. Mariann is the closest thing to a grandmother I'll ever have.

"You take care, Danielle." She takes my face in her hands. "Ask for help if you need it, you hear me." She kisses my cheeks.

I love that she didn't counsel me on my plans, that she didn't even give her two cents. She trusts that I know what I'm doing. That means a lot.

After Mariann leaves, I sit down and look at Nick. He's smiling.

"What?" I say with tons of fuck-you attached to it. This is my chance to let him have it. To say all the things I didn't get to yell at him when he left me in New Orleans.

"I'm proud of you." His solemn tone knocks me down a notch. "And I'm sorry."

I fall another level off my high horse.

"I never should've left you the way I did. Hell, I shouldn't have even gone to New Orleans in the first place. I put you and myself in an unfair, unwinnable position."

I recall the feels I experienced with Nick in New Orleans. The confusion. The fun. The only thing missing from my memories is love. I care for Nick deeply. I'm just not in love with him.

Before I decide how to respond, Nick continues.

"I was looking for something familiar after being away for so long. I needed to feel good again. The only way I knew how to get that was by seeing you. I had this fucked-up vision of how things would go in my head. I was chasing a feeling that you couldn't give me. Nobody could. That high isn't real. It's an illusion we created when we were kids. A standard that we've held ourselves accountable to. It doesn't exist, Dani. I'll always have love for you. I know now that we don't belong together."

Nick has just confessed everything I've ever felt and couldn't articulate. I want to reach across the table and kiss him or slap him. Maybe both.

"Thank you," I say instead.

We talk for an hour, then Nick walks me back to the lobby.

"Do you have a car yet?"

"No," I confess. "It's on my list of things to do before I die."

Nick pulls me into his arms and kisses the top of my head. "Quit making me love you."

"Why would I want to do that?" I flirt. Not because I want anything to happen.

Nick releases me and tells the doorman to get me a cab. "You need to get out of here before I take you back inside."

"That won't be good." I move away from Nick in a playful way.

The doorman blows a small whistle, and a yellow cab pulls into the small circular entrance. He opens the back door, and I step towards the car.

"Thank you, Nick. For everything."

Nick pulls me into his arms. I feel him sniff my hair. I take a huge whiff of him too. He no longer smells like my Nick. The days of car exhaust and jasmine are long gone. Hopefully, I don't smell like burnt coffee and sweat. We don't smell the same or even look the same. But we'll always share a connection. Everything we've been through brought us to this point. To the Nick Marino and Dani Batista standing in front of a five-star hotel, saying goodbye.

Matt

July 2013

I'm a stalker.

My skills scare even me. It didn't take long to find her. You can find anyone on the internet these days. Lucky for me, because actual stalking—like standing outside her house or watching her as she shops for groceries—that could land me in jail.

I monitored her social media for a month before I finally got the nerve to write a message. I debated for two weeks before I sent it. We aren't friends on Facebook, and her page is private, so I can't tell how often she goes on. Her profile picture is a meme that says not a day wasted. I can't help but think there is a double meaning in that.

My timing is purely selfish. I just graduated from law school. I'm working as an attorney for Nick's foundation. He made me an offer I couldn't refuse. An offer I would have been an idiot to refuse. I've settled into my new life and there's just one thing missing.

I met a woman last week I might be interested in dating, but I put the brakes on. In the back of my mind, I'm still holding out for

Dani. Waiting for her to call, message, text, post, tweet, something. I don't want to hurt another woman the way I hurt Samantha.

In the midst of the chaos that surrounded our lives, I gave her my heart. I can't love anyone until I get it back.

I told her this in a Facebook message. I asked her to meet me, if for anything, just to get closure. A chance to make amends. I sent that message a month ago. I hoped she'd at least write back a big fuck-you. Then I'd know the door can never be reopened. Silence is worse than her hating me. I've become insignificant. That should be good enough.

It isn't.

I want to talk to her, even if the words she uses are harsh.

I want to see her, even if the scowl on her face breaks my heart.

I just need to know if I still want her. If I still love her.

I'll sit at this keyboard for the rest of my life typing words she'll never read until the day I finally learn whether or not she wants me.

I'm a fucking poet.

A poet and a stalker.

Dani

September 2013

The sun shines through the blinds behind my desk, illuminating the picture of me and Marguerite at her kindergarten graduation. You don't realize how quickly life moves until you see it through the growth of a child.

I used to catch my mom watching me the way I watch Marguerite. It annoyed the crap out of me. She'd stare while I was doing my homework at the kitchen counter or reading a book and say, "Where has the time gone?" I'd make a snide remark about her being old because I was an asshole.

My mother's motto was "Not a day wasted." I have that saying printed and framed behind my desk because it makes sense to me now. I don't waste time, and I don't spend time being wasted.

I've made a lot of changes to my life. Mainly my social life. I can't have one right now, and if I wanted one, I wouldn't know how to make it happen. Some of my employees use online dating services, but I've pretty much stopped maintaining my social media accounts. The Facebook caricature I'd created with the short hair and piercings—it wasn't me. I was hiding behind the red hair dye and mascara. The party girl with her tongue shoved down her gay best friend's throat isn't how I want to present myself to the world.

"Miss. Batista." My assistant, Laney, walks into my office with files in her hand. "I'm sorry, I mean Dani." She looks up with a shy smile. She's only nineteen and already recovered from a heroin addiction. She's sweet and tries to do a good job. That's all I ask.

"What's up, Laney?"

"This is the paperwork on the two girls coming in today." She places the folders in front of me. "Here is the mail from Saturday, and this one just came via courier." She hands me a white envelope with the Anderson Investment Management logo in the top left corner.

"Thank you," I tell her as I stare at the envelope from AIM. "Tell the group I'll be about ten minutes late for our morning meeting."

"Okay." She nods and walks out of my office, closing the door behind her.

I slide my finger under the flap and open the envelope. I've been expecting this letter for a week. I don't know why I'm so worried. Not worried. Excited.

I gave Money Mark full control of the money left in my trust. I told him to invest heavy. I wanted the largest return possible. His eyes lit up like a gambler with an unlimited marker at a Vegas casino. That was seven months ago. This envelope is going to tell me if the gamble paid off.

When my trust was finally funded, it held three hundred and thirty thousand dollars. The quarter of a million dollars my father left me, plus another eighty thousand that Mark claimed was from his smart investing. After four years of living expenses and tuition, I still had every penny, plus more. Nick said this is how the rich stay rich. I didn't see how it was possible, but Mark rattled on about interest earnings and me not living an extravagant lifestyle. I guess I believed him. It wasn't like Mariann would have taken the extra money back.

The expenses to get Hope House running and up to code were way more than I expected. We opened our doors on January 1, 2012. Six years after my parents' murder. The moment I cut the ceremonial ribbon Mariann forced me to hang, everything I was working for finally came to fruition.

Until the electrical began shorting out, and the upstairs shower started leaking into the ceiling. The house was at seventy percent capacity when the plumbing started backing up. It happened the day a woman from social services was stopping by to check on one of the younger girls. She promptly had me shut down. It was all sorted within a week, but only half the girls came back. The money I get from the state and insurance companies cover the monthly operating costs. If I don't have tenants, I don't get paid.

We're still working out the kinks. That's what I tell people when they tour the facility. From the outside, it's beautiful. The house was remodeled to have a large open floorplan downstairs. The main room is modestly furnished with three small seating areas and a reading nook. The dining room is a long farm table with benches on both sides. Mariann donated it to me; it's one of the tables used at Lucy's wedding reception. The garden is my favorite thing. The water treatment, the flowers, the yoga area—they're perfect for relaxing, reading, or enjoying other people's company. Prospective residents, as well as administrators from treatment facilities looking for a reputable place to send their clients, are always impressed by the garden. I just need the inside to work as well as the outside looks. To do that, I need more money.

I open the envelope from Mark and hold my breath. I unfold the letter and scan to the bottom of the statement. I let out a little scream.

Laney is at my door seconds later. "Is everything okay?"

I look up with a huge smile on my face. "Yes, everything is amazing!"

I don't return to my office until after three o'clock. I've been on a high like you can't believe. Money Mark came through big. So big. I made sure he sent me proof that the money I earned was from investments, not Mariann. Even though she no longer has access to my account, I wouldn't put it past her to convince Mark to somehow fudge the numbers. She's already done so much for me.

"Dani," Laney pops her head in. "That social worker said she was emailing the paperwork. She needs it back by the end of the day."

"Okay, I'll do it now."

I open my email and find a message from Lucy. She tells me to check my Facebook. I haven't been on in over a year. Lucy just started using it and wants to friend me. It is easier to share pictures and updates, but I'm hesitant. I'm avoiding it because of one person.

Lucy said she posted a video of Marguerite's first soccer game, and I really want to see it, so I log on. I have eighty-seven notifications. I ignore them and search Lucy's page to watch the video. My fingers strum the keyboard as I wait for it to load. I watch it twice, then comment with a smiley face.

I decide to clear out the notifications while I'm here. Most of them are from games. Once they're deleted, I tackle the messages.

I click the little envelope, and my heart stops when I see Matt's name at the top of the list with the number eighteen beside it.

I'm afraid to open them. Once I do, he'll see they've been read. I look at the date; the last one was sent two weeks ago. I stare at the message window and debate what to do. Eighteen times Matt sat at his computer and wrote me a message. Do I even want to know why?

I click off Facebook and go through the mail on my desk. I separate them into piles: bills, checks, junk. Why did Matt message me? Could it be a mistake? Maybe he was trying to message another Dani. Maybe his account was hacked. I'll never know unless I read them.

I reach for my mouse and click on the Facebook icon. I'm about to log back on when my door opens, and Nick walks in.

His timing is impeccable.

Matt

December 2013

"So you're in love with her?"

"I wouldn't marry her if I didn't love her."

I make a grunting sound. Nick has never done anything he didn't want to do.

"Oh, are you jealous, Matty? You still think you were the love of my life? He rubs my shoulder and then slaps the back of my head, bringing some much-needed levity to the moment.

"Ha ha. Fuck you." I push him away. "You know what I mean."

"Yeah, I know. But you can't plan these things. I stopped trying to control fate a long time ago."

"I'm happy for you. For both of you."

Nick adjusts his teal-colored tie and straightens his tuxedo jacket. "What's up with you? Did you bring a date or what?"

"Nah, just flying solo." I almost asked my co-worker to come with me. We have drinks after work sometimes, but I didn't want her to read anything into it. "I'm cool with everything now. It's no big deal if I see her."

It hurt that Dani never responded to any of my messages, but I can't hold that against her. Just because I needed to write them didn't mean she needed to reply. Knowing she read them is enough for me. "I'm over it."

Nick walks to the bar and pours himself a shot. "Sure you are." He pushes a glass towards me. As I'm walking to the bar, the door opens, and K walks in.

"What's up!" His voice booms into the empty room. He looks twice as large as he did three years ago, if that's even possible.

We greet K with hugs, and then Nick pours him a shot.

"So, what's up? How's Arizona?" Nick asks as they clink their shot glasses.

K plays for the Arizona Cardinals. They have a bye this week, so he was able to fly out for the wedding.

"Hot as fuck, man." K laughs. "I don't want to talk about me. Today is about you." He holds his glass to Nick. I lift mine too. "I wish you both a long happy life and lots of kids." K shouts the last bit.

We take our shots and slam the glasses on the bar. This prompts the wedding coordinator to peek into the room.

"I knew using this room for the groomsmen was a bad idea." She walks to the bar and takes the tequila bottle. "Let's save this for the reception, okay boys?"

"Yes, ma'am," K says as he checks out her ass.

Some things never change, while others won't stop evolving. There are days when I'm going on hour fourteen at work, and I look at the clock wishing time would stop. I'd give anything for another few hours of sleep. Another day in the week. Nick once told me that time was on our side. Every second that ticks by is another second closer to our goals. I laughed him off. We were high, after all.

We never thought about what happens after we've caught up to the future. What the hell do we do now?

Ashley thinks I need a girlfriend. I do want someone to love. Not just anyone. I want the one person in the world I can't have.

I haven't seen her in person since the day I walked out of the bar. I haven't heard her voice or smelled her hair. She's an illusion now. Like an angel or a demon. I don't know her, yet she still means everything to me.

In the last few weeks we've had opportunities to see each other. I chickened out. I used work as my excuse. I have a big case, so I skipped the dinners and wedding showers. I didn't miss the boys' weekend in Vegas though.

I don't know what I'm expecting to happen. Hope for the best, expect the worst. There's no more putting it off. I'm going to see her today, whether I'm ready or not.

"Come on, let's go get you married." I slap Nick on the back and walk him to the door.

Dani

December 2013

I look at my reflection and try not to throw up. I've been waiting for this moment for three months. My hair and makeup are perfect; my dress is spectacular. I keep telling myself I have nobody to impress, but that's a lie. I've never been this nervous to walk into a room. The suspense is killing me.

The wedding ceremony is in a room adjacent to the reception. When the doors open, revealing the winter wonderland, it takes my breath away. I start down the aisle and see them standing at the altar. Matt whispers something to Nick. Something that makes him laugh. They will never change. I love that. When he finally looks up, we lock eyes, and everything I convinced myself was true becomes a lie. The feelings I swore didn't exist come rushing back with just one look.

After the ceremony, there are pictures. After pictures, it's the big entrance, and then we sit in our assigned seats. I spot Lucy, Johnson, and Marguerite walking into the reception. She walks straight over and gives me a hug.

"You look amazing." She stands back to admire the dress that cost a month's worth of groceries at Hope House. That fact causes me a tremendous amount of guilt.

"Hello, Miss Marguerite," I say to my feisty little cousin. "You are the most beautiful girl here."

She smiles with a slight eye roll. "When I get married, there better not be anyone more prettier than me."

"Margie, what did I say about being sassy," Lucy scolds her. She looks up with an exasperated expression. "We'll see you later." She drags Margie across the dance floor to their table.

I scan the room and find him at the bar with K. The music fades, and a voice asks us to take our seats. I watch him move across the room. The bridal party is seated at a round table in the center of the room. Easily accessible to everyone. I want to get up and talk to him, but I can't. Not yet. I never should've waited until today to say the things I need to say. I thought doing it here would take the pressure off. I'm starting to think I was wrong.

"Dani."

I turn around and find a woman who resembles Ashely standing in front of me.

"Ash," is all I can get out before I choke up. "You're so grown." I stand and give her a hug.

"Thanks for noticing. My parents still treat me like I'm eleven." She pulls out of my arms. "You look beautiful."

I dismiss her compliment. "Tell me about you. How is school? Did you graduate?" I hate that I don't know these things.

"I have one more semester. But I decided to go to nursing school. I was talking to Lucy about it, and she thinks it's a great idea."

"She's right!" I can't imagine a better nurse.

We catch up for a few minutes before she moves on. I promise to keep in touch. We have no reason not to be friends now.

The DJ quiets the room and hands a microphone to Mariann. She gives a brief thank-you to everyone for sharing this special day. Then the DJ introduces the best man. I steady myself before I look at him. For the next five minutes, I can gawk, and nobody will think anything of it.

Matt

December 2013

"I should've written something down. Something proper, using appropriate words to honor this occasion. I don't need a script when it comes to Nick. I've always been straightforward with him. I never had any problem telling him when he was acting like a jerk." The crowd laughs. It eases the pressure, just a little.

"We always tell each other like it is." I pause. Not totally sure if I should continue. This is the most selfish thing I've ever done. Me and selfish go hand in hand. "I've been best friends with Nick since we were five. We've gone through a lot together, and today won't change our friendship. Nothing and nobody will ever come between us. I love you, dude."

The crowd claps and Nick stands up to hug me.

"Love you, bro," he says and pats my back.

I warned Nick that I may stray during this speech, and he told me to do what I have to do. That's why he will always be my best friend. Nick returns to his seat, and the room quiets again. Before the DJ can cut me off, I keep going.

"When Nick told me he was getting married, I wasn't sure he was ready. Then I realized life isn't on a schedule. People fall in love whether the timing is right or not. Like me, she's known Nick a long time. They grew up together. More importantly, they grew into adults together."

The crowd awes, and some people clap, hoping I'll stop here, but I'm not finished. I look at Dani; a sad smile sits on her face. The next part of my speech is for her.

"Nick and I had a lot of firsts. We rode our first bike together. We even shaved for the first time using the same razor. Cut the shit out of ourselves." Nick brings his hand to his chin, where he has a small scar from that day. "We learned to drive in the same car and later crashed it together. Sorry Mariann." She shakes her head with a fake scowl.

I clear my throat and look at the champagne glass in my hand. "Nick and I are alike in so many ways. We even fell in love with the same girl."

A collective gasp sweeps through the room. A tear slips down Dani's cheek. I take a deep breath and look at Nick. He nods for me to keep going. He's the most selfless human being on the planet.

"I want to tell you I'm sorry, Dani. You were never a prize to be won. Loving you wasn't a competition. It was an honor. I'm not saying these things with any hope or agenda, other than to let you know that I love you, and I always will." I place the microphone on the table and walk out.

As the doors swing closed behind me, I hear the DJ move on to the maid of honor. "Don't know if you can top that," he jokes, and the room laughs.

I'm in the lobby of the Four Seasons, debating what to do. Should I go back inside? How do I face her now? Clearly, I didn't think this through.

"Matt!" Ashely squeals as she runs towards me. She leaps into my arms. "That was epic! I'm so proud of you!"

"Thanks," I huff and let her go.

"Don't look so worried. It's gonna work out. I know it will." Ash beams as we head towards the ballroom. "My brother, the best book boyfriend ever!" She holds up my hand as if I just won a boxing match.

This isn't a competition. I didn't hijack my best man speech to win Dani. I did it because I couldn't live another second without her knowing how I feel, and this was the only time I knew I'd have her undivided attention.

As I'm walking back to my seat, Haley stops me.

"Do you feel better?" she asks. Her tone is slightly irritated.

"I'm sorry." I give her a hug. "I didn't mean to ruin your wedding day."

"It was the worst best man speech I've ever heard." She pulls away, and a smile spreads across her face. "It was also the most romantic. You owe me."

"Send me a bill," I tell her as we take our seats at the bridal table.

Dani

I watch Matt and Ashley return to the reception. His eyes are on the floor to evade the attention he just drew to himself. These people don't care about Matt's speech now that dinner is being served.

A waiter places a salad in front of me. I look up to thank her and spot Lucy walking over. She's been seated in the corner near the kids' table, while I'm stuck at the half-filled singles' table. I sat here by choice. Mariann offered to seat me with Lucy, but I opted to be on my own.

She sits in the empty chair beside me. "How are you holding up?"

I shove a forkful of arugula in my mouth so I don't have to answer.

"Are you going to talk to him?" She taps her fingernails on the table until I finish chewing. She's annoying like that.

I take a sip from my champagne glass and set it down before I look at her.

"If he wanted to talk to me, he could've come over and said hi." That isn't Matt's style. Most of the speech he just gave was written in the messages he sent me months ago. I planned to reach out to him, but his last message changed my mind. He said he was done, that he thought he could finally let me go.

Lucy drinks the rest of my champagne. I'm sober, but I can have a glass of wine every now and again. Today of all days, I shouldn't be drinking, and Lucy knows that.

"Dani, he just spilled his heart out to you. Isn't that good enough?"

I accepted he was going to move on because it was the healthy thing to do. I was ready to come here, to see him, to give him the closure he needed. His speech didn't feel like closure. Who am I kidding? This dress, my makeup. It's all for him. Not to win him back, but to show him I'm okay.

"This isn't the time or place to have this conversation," I say.

"Matt doesn't seem to agree. Just think about what he said. If I were you, I wouldn't close this chapter just yet." Lucy takes the champagne glass and stands up. "Do you want to come sit with us? We can make room."

I push my wine glass away and replace it with a glass of water. "No, it's okay."

Lucy smiles. I love that she doesn't smother me. She always let me live my life, good and bad. It made me such a stronger person. Lucy goes back to her table, and I continue eating. Eating is the only thing I'm good at. I suck at relationships, I'm horrible at math. I'll eat the hell out of some food, especially a free gourmet meal.

The main course comes, and I do what I always do when I eat dinner. I check my Facebook. I'm addicted now; there's no use fighting it. I open the app and scroll through my newsfeed. It's mostly posts from the wedding. I decide to log off; I don't want to see anyone's comments on Matt's speech. Just before I click off, a little red 1 appears. I click it and see that I have a message from Matt. This all started with a message. It's only fitting that it ends with one.

I walk onto the veranda and find Matt leaning against the railing. His hands are in the pockets of his tuxedo pants, and his bow tie is undone. I had my fill of Matt during his speech. The slight scruff on his face, his sexy, confident stature. I can't look at him now that he's so close.

My stomach is knotted like I've just been caught cheating on a test or running a red light. I glance at Matt then look away. Too many feelings. Too many regrets. It's everything built up over the last three years.

Standing in the presence of someone you once believed to be the love of your life is a very tense situation. I find myself slipping back to my old coping mechanism. Sarcasm.

"I see you're still up to your old tricks." I hold up my phone. "Sending ambiguous messages rather than speaking to me face-to-face. That didn't work out too well for you the first time."

He grins and nods. "I deserve that. But then again, here you are." His tone is a tad more arrogant than called for.

"Wow, okay. So let's just go there. Tell me about the messages. What was the point?"

"You read them, you know." His smile fades slightly. "Why didn't you reply?"

"I didn't see them right away."

The first message was sent almost two months before I found them.

"By the time I read the last one, you seemed...done."

"I was, then I saw you today." He takes his hands out of his pockets and stands up straight. "Then feelings."

He kind of throws his hands in the air, like that's all the explanation I need.

"Feelings? That's it? There isn't something else you want to say?"

A gust of wind blows over the balcony, and I shiver.

Matt takes off his coat and pulls it onto my shoulders. I shrug my arms into the sleeves, and he places his hand inside one of the pockets to remove something. His phone, I think. He places it in his pants pocket. I close my eyes and absorb Matt's warmth. I start to plan on how I'm going to steal this coat.

"Do you remember the day I asked you to meet me in the parking lot?"

I open my eyes and look up at him. "Of course. That day changed my life."

He lifts my right hand and pushes up the sleeve. He stares at my freshly manicured fingers, and I doubt he's admiring my cuticles.

"That was the last time I felt honest desire." He rubs his thumb across my hand.

The movement gives me authentic chills. Not the ones I'm already suffering due to the foggy night air. Matt's thumb gives me I-never-want-this-moment-to-end kind of chills.

"The next day we took thizz, and nothing has ever felt the same."

Ecstasy is such a tricky thing. The feeling seems so genuine you start to doubt reality. How can I feel love towards someone I hate? Why can I smile when inside I want to cry? When the high fades and you're left in a puddle of despair, the only cure is another pill. When the pills run out, you look for anything to mask the pain. Whether it's another drug, or alcohol, or even love. Not just any love, obsessive, destructive love.

"It took me a long time, a lot of bad days and sleepless nights, to figure out why I did the things I did. Writing those messages helped me gain some clarity. I kept writing until I realized where I went wrong."

"Matt, it wasn't all you—"

"Let me finish, please." He places his hands on my shoulders. "I don't blame you for any of it. I don't even blame myself. It was thizz. It was the illusion that love should feel a certain way. When relationships are fostered in phony desire and desperation, you keep trying to connect on a level that just doesn't exist. I get it now. All of it. And I want to reset."

He wants a reset. As in, another chance.

Matt leads me to a chair, and I sit down. He doesn't sit beside me or stand above me. He kneels. Matt kneels on one knee and takes my hand. Every hair on my body stands at attention.

"We haven't been together in a long time. I don't know if we can make it work now, but I'm willing to try. I don't want the fantasy or the happily-ever-after. I want to live in reality with you." He pulls a box from his pocket and opens it. "I bought this a long time ago. I was going to give it to you for your birthday."

Sitting in the center of the box is a ring. The setting is a dolphin encircling a sapphire.

It's perfect.

Matt looks at my hand in his. "Say something."

I try to conjure fitting words for this moment. Something insightful or sarcastic. Words that describe what I'm feeling. I look into

Matt's blue eyes, the ones I fell in love with long before thizz was part of my vocabulary. The eyes I've never stopped dreaming about.

I know exactly what I want to say. I hold onto the words and enjoy what I'm feeling because the best part of anything is the moment before it starts. Right now is the start of my life with Matt.

epilogue
Matt

Sometime in the future.

I look at the bag of pills on the counter and sigh.

"Are you sure you want to do this?"

"Yes." Nick rummages through the drawers of his former kitchen. He uses the cottage as a gym now. It's a place for him and little Jake to spend man time. He pulls out a hammer and holds it up.

"Too much?"

"Yeah, unless you're trying to demo the countertop."

He reaches into the drawer again and pulls out a rolling pin.

"Dude, why do you have a rolling pin?"

"It's a fucking kitchen," he says matter-a-factly as he walks back to my side of the counter. "Look Matty, we're parents now. We can't be doing this shit." He lifts the bags and massages the pills.

Nick decided we should destroy what's left of the thizz when he found out Dani was pregnant.

We never held our annual thizz weekend. It seemed like a good idea in theory, but life kept getting in the way. In good ways.

Nick and Haley found out they were pregnant. The following year, Nick had the baby to take care of. The year after that, I was in the middle of a huge case. Then Dani and I got married. Then Ashley

271

announced she had gotten married in Las Vegas, and I spent that year helping her get divorced. And now I'm going to be a dad.

On more than one occasion, I've sat in my chair at work and wished I could pop a pill. Just slip into oblivion, even just for a night. So, knowing that won't be possible ever again; makes me kind of sad.

"I'm not saying we should take them." I try to articulate what I'm feeling. "Just knowing they were here, it kind of felt like security or something," I admit. "Knowing I could come here and take a pill is what kept me from slipping."

I never realized how often I thought about getting high until Nick told me his plan. Now that I'm about to lose any chance to ever take a ride on the blue dolphin, it's making me second-guess myself.

"Yeah, I get it. You know how many nights I've come out here and stared at this bag?" Nick looks at me with a solemn expression. "Too many, Matt."

"Okay." I step back as if the bag is going to explode. "Go for it."

Nick takes the first whack, then the second. I take the next three. When I hand the rolling pin back to Nick, he does a spin move and whacks the counter. The bag rips, and powder flies into the air.

"Oh fuck, don't breathe it," he yells.

Neither of us can hold our breath because we're laughing so damn hard. I open the windows while Nick grabs a dustpan and a broom. We clean the blue powder mess, laughing harder than we have in a long time. Nick tosses the bag on the ground and grinds what's left with his foot.

Once the cottage is clean and aired out, Nick grabs a couple of beers from the fridge. He walks to the counter and sits on the stool beside me. He takes a drink from his bottle and says, "That was therapeutic."

"It was."

I look towards the garbage can, where a few hundred dollars' worth of MDMA sits in the bottom of a trash bag. There was a time when we would've killed for those pills. Nick lived to sell them. Dani couldn't live without them.

"I'm proud of us."

"Me too," Nick says and leans on the counter.

We sip our beers in silence for a few minutes. Ecstasy fucked up our lives, almost got us killed, and nearly ruined my relationship with Dani. And we're still going to miss it.

"So, what's up with you this weekend?" Nick finally asks.

"I just came up to see you." I down the rest of my beer. "Why?

"Mariann took Haley and Jake to the city for the weekend."

He can't contain his grin now.

"What are you up to, Marino?"

Nick places his hand palm down on the counter

"One more time?"

A smile cuts across my face as Nick lifts his hand and reveals two blue dolphins.

One last time.

thank you

Murphy Rae, Indie Solutions: Thank you for another amazing cover. You get me.

Holly K.: You make editing fun. Kind of.

Facebook friends and family: Thank you for all the support and love you've given me over the last year. You are priceless.

My real life family: Thank you for never making me feel like I'm important.

Napoli Pizza: Thank you for delivering fast and fresh pizza so my family doesn't starve.

One quick note about a serious subject in this book: There is no formula for addiction. One person's typical Friday night is someone's last night on earth.

Say no. Go home early. Get help.

about
the author

Nicole Loufas lives in Northern California. She loves books, music festivals, and bloody mary's. She prefers gin to wine, and hates the smell of fried fish. She writes poetry in her spare time and books the rest of the time.

Check out Nicole's other books:

Thizz, A Love Story

The Lunam Series

The Excursion

www.nicoleloufas.com

Follow me: Facebook.com/NicoleLoufasAuthor

Join my Facebook Group: Nicole's Book Rehab

Twitter: @NicoleLoufas

Instagram: @nicoleloufas

Goodreads: Nicole Loufas

DON'T FORGET TO LEAVE A REVIEW!